HERO

HERO

THOMAS PERRY

THE MYSTERIOUS PRESS
NEW YORK

HERO

Mysterious Press
An Imprint of Penzler Publishers
58 Warren Street
New York, N.Y. 10007

First Mysterious Press edition

Interior design by Maria Fernandez

Library of Congress Control Number: 2023918645

ISBN: 978-1-61316-477-8
eBook ISBN: 978-1-61316-478-5

10 9 8 7 6 5 4 3 2 1

Printed in the United States of America
Distributed by W. W. Norton & Company

To Jo

HERO

I

Justine Poole sat at her desk in the middle of the big open office of Spengler-Nash Security and stared at her computer screen. The image was from a security camera on the corner of a house's roof. It was in color and it was clear. The equipment was high-end and well-aimed, focused on the front gate. The house wasn't visible from this angle, but it was obviously large, like the two houses partially visible across the street, and it had a high hedge that Justine guessed must keep it very private from the ground level. The gate was also high, flanked by brick stanchions with antique-looking lights mounted on the tops. This was during bright daylight, so the lights were off. The stanchion on the right had a keypad and intercom facing the driveway.

A young woman was pushing a baby carriage up the sidewalk outside the fence toward the house. Behind Justine, Rena Todar said, "LA Mother of the Year. That baby can't be more than three months old, but Mom's already wearing a crop top to show off her abs."

"Yes," Justine said. "I'm thankful that I have a lovely personality and don't have to cheapen myself with exercise and sensible eating."

"What is that, anyway?"

"Security camera footage Ben sent me to take a look at. It's a follow-home. She's about to get robbed."

As the young mother pressed a code on the keypad at the gate, a car pulled up in the street behind her and parked. The gate's electric motor rolled the gate open and the woman pushed the carriage into the driveway and punched in the code again. She turned to continue up her driveway as a man jumped out of the back seat of the car and ran to straddle the single track for the gate's wheels. The woman pushed the stroller toward the house, but the gate didn't close behind her.

"See?" Justine said. "He's standing in front of the electric eye so the gate won't close." The gate reversed its motion to reopen the rest of the way, and the car swung to get its nose into the driveway and stopped. The woman took a few running steps up the driveway, pushing the carriage ahead of her.

"Nice car," Rena said. "Brand-new Audi."

Now that the car was blocking the gate, the man was free to catch the woman, which he did in three steps. He put one hand on the carriage's push handle to stop it and kept his other hand in the pocket of his hoodie. He seemed to be holding a gun. The progress of the carriage resumed, but slowly, with the mother and the robber walking together toward the house. They passed under the camera and disappeared from its view.

The car's driver remained at the wheel, but two other men wearing hoodies now emerged from the car with their hands in their hoodies' pockets and walked quickly under the camera and out of sight. Justine said, "And that's that. If you fast-forward about ten minutes you see the guys reappear carrying big trash bags, get in, and drive away. What do you think?"

"I think that's a problem," Rena said. "There's a state law that you have to install the electric eye to keep a gate from closing if there's anything in front of it, but it might be worth thinking about rewiring around it at our clients' houses."

"That's a nonstarter." Ben Spengler had come out of his glassed-in office to the open bay. "As soon as we do that, somebody's kid is going to get squished in his parents' gate." Justine and Rena swiveled in their chairs to face the blond, heavyset man.

Rena said, "What good is having an unscrupulous employer if we have to follow rules like that?"

"Beats me," Spengler said. "Any other ideas?"

Justine said, "So far all that occurs to me is to tell them to look over their shoulders every fifty feet, or hire us to do it for them."

"That one sounds good. You can double my income. Which reminds me." He held up a sheaf of papers in his hand and shook it to make a shuffling noise. "I've got some last-minute changes to the assignments for tonight. One's for you, Justine. You're going with Marcia Min tonight. She's doing a surprise appearance at the Comedy Pit to try out new material. You're alone on this one, but the bouncers there know you, and they're competent." He walked away across the big room and yelled, "Baker! Mitnik! Fresh assignments!"

Two hours later Justine drove up to Marcia Min's building in her own small gray car. The policy at Spengler-Nash was that surprise appearances at clubs should be actual surprises, so the·celebrity needed to be spirited in. Justine liked it, because anyone who might cause trouble would not have time to dream up something ugly and get ready to do it. Justine looked up and could see Marcia's face in the window of her upper-floor apartment looking down at her. From so far away Marcia looked like a child—a sad, lonely one. She disappeared from the window and Justine returned her attention to the street, the sidewalks, and the nearby buildings. After about five seconds she talked into the speaker on her phone.

"This is Poole. I'm at the client's home and we're on schedule."

A female voice said, "Acknowledged." Neither of them said the client's name or the address or the destination, any of which would be inviting company.

Marcia Min was dangerously popular right now. Two years ago, she'd had a big national stand-up tour and a streamed television special, and then spent last year in LA shooting two full seasons of a television show based on her comedy, called *Shanghaied*. That title had made Justine wince, but she supposed the only people the world could be sure had never shanghaied anybody were the people who lived there, and a hit was a hit.

The whole country wanted a third season, even though only the first one had aired so far. The network had given Marcia's agent an opening offer for a third but it was insultingly cheap, so her agent had leaked a rumor that the show was being canceled. The resulting wave of online outrage had been so overwhelming that the network had been rocked back on its heels, but not so much that it forgot to use the public reaction as a chance to raise their advertising rates for the show's already-shot second season. Justine suspected that Marcia's sudden impulse to test new material at the Comedy Pit was actually a quiet reminder to the network that any time she wanted to go back to making a fortune on the live performance circuit, all it would take was asking her agent to hire a bus.

Justine saw Marcia come out the front entrance of her building wearing a pair of jeans and a leather jacket, trot to the car, and take the passenger seat. "Hey, Justine," she said. "You know where we're going, right?"

"Yep," Justine said. "We'll be there in fifteen minutes. I love that jacket, by the way."

"If you let my enemies kill me, you can strip it off my body before the cops arrive. You can have the bullet hole patched good as new."

"I'll keep that in mind," Justine said.

"Maybe we can even do a trade. I like those bodyguard suits you guys wear to some of these gigs. They have sort of an Anime Badass Motorcycle Emergency Sex thing going on."

"That's my world, all right," Justine said. "Let me tell you what I'd like to do when we get to the club. The bouncers are saving a parking spot in back by the dumpster. There are two bouncers, I think both of them hired since you played there. Ali is a slim, dark man about forty who's a lethal martial arts guy, but he looks normal. Bobby is a big guy, looks like a college linebacker. I'd like Bobby to go in ahead to block the view of you a little until we get to the stage. I'll be right behind you, so nobody approaches you that way. You step right up onto the stage. Barry, the manager, will be acting as emcee. He'll hand you the microphone and step away. The only lights will be on you, and I'll be at the front table to your center left. If you see a problem from up there, point at it."

Marcia said, "Sounds good."

"Great," said Justine. "Anything I should watch for tonight? Offended religious groups? Political stuff? Process servers?"

"Nothing so far, but it's not even nine o'clock yet. Maybe a scorned lover or two and some angry wives."

"If I see a couple of those, I'll try to fix them up with each other."

"That's actually a pretty funny idea."

"Consider it yours," Justine said. "We're six minutes out now. I'll be quiet so you can think."

Justine drove while Marcia devoted the time to scrutinizing her makeup, making tiny, invisible changes to it, and brushing her hair, but Justine knew her brain was running through what she was going to say.

Justine turned west on Sunset and pulled the car into the narrow driveway that led to the alley behind the Comedy Pit and into the small employee parking area behind the building. She parked in the only empty spot, and Ali the bouncer stepped up and opened the car door for her. "Hi, Ali," she said. "I'll leave the key in it."

"Thanks, Justine."

She looked to the side and saw Bobby beside the rear door of the building. He was wearing a black T-shirt and jeans. "Hi, Bobby. Are you going in first?"

"Sure. Unless—"

"Perfect," she said. She looked back into the car at Marcia. "Ready?"

"Eager." Marcia got out of the passenger seat and came around the front of the car. "Thank you for doing this, guys. I'll just piss everybody off a little and we'll be back out before the traffic light changes."

Justine looked at her watch. "Okay, Bobby. It's time."

Bobby waited until Marcia Min was close behind him before he stepped in, and Justine followed a step behind Marcia. Ali shut the door behind Justine and stayed in front of it to be sure nobody else got in. Inside there was only a four-foot landing before the beginning of the stairway down to the "pit." The walls of the staircase were red brick with the half-readable skins of peeled-off posters. The staircase was a dozen steps in a single flight. Five steps down the left wall ended, replaced by a stretch of open space with a steel railing, so Justine had a view of the crowd.

The thirty tables were packed with people, everyone's chairs turned toward the little platform that served as a stage. Justine had several thoughts at once. There were too many people, almost certainly a violation of the fire regulations, but she decided that for the moment she should let it go, because her job now was protecting Marcia Min for an appearance that would probably be fifteen minutes. The crowd also made her think that Marcia's surprise visit was a secret that had gotten out. This was a Monday night on a nothing week in mid-summer.

When she turned her eyes forward again, Bobby was taking the last of the steps down. He paused, standing straight and tall enough to obscure the two women behind him from the view of the audience. About three seconds later, the comedian on the stage gave a bow, said "Thanks for coming," waved, and handed the cordless microphone to Barry, who was already there to receive it. Barry yelled, "Give it up for Danny Rastow!" There was a roar of applause that Justine suspected wasn't entirely for Danny Rastow. It lasted a few seconds and grew as Danny Rastow jumped down from the low stage and out of the spotlight into near invisibility.

During the applause Barry stepped into the spotlight, leaving the area at his feet in shadow while a woman seated there got up and Justine slid into her seat. Meanwhile, Bobby the bouncer crossed the room in an aisle between tables, holding the attention of a percentage of the audience.

Barry said, "We have a pleasant surprise tonight. I just noticed that a dear friend of the Comedy Pit is here. Please welcome—Miss. Marcia." The applause began and intensified, a couple of screams were added, and Barry shouted, "MIN!" The audience roared. Marcia Min took two running steps out of the shadows. Her third step was a leap up onto the stage and into the spotlight, where she accepted the microphone and said,

"Thanks, Barry," words that were simply tossed up against the wave of sound from the audience.

In the previous second, after seeing Marcia make it onto the stage without falling, Justine had already taken her eyes and mind off Marcia Min and turned them onto the audience. Her eyes were busy scanning the people at the tables and the bar, looking for facial expressions that were out of place or out of proportion, or for any physical movement that might reveal a problem was coming.

Justine didn't listen to Marcia Min's new anecdotes and observations, because she was making an effort to keep her ears tuned to the sounds that weren't coming from Marcia Min. Her full attention was aimed outward from her spot in front of the stage, keeping the glare of the spotlight behind her so her pupils would be slightly dilated and sensitive to the shapes and movements in the audience and the periphery around and behind it, where trouble nearly always began.

The sets at the Comedy Pit were fifteen minutes. They might stretch it for somebody like Marcia Min, but not much, because it would take minutes away from somebody else's fifteen. Justine was aware that Marcia was getting big laughs, bringing the audience with her into the complicated, surprising narratives she liked to tell in these intimate spaces.

Justine had been assigned to protect comedians many times since her first one just after she'd turned twenty-one. That night she had made a mistake and had been glad that Ben Spengler had been there to correct her. There was a heckler in the audience and Justine had stepped away from the wall where she'd been standing and begun to edge closer to him, preparing to distract him and signal for the bouncers. Ben was suddenly beside her and whispering in her ear, "Come back." They had stepped back to the wall, the act had ended, and nothing bad had happened. Later he'd said, "Don't bother with hecklers. Humiliating them is part of the comic's trade. They practice it, test new put-downs, and so on. You're just here so nobody gets hurt—physically, not psychologically."

Justine saw something that held her attention and the memory was gone. There was a young woman with a black cloth bag between her feet under her table. Nearly every other face in the audience was up and looking at the stage, but hers was looking down. The man sitting beside her had the large-screen version of the latest iPhone, and he was looking at the screen. He must know that comedy clubs didn't allow anyone to record performances, so what was he doing? Justine scanned the room to locate Bobby, but he seemed to have gone upstairs to the front door. She looked at the young woman and saw her pull both feet back beneath her chair to shift her weight to the balls of her feet. That was bad news. Justine brought her feet back, too, and moved to the edge of her seat.

The young woman made a sudden lurch forward, and now she held something in both hands as she charged the low stage. At the same moment her male companion stood, his phone's camera following her advance. Justine sprang up, pushing off hard to pick up two steps on the young woman. The young woman had both hands palms-up to hold the object. Justine was only a half-step behind and gaining when she recognized the object as a cream-topped pie in a round foil pan. Justine's left hand pressed down on the woman's forearm so the pie tilted downward. The woman compensated by increasing her upward pressure, and Justine instantly lifted with both hands to amplify the woman's effort. The pie arced upward into the woman's face. The pan fell, leaving a mess of whipped cream and strawberry covering her hair and eyes, so she was forced to stop and paw at her face because she couldn't see where she was going. Justine gently sat her down on the floor in front of the stage.

The man took a step toward Justine, but when Justine turned her head to look at him, something about her made him freeze and back up.

Above them, Marcia Min was laughing, so the audience laughed too. "You baked that for me, hon? That was really thoughtful. I'd lick your face, but my time is up and I'm afraid I've got to go. Thanks, everyone!" She curtsied and threw a kiss, and then spun, stepped off the stage, and climbed the stairs quickly. Justine stepped up behind her so nobody else could follow.

As they emerged from the back door of the Comedy Pit, Justine said to Ali, "Thank you, Ali." She handed him two envelopes, one with "Bobby" written on it and the other with "Ali."

He said, "You don't have—"

"No, but Spengler-Nash does."

She and Marcia got into her small gray car, and Justine swung out onto Sunset and drove off. Marcia was laughing. "That was insane. You're just like a snake."

"Thank you, I think," Justine said. "Have you ever seen them before?"

"No, but since people learned I broke up with Allen last week a couple of online tabloids have been making a story out of it, saying he's devastated and I'm a cold-hearted bitch and all that. What they don't seem to know is that he was so heartbroken that he had to console himself in advance while he was in New York."

"Really?"

"Yep, with three different women—two models and an actress. Any publicity is usually good, but I hope this pie thing doesn't catch on."

"No hard feelings? Real ones, I mean?"

"None on my side, and he gets to keep the models and actress until they read about each other." She looked at her watch. "That was fun, but I'm tired. We're doing a retake tomorrow and I've got to go in for hair and makeup at six A.M."

"It takes the same time to get you home as it did to get you here," Justine said. "We'll be at your place in fifteen minutes."

⁓❖⁓

Ben Spengler watched the dark blue Mercedes crawl past Mystique Restaurant for the third time. There were two young men in the front seat and at least two in the back, and maybe another between them. Spengler glanced at his watch. It had only been five minutes this time. The intervals were getting shorter. He suspected it was because they didn't want to miss the moment when the high-value diners paid their checks and went home. Tonight, Jerry and Estelle Pinsky were in there meeting with some other charity donors about another idea for saving some part of the world, and the bodyguard keeping an eye on the Pinskys was Ben Spengler. He seldom gave himself client protection assignments anymore, but the Pinskys were old Hollywood, and they had been paying Spengler-Nash for security since practically his grandfather's time. Giving them the boss's personal attention was a courtesy.

The Mercedes was just all wrong. Those young guys couldn't afford that Mercedes unless they were cryptocurrency speculators or a singing group he hadn't heard of, and if they were, why the hell would they be circling Mystique? There were twenty clubs within a half mile that catered to people without gray hair, and at ten-thirty they were full of women who had made themselves beautiful to come out in twos or threes to meet somebody. He took out his cell phone and his finger moved down the contacts list toward the "P" for "Police."

He could call them now, but he had always resisted calling them until he was watching the suspect make an unambiguous move. Calling the cops too soon only irritated them. They needed to know whether they were being asked to arrest a few young men because some older guy disapproved of their wardrobe and posture, or if they were being invited to blunder into an ambush by a squad of terrorists carrying machine guns. He looked at the word "Police" again, and then touched the name below it with his index finger.

"Poole," said the familiar voice.

"Hey, Justine," Spengler said. "I'm on the Pinskys. They're in Mystique and I've got about four or five young guys in a Mercedes gliding past every few minutes. Have you still got Marcia Min?"

"I just took her home. She has a six o'clock call tomorrow. Where do you want me—the restaurant or the Pinskys' house?"

"The house would be best."

"I'll see you there," she said. "Let me know when they're moving."

"I will. Stay out of sight until we know what the plan is."

Justine was in her car looking at her phone for the fastest route to the Pinskys' house. She had been there a couple of times, but she was a night shift person, and she knew that sometimes the best route could be blocked by accidents or road repairs. Tonight, the GPS estimated the trip would take eight minutes.

The Pinskys lived in a big house in a part of Beverly Hills where nearly every house belonged to somebody who had screen credits, but theirs had been built forty or fifty years ago, before people had stopped feeling any discomfort about building a place that was as big as Justine's high school. She had studied the Pinsky house the first time she'd been assigned to work a party there. The lot had originally been part of the director Miles Moncton's ranch in the early 1920s, and she had seen an old picture of it online. There had been a few gentle hills covered with dry grass and a few California oaks scattered about fifty feet apart.

The hills were bulldozed flat at some point and the land cut into two- and three-acre parcels, but some of the old trees were still visible, probably spared to shade the houses. The road was now lined with fifteen-foot hedges like green walls, and at intervals there were iron gates blocking private roads.

She approached the Pinskys' address and saw that neither Ben Spengler or the Pinskys had arrived. She pulled up to the gate, looked at her work phone, and found the four-digit gate code. She pressed the numbers and the gate rolled out of her way. She drove in, pulling her car up the driveway and around the garage to the parking lot that had been built there for party guests. She put on her utility belt, picked up her flashlight, got out, and walked around the house to the front.

The Pinsky house was a long, low structure that had been a typical wooden ranch house of the sort that celebrities of the 1970s still had until Jerry and Estelle Pinsky had become concerned about the fires that had burned through some Southern California neighborhoods. They had hired an architect to transform the ranch into a simulated Spanish colonial adobe rancho with a red tile roof, white concrete-and-stucco walls, and a yard that was carefully re-landscaped to ensure that nothing that could burn was within twenty feet of the house. The wooden doors and window shutters had been reinforced with steel, and the outer walls were raised to ten feet. Low desert gardens ran along the inner side of the perimeter walls. Much closer to the house were the pool, spa, patio, and tennis courts—all things that didn't burn.

What Justine liked about it was that all the fireproofing had accidentally turned the place into a fortress. It was too bad that the rest of the world couldn't afford to do that, but the rest of the world hadn't produced three or four long-running television sitcoms and two dozen movies.

She knew exactly what the next step of her job had to be. She went past the front gate and moved along the perimeter to be sure that the crew stalking the Pinskys hadn't sent friends ahead to secure control of the place. Her search told her she was alone. She left the gate open to make sure the Pinskys could drive straight in without waiting, continue up the long driveway to the door beside the garage, slip inside the house, and engage the locks.

Justine knew where she wanted to be—close to the front gate on the inner side of the perimeter wall. That was where the gate's electric motor was, bolted to its own small concrete foundation and shielded from view by the gray steel housing that protected it from weather and dust. Justine stepped to the other side of the motor, sat down with her back against the outer wall, and looked at her phone. There was no message from Ben Spengler, which she assured herself meant that the Pinskys still hadn't left Mystique and Spengler was watching over them.

She put the phone away and checked her gear. She had three pairs of handcuffs on her utility belt, along with her Glock 17 and two ten-round magazines loaded with 9-millimeter rounds. When she'd left the car, she had also brought the tactical flashlight with its brutal eye-searing glare. She'd had no use for any of this equipment or place to carry it earlier tonight while she had been watching over Marcia Min at the Comedy Pit. The thought made her remember Marcia joking about the black Spengler-Nash outfit she and the others sometimes wore. She wished she were wearing hers now, instead of street clothes. She would have been more comfortable and harder to see in the dark.

Justine hated this part of the job—the waiting when she knew the threat was real and she was putting the body she lived in, the creature that she was, at risk. She also loved this part, when she was crouching in a well-chosen spot, knowing things the adversaries didn't suspect yet, and sure that the most crucial thing they didn't suspect was Justine Poole. She could feel her heart gradually increasing its beat, like an engine warming up.

She knew she must not stand up or try to look out through the gate. She needed to see her opponents well before a confrontation happened, but she also had to be alert to the possibility of an advance scout sent ahead to detect the presence of professional security. Just today Ben had sent her security footage to help her learn how the latest group of follow-home robberies were being choreographed. They hadn't had time yet to talk seriously about how to go about stopping one.

She knew that Spengler's method tonight would begin by following the robbers' Mercedes and taking good, clear pictures of it that showed the license plates. When the Mercedes reached the gate—closed or open—he would pull in behind it so he could block the robbers' escape and do whatever would get their attention away from the victims while the police caught up. Why hadn't he called her by now?

And here came the Pinskys. She watched the glow from their head-lights moving along the canopies of the trees, but she heard only the whisper of the tires on the pavement as their electric vehicle approached. The car began its turn toward the gate and a slight brightening appeared in the driveway that allowed Justine to see the paving stones. The car completed the arc and straightened, and its headlights shone up the driveway and lit the garage door as the car kept going. Jerry must have pressed the remote control in the car because the electric motor beside Justine turned and the teeth of its main gear meshed with the chain and the gate began to close behind it.

Justine rose to a crouch, keeping her head low and on the safe side of the motor housing, and waited. The garage door at the end of the driveway started to rise.

The Pinskys' car pulled ahead and its headlights illuminated the back wall of the garage. Justine could see their silhouettes through the rear window, Jerry's head on the left side, and Estelle's on the right. The lights went out. *Get out*, she thought. *Get into the house.* Didn't they know?

Outside the wall there was an engine noise and more lights. Justine returned her attention to the gate. The Mercedes arrived and pulled forward, and the first man was already out and running. He stuck his leg into the space in front of the moving gate in time to interrupt the beam of light to the electric eye. The gate stopped instantly and then began to roll back in the other direction.

The three passenger doors of the Mercedes swung open and men sprang out and ran to join the point man in the driveway.

Everything felt unsettled, almost unreal. She thought, *Act now or miss the chance to save this.* She stayed low, drew her pistol, aimed at the first man and shouted, "Hold it! Stay where you are or I'll shoot!" She held the tactical flashlight as far from her body as possible and pushed the switch, bathing the men in its wide, blinding glare. They all looked young and large, all wearing black masks and dark clothes.

The point man and one of his companions raised pistols she hadn't seen in the dark, and fired at her light.

She fired back, the shot hitting the point man in the chest, and as he collapsed backward toward the ground, she shifted her aim to the second gunman and fired. He had been the driver, last out of the car, so he was closest to her. He fell too, dropping his pistol on the pavement. A third man fired at her and she felt the bullet cut the air a foot above her ear. She fired in response and he went down, but she was sure she had missed him and he was just ducking. She turned off her light and sprinted for the gate with the vague idea of using their own Mercedes as a shield. Even though it was probably stolen, they might hesitate before damaging their means of escape.

As she ran, a volley of wild shots ricocheted off the inner side of the wall where she had been, and when she dashed behind the Mercedes, she heard the front door of the house slam shut. She inhaled and felt her lungs swell in elation. The distraction must have done it. The Pinskys were inside. She kept running past the rear of the Mercedes, made it to the gate stanchion and twenty feet past it along the outer wall, pivoted, dropped to her belly, and aimed her pistol at the mouth of the driveway.

She used her left hand to take out her phone and thumb-dial 911, then returned her eyes to the open gateway.

"Nine-one-one, what is the location of your emergency?"

"Five-oh-seven Mirabella in Beverly Hills," she said. "Five men with masks and guns are trying to pull a follow-home robbery of Mr. and Mrs. Jerry Pinsky, the residents. Two of the men fired shots at me so I had to defend myself. We'll need two ambulances."

"Your name, please?"

"Justine Poole, with Spengler-Nash Security. I have to hang up now." She did and saw Ben Spengler's car appear around the last curve in the road and then stop in the street blocking the Mercedes in the driveway. As he got out and crouched behind his car, Justine popped up, aimed her flashlight at the ground so he could see her, and waved. He waved back, so she advanced along the wall to within a few feet of him.

Spengler advanced to the other side of the open gateway and pulled out his pistol. He said, "I'm sorry, Justine. They looked like they were going to try to drive the Pinskys off the road for a carjacking, so I had to stay close, and then I got scraped from the side by another car trying to pull into my lane. What's going on?"

"There are five of them. They kept the gate from closing, I yelled at them to stop or I'd shoot, but two of them fired and I had to shoot them. There are three more of them inside the gate. They fired too, but didn't hit anything."

"Did the Pinskys make it into the house?"

"I'm pretty sure. And I called the cops."

"Good," he said. "All good." He edged up against the concrete-and-stucco wall and leaned out to get a view up the driveway where the two men she had shot were lying. "I see the two casualties. I don't see the three who are still lively."

They heard the scream of sirens in the distance. As the sound grew louder and more high-pitched, he said, "That sounds like good news. But this is where it might get hairy, so make sure they can see who the good guys are right away. Do nothing that might look like resistance."

The sirens trailed off, and the street was awash in light—blue and red lights spinning to splash bands of alternating colors over everything, glaring white headlights, flashlights sweeping from place to place. Several spotlights found Justine and Ben and stayed on them. A voice shouted, "Put your weapons on the ground, step back from them, and lie down!" Four police officers emerged from the glare and ran to them with pistols drawn. One yelled, "Face down on the ground! Now!"

Ben and Justine both lay on the ground with their arms out from their bodies as two of the officers dragged their wrists behind their backs and handcuffed them. As soon as she felt the cuffs click Justine said, "I'm Justine Poole. I made the 911 call."

Neither cop answered, which she supposed was an answer.

The cops frisked them and then helped them up. "All right, come with us. You'll have to sit in a car while we clear the scene." They took them to two different police cars and locked them into the caged rear seats.

Justine could see at least a dozen police officers gathered on both sides of the open gate where the Mercedes and Spengler's car were stopped. She said to the officer who was with her, "There are five of them. Two opened fire on me, so they're on the ground, wounded. I'm almost sure the Pinskys made it into the house while that was happening. They're clients of Spengler-Nash, and we were here to protect them."

The cop spoke into the radio microphone on his shoulder. "The female says there are five armed suspects inside the gate, and two are down. She thinks the intended victims are in the house." That sounded accurate to Justine, so she remained silent.

There was radio chatter, which sounded to Justine like acknowledgments, and then an older male voice said, "We're standing by for SWAT."

The cop who was with her got out and walked to join the others at the wall. Now that she was sitting alone in the back of the police car, she began to feel the letdown after the adrenaline rush of the confrontation and gunfight. She felt exhausted, almost sleepy, but tears had formed in her eyes. She had no way to wipe them, so she had to endure the feeling and wasted no more time thinking about it. She leaned back in the seat and tried to turn in a way that would not increase the tension on her arms and handcuffed wrists. She could see into the side window of the other car where Ben Spengler was, and he seemed to have decided on a similar position. He had been in the bodyguard business since before she was born, so she supposed this was another of the thousands of tiny bits of knowledge he'd accumulated the hard way.

The SWAT truck looked a lot like a UPS delivery vehicle, but bigger and darker. The cops in battle dress and body armor streamed out of the back doors. They all carried M4 rifles except one, who had a marine sniper rifle with a big scope. They milled around behind their truck for a few minutes while their commander conferred with a couple of high-ranking cops in black uniforms who had been among the last on the scene. Then the SWAT team formed themselves into a single big cartoon creature with twenty-four legs, twelve heads, and rifle barrels pointing outward in all directions and shuffle-footed through the gate, up the driveway, and to the house.

Justine listened for gunshots but didn't hear any, and she allowed herself to feel tentatively optimistic: the cops hadn't been under fire, so maybe the Pinskys were safe. She waited, but she was at the wrong angle to see the front door open, if it did, and there was no noise. Silence could mean the Pinskys were dead, so she tried to prepare herself for that kind of outcome, but she couldn't find a way of getting ready. They were a nice old couple who seemed to treat everybody kindly. Jerry had always called her "Kid," and Estelle seemed to call everybody under seventy "Honey." Maybe the closed doors of the police car had just kept her from hearing what was going on, and everything would all be okay.

The cops outside the gate began to move around, they holstered their pistols and spread into the street. Two SWAT team members, a man and a woman, came out of the driveway, each of them guiding one of the Pinskys to a waiting car, and then it pulled out and they were gone. Justine smiled, closed her eyes and whispered, "Thank you."

2

"...With live, late-breaking news. Tonight, television and film producer Jerry Pinsky and his wife were the latest victims of an attempted follow-home robbery in Beverly Hills. Police say the attempt was foiled by a member of the security company Spengler-Nash. The female agent fought off the alleged robbers in a gunfight while the couple took shelter in their house. Two of the suspects were hit by the agent's bullets, and three others tried to escape on foot but were captured by police."

Mr. Conger pressed the remote-control channel button, not because he thought the story would be better on a different channel, but because he couldn't stand to listen to the news anchor's comments. The disaster had happened. Hayzen and his squad of morons had let themselves be defeated by a lone bodyguard for celebrities and had run away to save themselves. For the first few minutes he had imagined the bodyguard and assumed he was a sixty-five-year-old retired male cop issued an old .38 revolver that usually served only to weigh down his belt so he needed to keep tugging up his pants. Mr. Conger had thought that was a devastating image, until he had learned who the bodyguard really was—a lone girl.

His people—and he—would shortly be this month's joke around town. The shooter couldn't have been anyone worse. Anybody else and the television stations would have reported the story once. Because this security guard was female, they had already started making her into a hero. They would repeat the story, and probably lead each broadcast with it, for weeks. Every time they did, people in town would have less respect for Mr. Conger. This woman would probably be the grand marshal of the Hollywood Christmas Parade.

Mr. Conger's mind foraged for ways to make this all right again. He hoped Hayzen had been one of the two men shot, and that he would die. He thought about that for a few seconds. That wouldn't be good enough. He wanted this never to have happened. The closest thing would be to erase the crew—have all of the ones who ran away killed. They would be gone then—nobody for him to think about and resent.

The cops had them, and they would interrogate them. They would be locked in a high-security part of Men's Central Jail on Bauchet Street the rest of the time, so it would be almost impossible to get near them, and it would be completely impossible to take out all three at once, which was the only way to avoid scaring at least one into telling the cops everything.

The option of killing them just wasn't available. Mr. Conger would have to make himself feel better some other way. He could assume the three failures would get their punishment in the natural course of things, without his controlling their fates. If one of the two men the woman shot died, he would have been killed during the commission of a violent felony. The other four would probably be charged with capital murder as though they'd killed him. The "felony murder rule" wasn't a fair law, but it was the law. In a way, the unfairness made it a better punishment for embarrassing Mr. Conger. It would be excruciating for the four to go to prison for life because somebody else shot their friend.

There was one thing that Mr. Conger really had to do. From one point of view, it was just a loose end, but to Mr. Conger it was already more than that. This woman couldn't be allowed to sit back now enjoying the admiration of the whole city just for ambushing two young men in the dark. Otherwise in a week there would be a GoFundMe page raising money to pay for therapy to soothe her rattled nerves or to send her to law school or something. He had to end this now. Killing her was the only way he could ensure that the three survivors would keep their mouths shut. He would show them that he was avenging their fallen friends, so he must care about them too. It also wouldn't hurt to remind them that he hadn't forgotten how to make people dead if they displeased him.

He thought about who would be right for this. It had to be somebody who didn't look the part. It couldn't be one of his thieves wanting to make extra money or some biker with tattoos on his face. Leo Sealy was the one who came to mind. He looked like a high school gym teacher or a personal trainer or something. Mr. Conger smiled to himself, because Leo Sealy had been both of those things—or pretended to be while he was doing a couple of jobs, anyway. In reality he was just a gym rat who didn't mind getting his hands wet for a price.

It took Mr. Conger a few minutes to find Leo Sealy's phone number, because it was one of those numbers that he had never put into a phone or a computer. He had to go to the bookshelf, take out the Bible, go to the annotations on the first book of Samuel—"S" for "Sealy"—and find the phone number he had written as chapter, verse, and lines. 21: 3:55 and 50: 0311 was 213-555-0311.

He took a burner phone out of his desk, inserted the battery, and called. He heard Sealy answer: "Yes?"

"Hi," Mr. Conger said. "I'd like to talk to you in private tomorrow, early, if you've got the time. Recognize me?"

"I recognize you. Where and when?"

"Same place as last time. I'll be there at seven."

"See you then."

❦

When Leo Sealy drove up Crystal Springs Drive into the parking lot for the Harding & Wilson golf course in Griffith Park, he saw Mr. Conger in the second aisle sitting behind the wheel of a black Land Rover with the motor running, presumably to power the air conditioning and the radio. As soon as Sealy pulled to a stop, Mr. Conger got out and walked to the passenger side of Sealy's car. Sealy unlocked the door, and Mr. Conger got in. "Okay. Drive."

Sealy drove out of the lot and up the road beside the fence along the edge of a fairway of the golf course, shaded by tall eucalyptus trees. There were only a few cars on the road this morning. Mr. Conger said, "Thanks for meeting like this. I've got a job if you want it. Last night two of the five guys doing a home invasion job for me got shot by a bodyguard at Jerry Pinsky's house. It happened in time to make the eleven o'clock news. Did you see it?"

"No, but I always record the news. I'll watch it later."

"Well, I want the bodyguard dead. It doesn't have to be fancy or clever, or look like an accident or anything like that. Just dead will do. Because you're the best, and because the bodyguard apparently knows how to use a gun for something besides a paperweight, the pay is a hundred thousand. I should mention the guard is a woman. What do you think, Leo? Do you want this?"

"Do you have a name or address or anything?"

"No, it just happened last night. The name hasn't been released, but she works for Spengler-Nash."

"That figures," Sealy said. "What are the terms?"

"Fifty right now, and the other fifty when it's done and I see it on the TV news."

"I'll take it. Thanks for thinking of me."

"Take me back to the lot. Your advance money is in my car."

Leo Sealy drove to the vast parking lot of the zoo up the street to turn around and drive back toward the golf course lot, where he parked beside Mr. Conger's car.

Mr. Conger took out his key fob and popped open his car's back hatch. "There's a golf bag with a few clubs in there. Take it home with you and count your money there." He got out of Sealy's car and walked with him to his own, watched Sealy lift the bag out and slip the strap over his shoulder. Then he closed the hatch.

"Thank you again," Sealy said.

"Don't mention it."

The two men returned to their cars and drove out of the lot in opposite directions. Mr. Conger felt better as he followed the road south toward Los Feliz. The morning was still young, and he had already launched a solution to a problem that would have irritated him more as the sun rose higher. He had turned the task over to somebody who would be able to accomplish the job. He felt as though his will had already been done.

3

The COVID-19 pandemic had been great for Leo Sealy. For Sealy's whole life up until then, if a man was walking around wearing a mask covering everything between his eyes and his chin, he'd better be in a hospital, or someone would call the police. After people started dying of Covid, a man with a mask was barely noticed.

Leo had hidden his face on a few jobs before then, but it had required specific conditions. He had noticed while he was casing one job that the target lived a block from a big construction site, so he had arrived wearing a hard hat and one of those stiff white round masks made to protect workers from inhaling dust. Another time he had done a hit in a ski town in the Sierras wearing a knit cap pulled down to his eyebrows and a scarf wrapped around his face. He liked the post-Covid world even better. A man wearing an KN95 over his face was a model citizen, and the death people were most scared of wasn't the one he had in mind.

People were herd animals. Anybody who wanted to move among them had to remember that. The herd was self-protecting and merciless. It was always detecting, isolating, and eventually ejecting any creature who wasn't quite right—the weak, the injured, the sick—because those conditions might be contagious, or weaken the herd. It was important for him not to seem to be any of those things, because they drew notice, and notice was always dangerous. "Another buffalo" was his term for the right look—one of thousands that looked about the same.

Whenever Sealy actually went out to make a kill, he liked to have two firearms on him. One of them was the killing instrument, and it was usually a .357 magnum revolver. When he used it, the brass casings stayed in the cylinder instead of being ejected all over the place. His second weapon was a reliable semi-automatic 9-millimeter pistol with a double-stack magazine that held at least fifteen rounds, like a Glock 17. That was the weapon to bring out if there was trouble, because it would be best for getting him out of it and on his way home quickly. He usually brought three extra loaded magazines for it in his car, but things had never gotten crazy enough to make him reload.

For Leo Sealy, everything was about speed. He was in, did the job, and was already out while bystanders were still paralyzed with confusion and shock. This required efficiency and economy of movement, and he knew he had to remain in motion no matter what. Even if he ever got unlucky enough to be shot, it probably wouldn't kill him, and if it did, he'd have nothing left to worry about. For him there was no stopping, no hands up, no being the lifer in prison who limped when he walked.

Sealy was thirty-six, and he'd learned the value of planning by living through unplanned jobs when he was starting out. He had walked close to the target and relied on his own agitation and ability to think faster than anybody who happened to be nearby. That had worked several times, but barely. Planning every move was better. It was what pros did.

If you weren't a pro you were an amateur. Most amateurs didn't think a killing all the way through. Most of them only thought up to the moment when the gun would go off or the knife plunge in. Then it was as though they woke from a dream. They had no idea what to do next. Each second that they put into thinking over their options after the fact, the more of those options disappeared.

The most dangerous person in this work wasn't the target, but the client. The client had a reason, often a justification, to get this person killed. If the target was the guy's wife or girlfriend, he already had one foot in a prison. If the target was a business partner or a competitor or an enemy, the client was on a very short list.

The client could almost certainly be broken down and made to talk. Every police department had at least one or two guys who were good at persuading the client that their only hope was to tell the cops all they knew about the "real" killer, the one who had taken a human life for mere dollars—like taking money was the height of perversity. It was like saying you shouldn't pay an exterminator for getting rid of your rats—that he should do it because he hated rats. Sealy supposed that reasoning would sound more sensible after about ten hours in an interrogation room.

His usual solution was to make sure the client didn't know anything about him that was true, so the client had nothing to offer the cops. Lying and minimizing contact had worked so far, but there was always some risk of an accidental disclosure. That was why he loved working for someone like Mr. Conger, who was never going to tell the authorities anything. Mr. Conger had a history that would make a scorpion get up and run, so nobody was likely to say anything about him either.

Having Mr. Conger pick him over all the people he could have was a big compliment. In Sealy's profession, the only opinions that mattered were the judgments of bosses and shot-callers. Many of them had spent their teens and twenties doing wet work themselves, and they knew what it took. Mr. Conger was one of those men, and one who was particularly feared.

Mr. Conger was unusual among bosses because he still knew how to fade in. He had a comfortable house and nice cars, but nothing that ordinary people didn't have. He had never done what some of the others did—try to build some stupid empire with a lot of flash and a string of clubs, getting his picture taken with music people. He seemed to Sealy to be like some of the old-time bosses that people had told him about. He invested in things like laundromats and hardware stores and gas stations and apartments, always with partners who did the work and paid him a cut. He kept those places separate from the illegal stuff, paid taxes on the profits, and kept everybody in the dark about everybody else. That made doing business with him a lot less uncomfortable than dealing with the adventurous ones.

Sealy drove back to his apartment in Van Nuys, brought the golf bag in with him, and found the money in banded five-thousand-dollar stacks of hundreds. He hid the money in his gun safe, which he'd bolted into the broom closet off the kitchen. He would figure out how to spread it around later. He knew that if he deposited that much cash in banks, ten thousand dollars at a time, it would be reported to the government, and smaller chunks would be reported as possible attempts to avoid the regulations. What he usually did was pay for things like groceries, restaurant meals, gas, haircuts, escort services, and clothes in cash, and run tabs at places like his gym and his cleaners that he paid off in cash, so over time the money would disappear into businesses that had no reporting requirements, or ones where the proprietor would simply pocket it. The rest he stored in safe deposit boxes. He put the golf bag in the clothes closet for the moment and turned to the process of finding out who he had just been hired to kill.

First, he would need to learn what he didn't know about the company the bodyguard worked for. Everybody in LA had heard of Spengler-Nash, but he liked to know whatever he could. The worst case would be that this woman was something Mr. Conger had not ruled out—an experienced armed bodyguard who knew what she was doing and was simply smarter than Mr. Conger's home invasion crew. If it was true that she had just survived a gun battle against five men, that would be his leading theory. He had to make that assumption until he knew something more encouraging. He hoped that she wasn't so smart that she already knew the battle hadn't ended yet, only paused until he found her.

Sealy expected that her identity would not be released today, but he also knew the cops wouldn't be able to keep it a secret for long if she'd shot two guys. Cops who shot somebody were usually kept anonymous for as long as possible, particularly if the shooting was found "within policy" after a preliminary in-house inquiry. A shooting by a security guard was a different story. The cops wouldn't give a crap about a civilian who was paid to protect millionaires.

4

Justine's mother had worked all the time, so her grandmother was the adult who had been around to raise her. Much of what her grandmother said was strange. "The cold is what we hate more than anything, the distance from others, being the one on the outside alone. The heat we love. The closeness, the touching and motion and feeling, the mind and pulse racing, and wanting more. It almost doesn't matter whether it's more fighting or its opposite, because there's always some of both and either can switch to the other with a look or a word. It's what we want above all other wants, and we're right to. But over time, heat burns. It leaves us with scars and calluses, so we're thicker-skinned and tougher, but less able to feel than we were when we were young and first stepped into the fire."

Justine remembered how her grandmother had stopped, her eyes fixed on the little girl's, shining like obsidian beads. The girl could see there was a frustration behind them. "When it's your time, move toward the heat and the light that's life. The cold is death. You may not remember who told you this, or know that it was true until you're old. You only need to remember which direction to take. Anybody who tells you different—priest, teacher, politician, boss—is your enemy and wants to fool you into working for his benefit." The girl knew even then that the way the old woman said it—that she would probably not even remember—was her way of making sure she *would* remember it forever.

Justine grew, and she got hurt sometimes. Her grandmother would take a quick glance and say, "You're all right." After this had happened dozens of times, Justine stopped letting the old woman know. All of the cuts, bruises, or burns would heal, because what she'd said was true again. What her grandmother had done was give her a kind of invisible armor that weighed nothing. The girl could have the armor because her grandmother had it first. The girl never heard her complain. Even the couple of times when the old woman hurt herself in the kitchen, she looked past the blood or the burned skin and said, "It'll heal," ran water over the spot, covered it, and appeared to forget the whole event. She hadn't even seemed surprised in the instant when the cut or burn had happened.

For the old woman the world was both a good and bad place in extremes. It was to be enjoyed, but she didn't trust it. If she shook a pill out of the pharmacist's bottle and, instead of the one she had chosen, another fell out first, she would make the effort to get the one she had intended. When the sharp-eyed young girl asked her why, she said she liked to be in charge. The girl knew her well enough to realize that the old woman couldn't be sure about the pill that had volunteered: this could be the one destined to get caught in her throat, or it could be the one that a benevolent deity had induced to jump in front to save her. She had little faith in benevolent deities, and if they saved people, she had no special right to be one of them.

At first the girl couldn't imagine why her grandmother thought there would only be one bad pill in the bottle, but with a little thought she understood. If there was a poisoner, he would want her to have only one fatal pill. That way, if she died, all the pills left in the bottle would be found clean and wholesome, so her death would be dismissed as natural.

Justine's relationship with her grandmother consisted of shared conversations that probably nobody else would have found important because the old woman and the young one were not really part of the current world. One had nearly used up her turn and the other was waiting for hers. The one who had to face the current world was Justine's mother, who worked and supported them all.

Justine was slipping into thoughts about how much of her relationship with her mother had consisted of missing her when she heard Ben Spengler answer his own phone again, which he usually didn't do unless somebody was sick. He said, "I'm sorry, Ms. Brellin. Spengler-Nash doesn't release any personal information about its employees. This is a private security agency, and that would cause an unnecessary risk to our clients as well as our employees. I'm sure you understand. And of course, this is a police matter, so there are strict rules about the information the police want released."

Justine was sure that if Ms. Brellin understood, she didn't care. Reporters needed stories, and anything that had even a remote connection to the entertainment business was like a magic elixir to them.

He said, "And these two gentlemen had three companions, also armed. Violent criminals often have associates who want revenge."

The next call came only five minutes later. Justine reached for the phone on her desk, but Spengler had disconnected it. "Spengler-Nash," he said. "This is Spengler." He listened for about thirty seconds, then said, "I'm sorry, Mr. Huebler. Television interviews are out of the question." He listened again, then said, "I've seen the technique. Everybody has. A darkened backlit face and disguised voice. Yes, it's pretty effective. But no, thank you." He listened again. "No, not me either, or anybody else in the company." She saw the muscles in his jaw tighten. "We don't have a 'side of the story.' And we're not interested in publicity, good or bad. Goodbye." He hung up.

She stepped into the doorway of his office. "I'm sorry, Ben."

"Don't be. We—particularly you—did what we were hired to do. This will cool off in a day or two. Once they're all convinced that we're not dumb enough to do what they want—which can only get us in trouble—and we haven't agreed to an exclusive for somebody else, they'll turn to the next story."

She said, "You know they're going to get something they can write. I'm grateful that it won't be from us. But this isn't the kind of story that stays hidden."

"I know," Spengler said. "But doing interviews can only get us in trouble with the cops. We depend on their patience and goodwill, and they have to sort out what happened and why, and the rest of this mess. So we've got to stay out of their way. And this stuff is why everybody here has a work name on their company ID. All we're doing right now is buying time until the cops hold a press conference."

Justine shrugged. "Thanks. I'm not sure what to do with that time."

"Reload," he said. "Not literally. But rest up. Your name will be announced or leaked, and a day later, your address and whatever else they can find will be on computer screens. These same people will be on your front lawn and banging on your door five minutes later."

"You think it'll be that bad?"

"A lone woman fights off five criminals to save an old couple." He amended it. "A famous, rich old couple, both of whom give money they got from producing beloved TV shows to lots of good causes. And once the camera gets a look at you, it will be worse. A lot of media people will make you their favorite human until too many people know too much about you for you to be safe. And what the hell are you even doing here? It's not even your shift, and if it was, we couldn't send you out to protect a client. You're the subject of a police investigation."

"Investigation?" she said. "Did anybody call it that? Won't they just check my record and ask the only nonsuspect witnesses—you and the Pinskys—what happened?"

"I don't know what the Pinskys told the cops last night. I know the cops asked them to hold off on any public statements for now, because I talked to Jerry and Estelle a while ago. Look, I'd like you to go home and pack a suitcase. You can stay at my place for a few days until we know where this is going."

"I don't know," she said. "What are you going to do?"

"I plan to hang out here at the office while you have my house to yourself. That big couch in my office is where I sleep best anyway."

She walked into the office and sat on the couch. "Maybe I should be the one to sleep here. I'd be surrounded by armed bodyguards twenty-four hours a day."

He thought for a moment. "You're right. It hadn't occurred to me, but this is about as safe as a place can be. We're on the fifth floor, and there aren't any taller buildings close enough to make a rifle shot practical."

She shrugged. "Sounds like my dream house."

"I'm not kidding," Spengler said. "Do it and we'll both sleep better."

5

There was no list of employees on the Spengler-Nash website and there were no photographs that had people in them. Leo Sealy had never expected there to be a "Meet Our Bodyguards" section, but careless mistakes could happen. This time they hadn't.

He took screenshots—a picture of the headquarters building on South Broadway above a description of the business they were in and a display of phone numbers for particular services. What they said about themselves sounded true. They claimed to be the oldest personal security agency in town, founded in 1922. They claimed to be the preferred provider in the Los Angeles area and demonstrated that they were reasonably ethical by not mentioning the names of any past or present clients.

He had heard from a man in the kidnapping end of the extortion business, who had been trying to hire him, that Spengler-Nash, in addition to protecting some of the most recognizable names in the entertainment industry, was retained to protect a steady stream of nearly anonymous executives of big companies. These were people who wanted to arrive in LA, do some billion-dollar transaction, and leave without having their presence noted by competitors or outside investors, or placing themselves in danger of attracting someone like Sealy's kidnapper friend. Many of these people were foreign nationals, and it was their home-country security companies that contracted with Spengler-Nash to make sure their paths in Los Angeles were safe, clear, and unnoticed.

Sealy looked up the address on Google Maps. It was in the downtown area near Clifton's Cafeteria and some former banks and other old buildings that used to be fancy and glamorous, but during his time in LA were always being ferociously remodeled, replaced, or converted, five or six at a time. The pictures on the Spengler-Nash website showed modern, high-tech communication and computer facilities, but the exterior didn't seem to have changed much since the 1920s. He corrected himself. At some point they had put in an underground garage, and that had to be modern, probably a conversion of a basement.

The company interested him. He forced himself to postpone thinking about the possibilities that might present themselves if he pursued a study of Spengler-Nash's clientele to look for profitable victims instead of hunting down this one Spengler-Nash bodyguard. Some day he might want to return to the idea, but not now. Sealy's self-discipline had brought him prosperity, and he had a contract to fulfill.

There were sure to be a dozen ways to find the woman who had the gunfight with the follow-home crew. There had to be a police investigation and that would mean she would probably hire a law firm. That would be another set of people who knew all about her—a bunch of secretaries, paralegals, and lawyers. One of the lawyers would probably be making public statements. What lawyer ever passed up an opportunity to be on TV? A press conference was better than a dozen commercials, and it was free.

Still, Sealy was betting on the cops. In a day or two there would be a press conference. If the police spokesperson didn't mention the woman's name, some reporter would ask. In fact, when a story like this was developing, it wouldn't matter if a police press conference wasn't about this case. Reporters would ask anyway, both on and off camera. They wanted the name as much as Sealy did.

Sealy set the DVR on his television system to record all of the local television news channels—2, 4, 5, 7, 9, 11, and 13. One of those stations would have the name soon. He also knew that while the minutes passed, Mr. Conger would be after the name using his own sources. He acted as though he could hire somebody to handle something and forget it, but he was a very smart man, and he never seemed to rest. He wanted things done promptly.

While Sealy waited for the afternoon news to be recorded, he performed random searches about bodyguard companies, Jerry Pinsky, Beverly Hills crimes, and follow-home robberies. He had completed his daily run early in the morning before the sun was up and the air was still cool, and then done his morning calisthenics, chin-ups, and push-ups. Now he had another long period of waiting, because the next round of local news would begin at five. He passed the time completing his weight training. After his survey of the five to seven P.M. reports, he had to wait again until 8:00 P.M., so he spent the time punching his heavy bag.

After the eight o'clock news Sealy was disappointed again. He spread the newspaper on the kitchen table and got out his gun-cleaning kits to care for his equipment. He wore surgical gloves and was always careful not to touch any part of a weapon, tool, or accessory with bare hands. When he had cleaned, oiled, wiped, and reassembled his guns he loaded a few spare magazines, never touching ammunition or magazines without gloves. His pistols were ghost guns, assembled out of factory-made parts except for the lower receivers, which had been custom-made without serial numbers by a machinist. Filing or drilling off serial numbers was ineffective, because even after the numbers could no longer be seen, it was possible for a crime lab technician to read one by detecting changes deep in the steel.

Sealy finished the cleaning, put away his equipment, and turned the television to watch the Channel 7 eleven o'clock news while the other channels were being recorded. It was an odd beginning. The anchor Mark Emery said his "Good evening" and then, "We begin tonight with a live report by Terri Marsten." There was Terri Marsten in her latest new suit, this one a light gray with the gold "7" pin on the left lapel. Sealy immediately recognized the building behind her and turned up the sound.

She said, "Mark, tonight I'm at the headquarters of Spengler-Nash Security Services. Just an hour ago we learned that the bodyguard who engaged in a gun battle with five suspects in an attempted follow-home robbery at the home of comedy creator Jerry Pinsky is Justine Poole, age twenty-nine, of Los Angeles. She is employed by Spengler-Nash and was assigned to protect Mr. Pinsky and his wife, Estelle, on their way home from a dinner meeting at Mystique Restaurant. Since the story broke last night, many have already hailed Ms. Poole's actions as heroic.

"Tonight we learned there have been negative reactions from others, including the Anti-Violence Coalition, which tweeted that Poole's actions were the worst form of vigilantism and that an armed private police force that protects only the wealthy and privileged is a threat to public safety. So far, police spokespersons have not responded. Nor has Benjamin Spengler, owner of Spengler-Nash. Back to you, Mark."

⚘

Justine set her overnight bag on the desk in Spengler's office, closed the blinds, and went into his private bathroom and changed into the sweatpants and T-shirt she had brought. It was too early for her to be able to sleep, but she lay on the big couch and pulled her blanket over her. Ben Spengler had been right. The oversized couch was as comfortable as some beds. She sat up again.

The late-shift people were on the other side of the building from Ben Spengler's office, where she could barely hear the hum of their voices, and words were too muffled to understand. The sound was reassuring to her, almost the way she had felt as a young girl when she would lie in bed and hear the steady, calm voices of her mother and grandmother coming from the living room. It meant that someone was awake and paying attention, so she could let go and sleep. She tried lying down once more and remembered that she had been up most of last night at the Pinskys' and then in the police station, and she hadn't stopped since then. She pulled the soft blanket up and closed her eyes.

⁂

Leo Sealy spent time considering his options and opportunities. He knew that the woman's name was Justine Poole, so he began by searching the internet for her. It didn't take long to realize there was something off about Justine Poole. She had no presence on social media—no Facebook, no Twitter, no TikTok, no LinkedIn, no anything. Google had over a hundred entries about her, but all of them had come from news stories or premature opinion pieces written about her by people who knew nothing about her or the shooting. There was nothing on the internet that had originated with a Justine Poole who lived in or near LA.

The news had said she was twenty-nine. He found a site that gave the names, addresses, and ID photos of ten women named Justine Poole, and another site with pictures of eleven others, and many of them were not the same women. There seemed to be at least twenty in all. About eighteen lived outside California, and the others he could find were too young, too old, or didn't fit. Nobody was going to be both a neurosurgeon and a bodyguard, or an airline pilot and a bodyguard.

He was beginning to think the reporter had gotten the name wrong. Was there an actual woman in America who hadn't signed on to a social network by age eighteen, let alone twenty-nine? Maybe she had been in the military overseas and hadn't been allowed to communicate on open sites. Her recent behavior under fire might fit with that theory. Or maybe she had married a Mr. Poole but kept everything online in her old name. A lot of women would certainly like to do that, and maybe a woman in the personal security business had the skill or connections to accomplish it.

He decided to set Justine Poole aside for the moment and looked at one more thing. The news woman had mentioned Benjamin Spengler, the owner of the security company. He wondered what role Spengler was playing in this mess. If the agency had been founded in 1922, he must be either the third- or fourth-generation owner. He was probably rich enough to be living on a yacht anchored off a Greek island, but the news reporters seemed to have been in touch with him as though he was in the office. Sealy went on several online directories to look for an entry for Benjamin Spengler. He could find plenty of references to him in articles, but nothing personal. He tried another way. He ran a search to find a photograph of Spengler from a newspaper article about a fundraising event for a children's hospital. He was a big man with blond hair and a beard, like an aging tackle from some old football team. Now

Sealy knew what he looked like, but what drew Sealy's attention was the article that went with the picture. He had given a donation that had made them name something the Spengler Clinic. That meant he had serious money. The money gave Sealy another idea.

He went to Google and typed in "Spengler Foundation." All those rich guys seemed to have a foundation. There was nothing. He tried Spengler Mansion, then Spengler House, but got nothing. Then he tried "Spengler Estate." That brought something, but not exactly what he was looking for. It was an article from the February 12, 1948, *Los Angeles Evening Herald* about the death of David Martin Spengler, the cofounder of the Spengler-Nash Guardian Company. He and his partner Francis X. Nash had been comrades in World War I, both members of the first force of Marines sent to France, and after the armistice founded Spengler-Nash Guardian in 1922. Nash had died in 1936, and Spengler had carried on without him. His estate, it said, included not only the company building on Broadway in Los Angeles, but also the family home at 567 Roe Street. Sealy took a screenshot and then left the computer.

He drove east and south into the heart of the old downtown and moved along Broadway to the Spengler-Nash building. He parked in an alley near the Grand Central Market and walked back. He needed this Justine Poole's address, and he needed it tonight. There was potentially a huge advantage to making his move now, before all of the news organizations found the address and converged there. Once that happened, there would be no easy way to get to her.

Leo Sealy had spent years working to make himself into a reliable operator anywhere in the country and a perfect operator for Los Angeles, where he knew the spaces and felt the pulse. Tonight he knew that if he got her address he would only have exclusive access to it for a short time, probably until daylight.

When he got to the Spengler-Nash building he saw a white panel truck pull up in front. The painting on the broad side said "Morgell," and underneath in letters only about five inches high, "Commercial Dry Cleaning." He timed his steps so he would pass near the back of the truck at the moment when the driver pushed his rolling rack out of it. Sealy could see that many of the clothes on hangers that the driver was delivering were black uniforms. Others were dresses, or men's suits. All of them had clear plastic covers and tags attached to the middle of the hangers. He paused as though to avoid a collision, but he was reading the tag on the end. Along the top was "Spengler-Nash." The next line was "William Finn," and the third an address on Santa Monica Boulevard, apartment 17.

Sealy stepped aside as the rack swept past him and then took two steps away. At the rear of the rack, pushing the rack toward the door, was the driver. He was about fifty and chubby with dark hair. As the driver passed the point where Sealy was out of his field of vision, Sealy spun, hooked his right arm around the man's neck, and squeezed, cutting off the circulation for a minute or so until the driver passed out, and then broke his neck. He dragged the body through the back door of the van and pulled it to a spot on the floor behind the driver's seat, went back out and rolled the clothes rack back into the van, closed the door, and sat in the driver's seat. He started the van and drove it around the block to a space along the curb.

He used the light of his phone to look at the tags, searching for the right name. After about thirty tags he saw it. There were three tags attached to stretchy black uniforms, but all they said was "Spengler-Nash" and "Justine Poole." Then there was a gray women's business suit, and it was the same, except that it also said "5794 Ashburton St., #8." He used his phone to take a picture of it, looked to see if the shot was clear, then pocketed his phone, got out of the van, and walked to his car.

He drove about a mile, parked, and studied Google pictures of Justine Poole's building and the neighborhood around it. The streets were lined with well-kept smaller houses and, on her street only, a couple of other fairly new apartment or condominium buildings. Hers had an underground parking lot with a barred gate across the entrance, and an eight-foot pedestrian gate that led to a walkway along the side of the building. He assumed that after his visit the police would take a look at the recordings from the security cameras mounted along the front to identify the cars that had passed by that night, so he had to be sure his would not be one of them. He parked on a side street three blocks away in a row of other cars and walked.

He wore dark clothes, a baseball cap, a surgical mask, and sneakers. He had clear surgical gloves on his hands and kept his hands in his jacket pockets. He knew from the photographs that the building had a pool, a spa, and a big patio with two stainless steel propane grills. He approached the building from the alley behind it, stepped to the wall surrounding the pool area, pulled himself to the top of it, swung his legs over, and lowered himself instead of dropping, to prevent even the smallest sound. The windows in the building were all dark. The whole neighborhood was almost certainly asleep at this hour, and he didn't want to wake anyone.

Sealy stood still and studied the building. When a man who made his living murdering people studied a building, it was a particular kind of view. He looked for openings and irregularities in walls that could be handholds or footholds, vents that could be wide enough for a human body if the covers were unscrewed. He liked louvered kitchen windows, because the frames could be bent with a knife and the strips of glass removed. He liked sliding glass doors on patios and balconies, because most of them had only a single latch by the door handle, which was really only a hook that went over a bar. Other sliders had deadbolts, but their owners were lazy about setting them.

Tonight, he was interested in balconies. The parking garage was about a half-story above ground level, so the second-floor balconies were an extra six or seven feet up. He stayed back near the wall beyond the pool and walked along beside it looking at the balconies. Each was about six feet by three feet of flat space with a steel railing. There were eight condos, four on each of the two floors. Numbers one through four would be on the first floor. Numbers five and six should be on the second floor, at the front corners. Eight should be on the back right corner. He stopped and looked at that balcony and was satisfied that it was the one. No security expert, especially a woman, would live in a ground floor condo in a big city. If she had enemies, she would want her windows to face the pool rather than the street, so she couldn't get popped from a parked vehicle while looking outside to check the weather.

He saw his way up. He didn't like it, but he could do it. There was a ladder made of steel bars built into the left side of the building so repair men could go up to work on the central air conditioning or patch the roof. It was not close to the balconies, but he could see that there was an architectural detail, a recessed line about an inch wide and an inch deep running around the building just below the level of the balcony, and another about six feet above it.

Sealy walked to the enclosure where the pool motor and filters were and found the leaf skimmer. It was about twelve feet long. He unscrewed the net and then collapsed the pole so it was only around four feet long. He judged that with the pole at three times its extended thickness, it would be strong enough. He slid it into the back of his belt, so it was out of his way, and went to the ladder. He climbed to the right height and stepped off the ladder to the wall, sticking his toes into the lower groove and gripping the upper groove above his head with his fingertips.

As he edged along the wall he felt fear, and it made him angry that he had to take so much risk for this. The anger made him more determined than ever to kill this woman. He hated her. He hated her most of all when he came to the corner of the building and had to reach around it and set his right hand and right foot in the continuation of the grooves he could only locate by feel and ease himself around. Six feet beyond it he arrived at the first balcony and climbed over the railing.

He began to pull the aluminum handle of the pool skimmer out of his belt so he could lay it from the railing of this balcony to Justine Poole's balcony, but then he noticed something that surprised him. The sliding glass door beside him was not closed. The screen was closed, but the glass door was open to let the night air into the bedroom.

Sealy leaned the aluminum pole against the wall, took out his pocketknife, and opened the blade. He tested the screen and realized it wasn't even latched. Why should it be? he thought. Few people could even get up here, and nobody but him would want to. He remained still for a moment, listening. Then he slowly moved the screen to the side on its rollers and track, stepped into the room, and slid the screen shut.

He gripped the knife as he looked at the couple on the bed. If he had to kill them, it would be with the knife, and the big danger was to have a loose hold on the knife so it slipped and cut his own fingers. The two people were older, the husband bald and the wife's bleached blond hair cut short. Both had sleep masks over their eyes.

He didn't hurry as he walked past the foot of the bed. He loved the way this condominium building had been constructed. They had used rebar and reinforced concrete instead of a cheap wood frame, so the floors didn't creak. He made his way out of the bedroom and then across the living room. He unlocked the door, opened it slowly, and stepped out. He made a point of not resetting the hand lock in case he needed to get out through this condo later.

He moved to the door with a metal "8" on it and looked at the lock. It was the same model as the older couple's lock, which was crap. He reached into his pocket for his wallet and found the membership rewards card from a liquor store that he had discovered to be perfect for this purpose. It was thinner and more flexible than a credit card, so he could get it into the narrow space between the door and jamb and bow it a little to slip into the depression where the plunger went into the frame. He worked it for a few seconds and opened the door.

He pivoted into the condo, shut the door, and stood still. He reached for the revolver he preferred for killing, but left it in his jacket pocket and instead took out the semiautomatic and attached the silencer to the muzzle. He was going to have to kill at least one, maybe two, people and get out before the noise woke the neighborhood. A silencer wouldn't be silent enough, but it would help. He looked around the living room for something else to help muffle the sound. He felt the pillows on the couch until he found one he could wrap around the pistol. Sealy held it in place and moved slowly toward the rear of the condo, then stepped into the bedroom with the bulky pillow-wrapped pistol aimed at the bed.

The bed was empty. The blanket and sheets were tight and neat across the mattress, the way soldiers did it. She was not home. He stepped closer and verified what he thought he had seen in the dim light from the window. There was only one nightstand and one pillow. He went to the closet and opened it. There weren't any male clothes and not enough female clothes for two women.

He stepped out to the hallway to look for a second bedroom. There wasn't a second bedroom. One woman lived here, but she wasn't here now. He decided to search the condominium and see what he could learn about her.

He returned to the bedroom, opened the drawer of the nightstand, and found a flashlight. He looked at his watch. He could afford to give himself an hour.

6

Sealy searched the condominium for anything that would help him find Justine Poole. There were a desk and a filing cabinet in an alcove off the living room. She had kept the desk's surface clear, but the filing cabinet gave him hope. The file drawers were probably full of folders that held pay stubs, receipts, and bills with notations and check numbers written in. He opened the bottom drawer first. It held three blue folders with labels that said "Taxes" and a year. Copies of tax returns would have Social Security numbers, birth dates, accounts. He opened them, but there was nothing inside. Had she scanned them into her computer?

He looked at the front of the first blue folder again. The name on the folders wasn't hers. The taxpayer was a woman named Anna Sophia Kepka. He looked at the other two folders. They were for this Kepka woman too. Had he broken into the wrong condo? He went back into the bedroom and opened the closet. He turned on the flashlight and ran it along the rack of clothes. He found a woman's suit, navy blue, with a laundry tag on it. He looked closely at the tag. The name was Justine

Poole. Anna Kepka could be a current or former girlfriend, a relative or something.

He opened the file cabinet again and went through the other drawers. There was a pink slip for a car, and it was in both women's names. He found the deed for the condominium, and again there were both names. He found printed copies of a MasterCard and a Visa, front and back. He set them on the desk and photographed each of them, the pink slip, the deed, and the car registration. He didn't want any of this crap. He wanted things like bank statements, restaurant receipts—things he could use to find her. He used the flashlight to look for other places where she might keep such things and noticed the black shredder she had beside the desk. It fit his growing impression that she didn't like allowing clutter and piles of paper to build up.

What he needed most right now were photographs of her. He moved the beam of the flashlight to sweep the walls for framed pictures, searched the desk and the file drawers for an envelope or file of them, then looked for a passport, for an album, and then for a zip drive or other digital storage device, but found none of them.

She had gotten herself into trouble firing a pistol, but he had found no pistol here. He supposed the police must have taken her gun for ballistic testing, and if she had another, she had taken it with her. He'd found no ammunition either, but if she knew she might be in danger, she had probably taken her supply with her. He supposed it was possible that Spengler-Nash issued its agents firearms and had them turn in their weapons at the end of each shift. If that was the system, the gun wouldn't even be hers. Bodyguards didn't have any responsibility to protect any-body when they weren't on the clock, the way LA cops did.

Sealy checked his watch. He had already used up his hour. He took a last walk through the condo with the flashlight and made a video of the trip with his phone. He didn't expect to be able to come back, but if he did, he would have a record of where everything was. As he passed through the little office area, he noticed the shredder again. He stopped and lifted the motorized part that held the blades and looked down into the wastebasket part. There was only a small mound of shredded paper in it. He returned the flashlight to the nightstand beside her bed, went to the front door, opened it and relocked it, then went out and closed it.

He went down the hallway to the stairs, descended to the underground garage, cut across the empty space marked 8, walked between the electric eye and its beam projector, there to detect a car ready to leave, and watched the bars of the garage door swing upward out of his way. He kept his face turned away from the building so the security cameras wouldn't get his image. He walked at a brisk pace until he reached his car.

By the time he was inside it and starting the engine, he knew where he had to go next. This young woman had been with Spengler-Nash for a while if they'd trusted her to protect big clients like the Pinskys. Anybody who knew much would know her troubles were not over. She was too smart to be at her condo. So where would she be?

⚘

Sealy drove to the address on Roe Street he had found for the Spengler house. It looked nearly the way the picture taken in the 1940s had looked, a two-story structure inspired by a 1920s architect's idea of an early Spanish hacienda. It had a red clay half-pipe roof and white stucco walls arranged in a rectangle around a courtyard with a fountain and garden. The only windows he could see were on the second floor, and they were a foot wide and a foot and a half high, too small for him to squeeze through. The picture he had seen of the inner courtyard side showed walkways along the first and second floors, with the doors to bedrooms along the walkways at intervals. He couldn't tell from here if that was still true.

There was a long cobbled driveway that began on Roe Street and ran about three hundred feet up the lawn before it widened to a broad parking area, then continued along the side of the house to another paved area in front of a garage with five doors.

The part that surprised Sealy was that a house like this still existed. It was at least five acres in one of the most desirable parts of the city, all lawns and mature shade trees. He left his car around the nearest corner and walked across the lawns of two other large houses to get to the Spengler house. There was no fence or wall, probably because the empty land around it served as a security feature. If Spengler was expecting trouble, he would see it coming, and no burglar wanted to carry stolen goods the length of a football field to get it to his car. There were too many other houses that looked easier to rob.

He knew that he was trying to penetrate a place that was likely to be difficult and risky. The owner of a security company had no reason to live in a house that wasn't thoroughly wired. He was almost certain to have all of the standard devices—security cameras, perimeter door and window alarms, glass-break detectors—and might even have some of the more troublesome stuff—dusk-to-dawn motion sensors to light up prowlers who approached the building, infrared body heat detectors, interior electric-eye beams across doorways, trap alarms wired into any interior door, pressure pad switches under carpets, big batteries and automatic generators that would kick in if he cut power to the system. None of this equipment was hard to get, and most of it was probably not expensive if you already had installers on the payroll.

The first step was for Sealy to see what obstacles he could detect from outside the range of cameras. He kept his cap and mask on as he walked around the edge of the vast yard. He saw the security cameras set at regular intervals under the eaves of the house, a transmitter near the peak of the roof to send an alarm signal by cellular transmission to—where?—probably to both the cops and Spengler's own security company. That meant Sealy couldn't just cut some wires in the phone company circuit box and isolate the place. A minute later Sealy saw a second transmitter on a different section of roof, meaning an intruder prepared to take out one transmitter wouldn't have time to disconnect the other in the fraction of a second it would take for it to report the state of the system, including the loss of the first transmitter.

Sealy was not a man who accepted obstacles as defeat. As he walked, he thought of ways to overcome them. Strong defenses could be made irrelevant by luring defenders outside the perimeter. Alarms could be circumvented, and houses could be entered through openings where alarms had not been installed.

The fact that this was an old house encouraged him. Air conditioning existed but wasn't common in 1922, so Southern California families kept doors and windows closed in the mornings to hold the cool air in, and opened everything late in the day to cool the house again. Houses had open vents to prevent attics and kitchens from collecting heat, and windows were installed on opposite sides of rooms to let cross-breezes pass. He continued walking in a wide circle at the edge of the property, studying the house for vulnerabilities.

Sealy reached the big, rounded archway that served as entrance to the courtyard. He stood two hundred feet away, remaining still for a long time, staring through the opening. There were two trees in the courtyard that had grown much taller than the architect could have anticipated more than a hundred years ago. They were taller than the roof of the house, jutting up so the canopy of foliage must shade the house in daylight.

There was a high wrought-iron gate across the arch. It had hinges built into the left side of the portal and a frame with a latch and rings for a lock. He decided to stay away from this entrance for the moment. If Spengler was hiding the woman who worked for him here, he would be making it as hard as he could to get to the house. This entrance looked to Sealy like a trap, an obstacle that he could probably climb over, but while he was doing so, he would be in the open and in no position to defend himself from someone in the courtyard.

Sealy moved so he could see the right side of the portal and looked at the windows of the row of rooms along the walkway on the left side. On the second floor one of the windows seemed to have a faint light behind it, from something like a plug-in night-light in the suite's bathroom, or even the screen of a cell phone or tablet. Sealy's heart began to beat faster and he felt the muscles of his arms and legs tightening on their own as he studied the walkway. The other windows were all dark. Maybe the light meant this was the bedroom Spengler had Justine Poole staying in, but maybe Spengler was only making it look that way so an intruder would climb the open steps to the second-floor walkway and make his way along it toward the room, while Spengler sat in some dark corner watching his progress through a rifle's scope. Sealy decided to keep walking.

Sealy walked past the archway and saw no promising way of entering the building until he reached the common part of the house, directly opposite the arch. It contained the living room, dining room, kitchen, pantry, and probably other things. There was a wide brick chimney at this end, and Sealy stared at it from the same distance. He saw something that interested him. It was too far and the night was too dark to be sure.

He assumed he couldn't prevent his image from being picked up on the security cameras. All he could do was to hope that nobody in the house was up at three A.M. watching the monitors. Since he'd been here for a few minutes without a response from the police or Spengler-Nash, he decided to take the risk of moving closer. He adjusted his mask to be sure it covered as much of his face as possible, pulled his hat brim down, and bent low to advance. The chimney was wide and tall, and when it came down to the level of about six feet, it jutted out on both sides, presumably because the fireplace inside the building was large.

Sealy leaned closer and touched the brick structure. He had been right: set into the outside of the lower part of the chimney was a steel rectangle about three feet by two feet, with four wing fasteners to hold it in place over an opening. It was an access hatch so the fireplace could be cleaned from outside. Most of the ones he'd seen on modern houses had been only about one foot by one foot, but this chimney was older and larger, and the door was too. He tried moving the first wing fastener and found it was easy and silent, so he undid the others. He took out his pocketknife and ran the blade along the edges, inserted it, and opened the hatch. He was looking past a couple of logs resting on two andirons into a large space where a long couch and three armchairs were arranged around a Persian rug. He listened. There were no sounds—not an electronic shriek or the thud of a running footstep.

He had found a way into the Spengler house that had not been wired into the security system.

✣

He's in, Ben Spengler thought. The man had found the clean-out door in the chimney. Spengler had expected him to either try to get in through the garage, or remove one of the screens covering the vents that led into the space under the house, but the chimney clean-out was okay too. Spengler was at the desk in his master bedroom on the second floor looking at the security monitor, watching the shooter crawling out of the fireplace into the living room. In a moment the man would be directly beneath him.

This morning Spengler had been in the midst of talking Justine into sleeping at his house to stay safe when it had occurred to him that his impulse was misguided. Keeping her hidden was a necessary tactic for now, but adopting this as a strategy would make her less safe in the long run, because it kept her potential killer safe too. The best strategy wasn't to keep the killer away. It was to meet his first attempt on her life and capture or kill him.

Spengler had realized right away that a killer would be sent out to find Justine. This year there had been a dramatic rise in follow-home robberies. He had assumed at first that they were the old kind, crimes of opportunity: a group of young guys see a couple at a restaurant wearing expensive jewelry and watches, or maybe driving an expensive car—Lamborghini, Ferrari, or Bentley—and follow them. But this one was different.

Jerry and Estelle Pinsky dressed simply. Young guys like the five robbers were unlikely to have recognized Jerry from his stand-up days forty years ago, and during his writer-producer days he'd been invisible. The car he drove wasn't as fancy as the one they were driving to rob him. This crew of robbers weren't on their own. They'd been working for somebody. There was a boss behind this—somebody who could pick victims, fence stolen goods, and drain credit card accounts without getting cheated or caught—and he would want to be sure the bodyguard who had killed two of his men got killed too. That meant the man in Spengler's living room right now was probably a pro. He had been good enough to get in. Now it was time for Ben Spengler to make sure he didn't get out.

Spengler watched the man's progress on the monitor. Yes, he was definitely a pro. He took his time, crawling across the big carpet, gently touching the few feet ahead of him first to be sure there wasn't a pressure pad under it. He took the most direct route to get to the bare hardwood floor before he stood up and walked along the wall. He was clearly searching for electric eye transmitters and receptors on the walls, trying to identify them before he passed between a pair, interrupted the beam, and set off an alarm. There were a few installed in the walls and plastered over except for the lenses, but Spengler had kept those alarm circuits disarmed for the night to keep this intruder moving in the direction he wanted him to go.

Spengler had two cameras trained on the staircase, and he watched the man ascend. The man set his feet on the space between the stair runner carpet and the wall, which avoided any pressure pads underneath, and kept his weight on the side of the step that was most firmly anchored and least often used, so it didn't creak.

Spengler decided it was time to move, before the man reached the upstairs hall. He turned off the monitor and walked along the hall to the old servants' staircase, a narrow series of steps on the other end of the house from the main staircase, designed so domestic workers could come up and down without being noticed. He went down two steps and waited.

About a minute later the man reached the upstairs hall. Spengler knew enough not to come out of the stairwell to look, but he could listen. The man was walking along the corridor trying the knob of each door. He would turn the knob, push the door open, probably only enough to see the bed, and close it again. As Spengler had predicted, he must be searching for the one where Justine was sleeping, thinking that she would be behind the door that was locked. He reminded Spengler of a nonhuman predator—or maybe a half-human beast—sniffing its way through the house, trying to smell fear in the air to find its next kill. The image brought Spengler a chill along the back of his neck, and he gave his head a little shake to clear it.

He heard the killer reach the room with the locked door, which was only a few feet from the stairwell where he was crouching. Spengler listened more intently, and heard the sound of the door's slight bump against the jamb when the doorknob wouldn't turn, and then fabric sliding an inch or two on the hardwood floor as the killer knelt, and the faint hiss of the man's breathing, almost a purr to comfort himself while he prepared to pick the lock.

Spengler felt an overwhelming urge to take a step out of the stairwell and shoot the man. As he thought about this man, he couldn't help feeling rage: the man was so eager to kill Justine, that brave young woman, in her sleep. Spengler wanted to shoot, but he knew that shooting even an armed intruder like this killer from behind would strike the police as very questionable, particularly after Justine's shooting. He had to try to make a citizen's arrest before he did anything else. He also knew that if he waited it would never be this easy again. This was when he had planned to make his move. In a few more seconds the shooter would make the pins in the lock line up, turn the knob, open the door, then step inside.

Probably he would close the door behind him. It would prevent any defender of Justine's from seeing where he was at a glance, and muffle the sounds of her death if he made it close enough to cut instead of firing. Spengler heard the click. He heard a shuffling sound as the man rose to his feet, and then the same faint sliding of metal against metal as the doorknob turned. The door swung open, and then it closed. Spengler let three seconds pass while he listened for the man to emerge, then took the last step up into the hall and two steps to the door.

He reached up to slide the deadbolt he had installed near the top of the door to the locked position. He had known the killer would arrive in darkness, and would almost certainly not see a bolt above his eye level anyway. He pulled from his pocket the six-inch spike and inserted it into the hole he had drilled in the jamb near the bottom of the door, and then inserted the second spike into the hole he had drilled on the hinge side of the door. The killer was locked in the room.

Spengler turned, stepped into the servants' stairwell, and closed the door to muffle the sounds he would make while he descended the steps. He reached the hall by the kitchen, and then headed into the dining room. He opened the French door and went outside into the courtyard garden. He took his phone out of his pocket and pressed 911. When the emergency operator came on, he said in a deliberate but quiet voice, "My name is Benjamin Spengler, and I'm outside my house at 567 Roe Street. An armed man has broken into my house and is in the upstairs hallway searching the bedrooms. Please send police. I can't speak any longer or he'll hear me." He ended the call. He nodded to himself as he put the phone away. Let the cops handle the rest of this. They deserved the credit.

Leo Sealy stood by the door and counted while he strained his eyes in the dark room trying to make out what was in it before he went deeper into it. The room was the most profound darkness he'd been in since he'd arrived. He couldn't hear the sleeper's breathing, so he couldn't use it to find the bed. He guessed the quiet sleep-breaths meant he had probably not accidentally entered a man's room. He decided he had waited long enough for his eyes to adjust and they hadn't, so he started to move, taking small, slow steps toward the space where he thought the bed would be, moving his hands back and forth ahead of him to detect obstacles.

He found the bed with his knee, having already passed his hand over it without touching it. He stopped, left his knee touching the mattress so he could feel any movement, and listened, but nothing happened. He moved along the mattress clutching the knife. He would find the head-board and move his left hand slowly down from there so he could grasp a handful of her hair, jerk her head back, and bring the razor-sharp blade across her throat with his right. If her position made that impossible, he could drive the blade downward into the space under her rib cage and thrust it up to the fourth rib.

After three steps he touched the headboard. He moved his left hand downward farther and farther, and felt bare sheet. He moved the hand to the side, then down, and then ran both hands across the bed. It was empty. She wasn't here. He felt rage, frustration, and then a deep uneasiness.

He had been primed and ready to kill anybody he met in the house, but hadn't been prepared not to meet anyone. He had expected that the room where he'd find Justine Poole would be locked, and this one had been the first locked room he'd found. As he'd entered, his heart had been pounding and he could barely restrain his energy, but he had done it. He took out his phone and used the faint light of the screen to verify that this room was empty, and noticed that the screen said 3:09 A.M. He put it back in his pocket.

There would still be a couple more hours of darkness. He was realizing now that this house was an even worse place to do a job than he had expected, but he was well into it now. He'd eliminated about a dozen rooms, and there were only about two more in this main part of the building. If she wasn't in one of them, she would have to be in one of the rooms on the walkways along the courtyard.

He grasped the door handle, turned it, and pulled. The handle turned easily, but the door didn't swing inward. It didn't budge. He pulled harder. He placed his left shoe against the wooden jamb to get the force of his leg and back into it, but the door was stuck. He couldn't believe it. He began to sweat, and that made his gloves cling to his fingers. He pushed the door to loosen whatever was stuck, but that changed nothing. There must have been some malfunction in the old lock that had disconnected the knob's shaft from the piece connected with the bolt, and left it locked.

He took out his phone again and knelt to examine the hinges. He used his knife to pry the pin that held the bottom hinge up and out. There were two more hinges, and a few minutes later, he had them out. The doors in this old Spanish house were not like modern doors. These were two inches of solid oak, fitted tightly, so Sealy understood the three hinges instead of two to hold the weight. He grasped the top and center hinges and pulled, trying to wrench open the door from the hinge side. The door didn't move. Maybe he needed to turn the knob at the same time. He tried that, but it had no effect.

He moved to the window and clawed aside the blackout curtains that were keeping the darkness complete. The world was still dark, but he could make out some shapes. Outside the window was a ten-foot margin of sloping roof above the courtyard. He knew that if he triggered the alarm he would never be able to turn off the alarm system. All of the window frames were sure to be wired, but there was no piece of electronics on the ceiling above him, and that was where glass-break sensors were placed by installers. He put his face close to the glass, but couldn't see any trace of the conductive tape that alarm companies used to wire the glass in windows, so the only live trigger was the frame. He went into the bathroom, found a pile of towels, picked one the right size, took it to the window, and stuffed it into the recessed area that held the window. Then he stepped up to it, raised his foot and delivered slow, hard pressure to the center of the window pane. The glass made a popping noise and buckled outward. Sealy crouched and listened for gunshots, voices, or footsteps. When none came, he used his phone screen to look at his foot and leg, but saw no blood or cuts. He waited a few seconds, then removed the towel to look at the window. The glass had fractured into large, jagged triangular pieces, so he spread the towel on the floor and lifted the pieces out of the frame onto the towel.

⚔

Outside in the garden, Spengler stood still and listened. This intruder was more troublesome than he'd expected. He had anticipated that he'd be like most of them, who would have resorted to trying to kick the door open or fire holes in it around the lock, and when neither worked, decide his only chance was to wait for the cops to open the door from the hallway on the idiotic theory that he could shoot his way out. Now Spengler heard noises that sounded like the man was clearing glass. This was not good. He had hoped the man would stay in that room until the police arrived. He clearly wasn't going to do that. Spengler looked around him in the garden for anything he could use, but found nothing at first. Then he remembered the curtains. He opened the French door, stepped inside, and used his pocketknife to cut a length of the curtain cord. He stepped out again, coiling the cord. Now at least he would be able to hog-tie the man while he waited for the cops.

Upstairs, Sealy worked to pull out the small pieces of glass still stuck on the edges of the window by the hard, ancient putty. Then there was nothing left but the frame. He draped a second towel over the lower edge to protect him from any remaining glass, moved the only chair beside the window and crouched on it so he faced away from the window, extended one leg through the opening, then the other, then pushed off the chair to raise his upper body off the seat and walked on his hands to push the rest of him through the opening. Now he was on the roof feeling the cool night air, and it made him feel energized. He crawled a few feet to the side, then eased himself feetfirst down the sloping roof toward the edge. He had to get as low as he could. When he neared the edge he paused, keeping as much of his body in contact with the roof as possible. When he was ready, he turned so he was on his belly. He began his slow slide, moving an inch or two at a time. He felt his toes come off the roof, then his knees. Now his weight dragged him downward and he was trying to hold on to each of the ceramic half-pipes that made up the roof to slow himself. Then he was at his hips, with his feet and legs hanging. He needed to keep slowing his slide by pressing down on the roof, but he was still moving. He slid the last few inches and managed to slow his descent, then dropped. In the second of his fall, he saw there was nothing right beneath him, and prepared himself to try to land on his feet. He managed to absorb some of the shock and roll to the side like a parachutist, got up, and took two staggering steps.

He heard a calm, quiet voice behind him. "I've been waiting for you. Toss your gun on the ground. Ten feet will do." As Sealy took the revolver out of his left pocket and tossed it, he ended up facing the man. It was not possible to see him because he was somewhere in the deep shadows under the overhanging section of roof.

The man said, "Good. Lie down with your arms away from your sides." Sealy bent his knees as though to lower himself to the ground.

The phone in the man's shirt pocket came to life. There was a buzz that seemed loud in the night silence, and the screen lit up.

Leo Sealy dived to the side, pulled his semiautomatic pistol out of his right jacket pocket in midair, and fired at the lighted screen. There was a muzzle flash from the man's own gun, but the aim was high. Sealy hit the ground, fired three more rapid shots where the muzzle flash had been, and saw the man was on the ground too. He fired once more at the prone figure, and saw the man's head jerk an inch. He realized the man had probably already been dead, because he had not even tried to move. He was dead now, anyway.

Sealy hadn't forgotten Justine Poole, and he knew where she must be. He sprang to his feet, ran the rest of the way to the stairs and took them three at a time, ran along the walkway, crouched, and peered in the window. There was a lump under the covers of the bed, so he fired through the glass. The lump didn't move. He went to the door and tested the knob. It gave. It was an open door, but this time maybe it was Justine Poole's trap. He went inside low and ready to fire, but he saw no woman to kill. He kept going into the bathroom and saw he had been right. There was a plug-in night-light.

The gunfire had started the clock. Time was going by, so he had to keep moving. He pivoted on his heel, hurried to the window, and scanned the other windows overlooking the courtyard. No door had opened, no window showed light or motion. He left the room and trotted back along the walkway, staying low and moving fast as though he were under fire. Justine Poole could have been hiding in a different room and now be somewhere on the grounds aiming at him.

As he ran across the courtyard to snatch up his revolver, he came near the body again. He had heard no sound on his run, so he dared to squat beside it for a second and use the light from the screen of his cell phone to look at the man's face. It was streaked with blood from his first shot, and the last had left an entry wound hidden by the hair, but he recognized the man. On an impulse he took a photograph with his phone. He looked at the screen and saw it was 4:21 A.M. He had to get moving again. He jumped to his feet and ran to the arched opening of the courtyard, climbed the gate, and dropped to the outer side.

His car was far away. He ran toward it, crossing the vast lawn of the house, then sprinted along the stone wall of the next house, which had a two-foot apron of concrete outside it that gave him a clear path. After that he veered outward to stay as far from the houses as he could. The owners of these houses had probably heard the shots. They also probably had live-in servants. He couldn't afford to have any of them see him. He had just killed Benjamin Spengler.

7

Justine woke at twelve minutes to six, when the police arrived at the Spengler-Nash office. She heard men talking, but didn't recognize the voices. She got up from the couch, pulled two of the blinds on Ben's office window apart, and saw two large male cops in suits. She had never seen police in the building before. She knew cops had been here a few times in the past nine years, when they'd come to talk to bodyguards who had reported something or had been in altercations to protect a client, but she hadn't been present.

Then she heard someone say her name. It confirmed her fear that she was the subject of the visit. She couldn't take the chance that she would miss something she needed to know, or worse, have them interrupt her when she was getting dressed, so she quickly slipped off her sweatpants and T-shirt and put on her Spengler-Nash outfit. It wasn't a uniform, because uniforms had insignia and names on them. Her term for it—outfit—was more accurate. It was just a pair of tight black pants and a tailored jacket of the same synthetic fabric that had two inner pockets designed to conceal a small handgun close to the body.

She opened the door and walked toward her desk, which was near the spot where the two police officers were talking to three of the night men, who were sitting in desk chairs with their bodies leaning forward. Two of them—Baker and Harris—had their heads in their hands. She couldn't identify what was going on, but Decker turned and saw her. "Justine," he said. "We just got really bad news."

Baker said, "The worst."

She felt light-headed for a half second and found herself holding the back of a chair. "What happened?" she said. "Is somebody hurt?"

Decker said, "It's Ben. The police found him at his house."

"Found him?"

"Mr. Spengler is dead," one of the cops said.

Justine looked at the officer, and he began to grow blurry, which meant the tears were starting. Of course a cop would tell her straight out. Cops were all trained to know the best way was just to spit it out and not make things into a guessing game. "How?" Her face was wet. She used her palms to smear the tears off to the sides.

"He was shot. Forensics and homicide people are there now. He had a gun, and it's been fired. That's about all we know yet."

Justine shook her head. "Really bad news" didn't cover this. There were no words for this.

"Do any of you have any idea why this would happen now?"

Justine looked at the three night men. "Didn't any of you tell them?"

Baker said, "They just got here."

Justine turned to the two cops and said, "I think this is about me."

"Why would this be about you?" the cop said.

"The night before last Ben was keeping an eye on Jerry and Estelle Pinsky, and noticed there was a carload of young guys circling the restaurant where they were. Ben knew I would probably be ending my assignment, so he called and told me to wait at the Pinsky house in case it was a follow-home. You don't know about this? Ben and I were in the Mid-Wilshire station for hours answering questions about what happened."

"Even if you were, can you tell us again?"

"I drove over there, parked in back to hide my car, and made sure nobody was waiting for the Pinskys. When the Pinskys arrived, the carload of robbers pulled into their driveway behind them and got out to rush them. I turned on my tactical flashlight and told them to stop. They had guns, fired at the light, and I shot two of them. At least one of the other three fired at me, so I ducked and ran, then called the police from outside the gate. Ben and the police arrived within about a minute of each other. The three ran, and the police caught and arrested them. One of the two I shot was dead, and the other died in the hospital."

"And you think this was the motive for Mr. Spengler's murder?"

"Yesterday, Ben Spengler warned me somebody would want to take revenge on me for shooting the two robbers. He wouldn't let me work and he wanted me to stay at his house last night, in case somebody connected with the robbers came looking for me at my place. When I told him I thought I'd be safer here surrounded by the rest of the staff, he said I should sleep in his office. If only I had just stayed at his house, at least it would have been both of us against whoever did this. He wouldn't have been there alone."

The other cop was older, and he had gray hair and sad eyes that looked sympathetic. "You all seem to be hit pretty hard by this. I take it Mr. Spengler was a good boss?"

"Hell yes," said Decker.

"More than that," Harris said. "A friend."

"An older friend, like a coach or an uncle that makes you want to be like him," Baker said. "He taught us how the job was done, and he was out there with us when something went wrong or we were short a man, or sometimes like this last time, when it was old clients who liked having the boss take care of them."

Justine said, "He said that the people who were behind the robbery would be looking for me. I think he was right, and they went to his house to find me, but found him instead."

"Were you and he especially close friends?"

Justine decided to pretend this wasn't just a way of asking if she'd been sleeping with the boss. "He was especially close with all the people he trusted to protect a client. He needed to be sure he knew you. But I don't think I was closer than anybody else."

She saw one cop's eyes were on her and the other was looking only at the others, searching for some sign that they thought she was lying.

A third plainclothes cop, this one older than the others, came from the communications room, where he must have been asking the same sorts of questions. He said to the others, "They want us at the scene."

Justine watched the other two follow him into the hallway and then walked to the window and looked out. After about a minute she saw the three cops emerge from the building and get into a plain blue car that was parked at the red "No Parking" curb in front of the building and drive off.

She turned away and looked at the three men from the night shift. She cleared her throat so her voice would be loud and strong and wouldn't break. "I'm so sorry," she said. "If I'd guessed, I would have been there instead of here."

8

It took a moment for Leo Sealy to wake and see where he was. His phone rang again. He snatched it up and looked at the screen. The caller's number meant nothing to him, so he considered declining the call, but he couldn't do that in the middle of a job. He pressed the green oval. "Hello?"

"Leo." It was Mr. Conger. "There's something wrong with your phone. It sounded like it rang four times, but then when you picked it up we didn't get connected. Or maybe you should set it louder."

"Yeah, the settings sometimes change when I carry it around in my pocket. Sorry."

"Get one that doesn't do that," Mr. Conger said. "Or check that the ring is on before you set it down."

Sealy sat up in bed. "I'll be more careful."

"You got Spengler last night, didn't you?"

"I had to," Sealy said. "I know that wasn't the job, but the woman wasn't at her condo, so I went to his house to see if she was staying there."

"I can guess she wasn't, since they only found one body. It's all over the news. You got Benjamin Spengler."

"Yeah. He fired and I fired. Now we're both home, but I'm the only one taking phone calls."

Mr. Conger chuckled. "I can't tell you how good this is. I didn't ask for this, but after it happened, I realized what I got. Ben Spengler was the big fish. This Justine is just some girl who was working for him. What I hired you for was to make sure everybody knew that when somebody messes with one of my crews, I don't just shrug it off."

Sealy felt uneasy. Mr. Conger sounded satisfied, but Sealy had yet to earn the second half of the money for killing the girl. That wasn't small change. He said, "I'm still after the girl. I just had to get some sleep. I was up all night."

"I understand. What you did last night bought us some time. The three guys who are sitting in cells right now are going to get asked about who they think did this to Spengler. That will tell them that I'm not forgetting about their dead friends, and I won't forget about them either."

"I'm glad that getting Spengler will help."

"It will," Mr. Conger said. "It already has." Sealy heard a tightness in Mr. Conger's voice that meant he was smiling. "When my guys hear about it, they're going to think if I got Spengler, a guy with seventy bodyguards, I can get anybody. And I still want the girl. Happy hunting."

"Thank you."

Mr. Conger hung up, and Sealy wondered if Mr. Conger had heard his last words, but he knew Mr. Conger didn't care what other people said. He cared what he said.

Sealy swung his legs off the bed, stood up, pulled the covers tight and tucked them in, folded the sheet over the blanket the width of his spread fingers, fluffed up his pillow, and gave the blanket one extra tightening tug so it was perfect and he wouldn't be tempted to return to it. He showered, shaved, brushed his teeth, and dressed in clean clothes. He loaded his laundry into the washing machine, made sure it included the clothes he had worn last night, and started the wash. He had handled his revolver and fired his semi-auto pistol several times, so he had probably covered himself with powder residue and heavy metal traces. It occurred to him to add the running shoes he had been wearing, so he paused the machine and tossed them in too.

⚔

The next step was to get a look at Justine Poole, but he hadn't found her yet, so he would have to try other approaches. He was fairly sure that the second name on the condominium and car ownerships had to be her mother. No doubt she had helped her with the down payments, and who else would do that? He opened his laptop and typed in the name Anna Kepka.

There was a long column of entries, each referring to someone with that name. The entries were in the hundreds, but few of them included a picture. Maybe one of them shared a resemblance with Justine Poole, but there was no way to know which one. None of them had the same address as Justine Poole, which seemed to bolster his view that she had just given her some money, and lived somewhere else—maybe with her second husband, Mr. Kepka. He couldn't find a local address for any of them. By the time he had read each of the entries, he felt frustrated and tired of the search and eager to know if any news of Justine Poole had come up.

He turned on the television and scanned the morning news shows he'd recorded. There was footage of the house where he had killed Benjamin Spengler, now in bright sunlight and crawling with cops and forensics technicians. He watched and listened, but the television reporter knew nothing but the name and the company.

His conversation with Mr. Conger had focused his mind. He felt more eager about killing the woman now than he had before. He wanted to get back into the hunt.

⋆⋆⋆

It was just after one o'clock when Ben Spengler's brother and sister emerged from the elevator and walked into the Spengler-Nash office. Justine had never seen them before, but they looked like Spenglers. The man was tall and straight like Ben, but he had a flat stomach and thin arms, and that was not like his brother. Ben had always carried more weight—a bit of a rounded belly, probably from sitting in the office on the phone or in the car watching over a long succession of clients, all the time drinking coffee and eating snacks that came in shiny bags and turned his fingertips orange. He'd looked as though he had not been in full sunlight in years. The brother had an even tan, which looked good with his slightly overlong graying hair. The sister had hair that was between light blond and white. She was tall too, fashionably thin with ice-blue eyes and a mouth that seemed to have been pouting for decades.

Justine was at her own desk near Ben's office, going through some of the fragmentary staffing plans Ben had left for this evening's jobs and acknowledging some of the "Here I am" calls and texts from the people out on the day shift. She had been crying on and off for three hours, and now her throat hurt, but she had forced herself to feign a normal voice when she was talking to colleagues. She knew somebody had to go and greet the siblings, and she happened to be the only one who could see them at the moment. She kept the channel open and the radio hot on the desk, but took her phone with her as she stood up and walked to the threshold of Ben's office.

She tried to manage an expression that showed sympathy, but she suspected it was closer to the grief she felt. "Hello," she said. "Are you—"

The male sibling interrupted her. "I'm Walker Spengler, and this is my sister Evelyn Hawley. We're Benjamin's family."

"I thought you must be. I'm terribly sorry for your loss. Ben was a great friend and teacher to all of us. We miss him so much already. I'm Justine Poole." She held her right hand out.

Walker Spengler and Evelyn Hawley looked at each other, and then focused on her face. They didn't seem to see her hand.

Justine extended the movement of her hand to sweep in the direction of the outer office. "Would you like to meet some of the other employees? We all loved and admired Ben so much, and I'm sure they'd like to meet you."

Walker looked at his sister, then said, "Yes. I suppose this would be the time to start. Assemble the others in the outer office."

"All right," Justine said. She walked out across the big common office toward the hall that held the ready room and the communications room. She was thinking about Evelyn Hawley. She apparently preferred to make her brother the barrier between her and the distasteful world. Walker's tone was imperious, but before he said anything he looked at his sister for—what? Permission, or possibly agreement. Justine guessed that Evelyn Hawley was in her late fifties, but she'd had some work done to the skin around her eyes, chin, and forehead. Justine had spent much of her working life protecting women, and most of the women who could afford to hire Spengler-Nash had endured the same repairs in their early fifties. The doctors must have been the best, but Justine wondered if there might have been accidental damage to some facial nerves or an off-target Botox injection, because Evelyn Hawley's face was almost without expression.

Justine stuck her head into the ready room, where the dozen men and women who were about to leave for afternoon assignments had been making last-minute preparations and checking for updates on clients' plans. She said, "Ben's brother and sister are here, and they want to meet everyone in the main office."

The group got up and headed for the glass-enclosed office that had always been Ben's. Justine kept going to the communication room, where Lydia and Stephanie were monitoring the computers and phones and Mick was on the radio. When she gave them the same message, Stephanie stood up, but Lydia said, "I need a minute to forward every-thing to a front office phone."

"You can use the extension for the phone on my desk," Justine said. "It's close enough to the front of the room so we'll hear it."

Mick turned a switch on his console, picked up a handheld radio, and joined the others as they hurried to the open bay, where the first group had gathered. They were all taking their turns shaking hands and saying the usual inadequate formulas of condolence.

When they were assembled, Walker Spengler said, "Thank you all for your kind words about our brother. We wanted to let you know who we are, and not leave everyone in a vacuum, wondering whether there was a future for Spengler-Nash. We're going to retain the business our family has had since 1922—at least for now. For you that means keeping things on a business-as-usual basis in spite of disruptions. We'll begin the search for a properly qualified person to replace our brother as soon as we can." He glanced at the clock on the wall and then surveyed the group. The bodyguards among them were dressed in clothes intended to make them fit into a variety of activities, from afternoon parties to airline travel. "I can see you all have things to do, so I won't delay you any longer."

The group began to disperse and he and his sister exchanged a look. "Oh, Miss Poole. Can we talk for a minute?"

She stood still. "Of course."

He and his sister went into Ben's office and Justine followed. Walker paused to close the door behind them while Evelyn sat behind Ben's desk, her hands folded in front of her. Walker stepped to the end of the desk and remained standing with his arms folded across his chest.

Justine waited.

Evelyn looked up at Justine.

"Justine," she said. "May I use your first name?"

"Sure," Justine said. She didn't say, "I'd like you to," because it implied a level of friendliness, and nothing about this felt friendly.

"As you must know, we've spent the better part of the past twelve hours learning all about what happened to our brother Benjamin." Her forehead remained an empty, unreadable surface, but she was able to make her eyebrows lift slightly as she stared into Justine's eyes.

She went on. "It's a tragic story. Everybody has lost. I don't pretend to know what your relationship with our brother was. I'm sure you sincerely miss him and feel grateful that he went to such an extreme as to lose his own life in an effort to divert your enemies away from you after your shooting."

"He was a special person," Justine said. She resisted the impulse to correct Evelyn. She had seen Ben be heroic a dozen times. The fact that she had risked her life to back up Ben this time didn't change who Ben was. Explaining the nuances and complications of the bodyguard business to a woman like this was probably impossible and would have been pointless. And yes, Ben had probably gotten killed because the killer had been looking for Justine.

Evelyn said, "You'll be getting a substantial payment as soon as the technicalities are taken care of. There will be papers to sign first, of course. Lawyers insist on that."

"Papers? What papers?"

"Well, you and Benjamin were close. You're an attractive younger woman. You will have to agree not to file any lawsuits against his estate or the family company."

"Why would I do that?"

"A common law relationship, or damages for his pressuring or coercing you. In your profession I'm sure you've protected people who have been sued, and you know the sort of thing."

"We didn't have that kind of relationship," Justine said.

"I'm relieved for you when I hear that. It spares you so much pain," Evelyn said. She looked up at Walker, a silent communication passing between them. "Legal is preparing a standard NDA, to assure our clients that their privacy is protected, as well as any company proprietary information. The lawyers will be calling you to a brief meeting. Once you sign the papers you can go home with your severance check."

Justine stood staring at them for a second. "Don't do this."

Walker and Evelyn exchanged another glance. Evelyn tried to assume an expression of motherly concern. "Surely you understand that we have a responsibility that we never wanted or asked for. Your continued presence here puts our employees at risk—exactly the same risk that our brother faced. How can we expect them to take that on?"

Justine said, "I'm asking you not to fire me."

"We don't want to fire you. That's why we're presenting you with this alternative. You get to walk away with a generous severance package and tell outsiders anything you want—that you're taking time to mourn Benjamin, that you're rethinking your future goals, that you're going back to school. Then you become silent. It will be a couple of years before people realize you must have decided not to come back. It's a very gentle, quiet process."

Justine said, "The police are still investigating what happened at the Pinskys' house. What I did was the only thing possible, but when two people get shot it's a very big thing, and the authorities need time to learn everything about it. If I'm suddenly no longer with Spengler-Nash, no matter what we say, the police will interpret this as a termination. They, and I, think of a professional bodyguard protecting a client with a gun as a regrettable but legal act—protecting others is one form of self-defense—but any shooting can easily slide from self-defense to manslaughter. If I get fired, it will mean to them that I must have done something wrong. They can even decline to make a determination, which means this could hang over me forever."

Evelyn's gaze was bright and piercing, and it looked to Justine as though she was pleased. She said, "Well, then. This is another very strong reason to be mindful about the way your departure is handled."

Walker took his cue. "Speaking of departures, I'm sorry, but we really have to be on the move now. We've got a meeting with the funeral director." He assumed a sad half-smile. "You understand."

As Evelyn stood and followed Walker to the door, she said, "Before you leave, please don't forget to be sure your contact information is up to date. The lawyers will need to reach you for the papers and so on."

9

Justine stood by the window of Ben's office and watched the Spenglers make their way past the desks and into the hallway toward the elevators. After a few seconds she heard the *ding* and the elevator doors opening, then closing.

The early shift bodyguards had gone. They were all probably a little bit late because of the visit of the Spengler siblings. It probably wouldn't matter because the clients today were mostly the sort who liked to take their time showing up to events. She knew because she had worked with all of them on the night shift. It occurred to her that she had been strapping herself into party dresses with pepper spray, tasers, and handcuffs hidden in them since she was twenty. She was a favorite for actresses and female executives because she could accompany them into restrooms and dressing rooms, and she was a favorite for some males because she could make herself look like a date.

As she left Ben's office and walked toward her desk in the open bay, she realized that this would probably be her very last few minutes in the Spengler-Nash headquarters. She turned fully around, looking at the space and letting her eyes pick out swirls and arches in the grain of the woodwork that she had been looking at for nine years. There was no use trying to memorize the look of the old office. In a month the details would probably be smoothed out of the image in her mind anyway.

She had felt the shock of Ben's death like a devastating wound, the kind that left a person breathless and in pain, and then the deep sadness for him and—she had to admit it—for herself had taken hold of her for hours. She loved him, and he was gone, taken away from her. She had not been able to stop crying at first, and then had forced herself to stop by throwing herself into work. She had goaded herself into a manic fervor, trying to assume the tasks he would normally be doing, as though keeping his company running smoothly was keeping him in existence. It was not some magical way of not letting him die. She wasn't crazy. In keeping this day's operations on track she was preserving his work, his accomplishments, intact. This was the only favor and tribute she could give or he could receive. That had ended with the visit of his brother and sister. She hated them. She hated them so much that she knew she shouldn't sit here thinking about them.

She tried to remember why she had decided to take such an outlandish career. She had been nineteen, going to the California State University at Northridge, chosen because it was close. She was poor. Her mother and grandmother's combined savings and the surplus they could produce by denying themselves more than she could bear to know, together with the student loans she was piling up, kept her there. She had needed a summer job that paid more than she had been making as a waitress and barista. She had seen the Spengler-Nash ad for someone to do research and reporting. She remembered wondering what that meant, but the pay looked great to her after the jobs she'd had for the years of high school and college. This might be a chance to work harder and do better, so she was interested.

She sent in her application, got an interview with Benjamin Spengler, and listened to his description of the job. It was office work, eight A.M. to six P.M. five days a week. He asked the usual questions, like "Do you have your school ID on you?" She figured a security guy was supposed to be suspicious so she'd shown it to him. He'd said, "What's your major?" She'd said, "I don't have to declare one until fall."

He'd asked some questions she was pretty sure he wasn't supposed to ask. "Do you get offended if a man where you work asks you out?"

"Only if he's an asshole," she said.

"How do you tell?"

"If it's the second date, I'll know. Or if he's cheating on somebody, touching me when I don't want him to, the usual stuff."

"Do you have a job now?"

"I've got two now—one at a restaurant on weekends and one at Northridge serving coffee."

"When does that one end?"

"When school ends on May 10."

"What will you do if this job starts April 25?"

"Do all three until May 10. I can shift the Northridge job to weeknights."

"You're hired. You start May 11."

The job started and it didn't evolve over time. It changed in abrupt shifts. One day they needed an extra female on a job, and she was called away from her desk, given a nice outfit and a radio, brought to a giant wedding, and told to watch for crashers. Another day the martial arts sensei the company retained came to start another round of classes, and she was told to join in to fill out the class and do her regular work later.

The Spengler-Nash office was in downtown LA, so getting there brought its own set of problems, a question of driving her mother to work early and then heading south on whichever route was least jammed with traffic, or starting on foot, then making the transitions among the tangle of bus routes to Broadway.

She did the job for two more summers. When she came to work the second summer, Ben Spengler said, "Haven't you turned twenty-one yet?"

"I have. About a week and a half ago."

"Happy birthday. You start firearms training on Thursday."

"As what? A target?"

"Good question. Here's the first thing you need to know about guns. If you need one, the job is crap."

"Even this job?"

"Especially this one."

Justine liked the agents at Spengler-Nash. They all seemed to be ex-somethings—ex-cops, ex-military, ex-intelligence—so the ones who told stories had good stories, and even the ones who didn't tell stories knew things they could teach her. She liked the jobs that she increasingly got, going to fancy parties at night and spending days on yachts and golf courses and horse trails. And as she worked, the company trained her. She learned defensive driving and became adept at evading pursuers and spinning a car to change directions. She learned the private, invisible ways that important, vulnerable people entered and left certain buildings in Los Angeles, how to get access and how to guide clients through them without attracting attention.

When she graduated from Northridge, she had to scrounge extra tickets from classmates to let six people from Spengler-Nash see it happen, and two more were there working because the commencement speaker was a client. The following Monday, Ben Spengler had her on the schedule to work.

She stayed. She knew that this was a detour from the route her life should be taking, but she was making good money and she was in her early twenties and change was always far away; the sunny days all seemed endless and beautiful, and the supply of them was infinite. Her nights were spent in the company of glamorous, intelligent people, and the supply of them seemed infinite too. She went with them to events that she could never get admitted to alone. People liked her and praised her, and there seemed to be no reason to do anything else.

She'd known even at the beginning that it was time to leave, but she had not decided what to do or where to go. She had been accepted to graduate programs at three universities, but had not returned any of the enrollment forms sent with her acceptances. She had not told herself that she was making a permanent, lifelong decision to stay at Spengler-Nash, only that the idea of rushing away from what she was doing in Los Angeles to an unfamiliar city to face more years of earnest drudgery seemed insane. It was always too soon.

She knew that she was not being entirely honest with herself about the other reason she had let it go on so long. When Ben's awful brother and sister had grilled her about her relationship with Ben, she had lied. She had not had a romantic relationship with Ben, that much was true. But the rest of the truth was that if he had given things an ever-so-slight push in that direction, she would have. When she had started working at Spengler-Nash during college breaks, she had been disappointed and bored with the male students she had dated. Even the graduate students seemed to still be boys, and Ben was something else, something she'd mostly imagined, because she'd grown up in an all-female household—a reliable, strong, and good man. The contrast was clear and vivid, demonstrated before her eyes every day.

Soon the fantasy of a relationship with him had died from neglect. A few times in later years during odd moments, or when she had just broken up with a boyfriend or Ben had done something that she particularly admired, she would think of the possibility again. As she approached thirty, the difference in their ages seemed to her to matter less. They were both adults, and he'd always treated her like one, but he had never let things go beyond business. It occurred to her that the one person she would have turned to in such a disaster—if a protector, teacher, and friend had been murdered—was Ben. Who did this to him? There were people at Spengler-Nash who had worked in law enforcement. She could use them to help her find out.

No, she couldn't. Justine stared down at her desk. She had just been told by the new owners that Spengler-Nash was over for her, and she was expected to stay away. As she opened the drawers and packed the few possessions that she'd kept at work into a box that had held printer paper, her mind revisited the central facts. Ben had said she was in danger, and now she was alone. The police still had her Glock 17 pistol. The Glock actually belonged to the company, so the police would probably never release it to her. She couldn't sleep in the office again tonight, and Ben's house was now a crime scene.

She picked up the box and walked across the large room full of desks to the hallway. She stopped at the doorway to the communication room and stuck her head in. The two dispatchers on duty, Dave and Cindy, had earphones on, and they looked busy. She called out, "I'm leaving." They looked up and saw her, but both were listening to the constant chatter of updates from the on-duty bodyguards. They gave friendly smiles and waved, still listening to the electronic chatter.

Justine had an urge to say, "No, you don't understand. I meant forever." Then she thought, *Why?* She turned and walked through the ready room, smiled at the people coming in from the locker rooms, and responded to their "See you tomorrow" promises with smiles and nods.

She kept going to the elevators, rode one down to the underground garage, put the box in the trunk of her car beside her overnight bag, and stared at it for a moment. It occurred to her that when she got it home, she was going to wonder why she had bothered to take any of the things in it. She saw the trash can in the place where it always was, picked up the box, held it over the can, turned it over, and dumped the collection of old hair ties, half-used pencils, dried-up pens, sticky notes, rubber bands, paper clips, old hairbrushes, out-of-date schedules and calendars, and other by-products of office work. She considered breaking down the cardboard box to throw it away too, but instead left it intact beside the can. It could still be useful to somebody who still worked here. She got into her car and drove out of the garage.

She glanced into the rearview mirror as she pulled away and saw the old five-story brick Spengler-Nash building one more time. She remembered Ben telling her, "LA is a place where everything is for sale and about to get torn down and replaced. Every building is a placeholder for the next building. The only exceptions are City Hall and Spengler-Nash."

She felt as though she was waking from a long dream to find that Ben Spengler, the reason why she had ever come to Spengler-Nash, the man who had kept the dream going, was gone. There was no Spengler-Nash without him, and now she was alone and in trouble. For the first time since she was a child, she began to feel afraid.

Could she go to the police and ask for some kind of protection? They would probably relish the irony after all the clients she had protected. She couldn't do it anyway. She would have to tell them that the reason she needed help was that she'd been fired, so her former colleagues couldn't help her. That would make the cops think she must have been in the wrong when she'd fired her weapon at the two robbers. It would also let them know she was no longer working in the profession. That would void her reason for a gun permit, and if she had no protection, she would need to have a gun.

She would have to buy one, but that was going to be tricky. The state of California required a gun buyer to prove residence and had a ten-day waiting period before she could take possession of the weapon. After the ten days she would have to accomplish the very dicey business of substituting the new gun on her carry permit, which was borderline fraudulent to begin with. Virtually no carry permits were approved in Los Angeles County, but it was legal to carry in Los Angeles if a person had a permit issued in another county. Spengler-Nash's employees who were armed had permits based on their supposed main residence at a ranch the company owned in Kern County. She would have to lie, change nothing on official paperwork, and keep the permit she had.

To Justine's growing uneasiness was added the maddening knowledge that being unarmed was her own fault, another proof that she had been asleep instead of anticipating what could happen. Many of the body-guards she'd worked with—especially the men—owned more than one pistol. They liked guns, some of them maybe too much.

Justine wanted to drive home to her condominium, but she knew it would be insane not to begin dealing with her vulnerability immedi-ately. She drove to Burbank and parked near the gun store where she had bought ammunition and gun cleaning supplies a number of times. She walked in and picked out a man about sixty behind the counter. She said, "I would like to buy a Glock 17."

"May I see some identification, please?"

She gave him her driver's license to supply a government-issued ID, and her car registration because they were both in the name she was born

with, Anna Sophia Kepka, and had the same address, and then filled out
the forms he gave her on the glass counter. She used her Anna Kepka
credit card to pay the $625 plus tax for the pistol and added in the cost
of two fifty-round boxes of 9 x 19-millimeter ammunition. She left her
phone number so the store could call her when the government clear-
ance came through so she could pick up her purchases.

When she left the store and got into her car, she felt a bit less panicky
because she had done something in her first hour out of the office. Her
mind instantly reminded her she would be stupid to soothe herself with
such a small step. She was still unarmed and about to drive toward her
home, which was certainly no safer than Ben Spengler's, and a hell of a
lot smaller. She sat in the driver's seat and studied each of the cars parked
within her sight, paying particular attention to the ones in her mirrors.
Then she started her engine and pulled out, her eyes flicking back to her
mirrors long enough to be sure none of the cars pulled out to follow.

10

Leo Sealy drove to Westwood, partly because it was nowhere near his home or his destination, so having his picture on security footage and receipts in his pocket might actually be helpful. He parked in the municipal parking structure on Broxton. When he walked out of the parking structure, he looked at the spot where he wanted a restaurant to be and the Broxton Brewery was there, so he went in to eat dinner.

Looking so hard for Justine Poole was turning Sealy into a nocturnal creature once again. He'd always found it safest and most comfortable to do his killing at night, and he hoped that this night was going to be another profitable one. But where was Justine Poole? She hadn't been to her condo, and she hadn't been in Benjamin Spengler's mansion, so where was she?

He thought about what he would be doing if he were Justine Poole. There were two leading possibilities. One was to get out of Los Angeles, and the other was to stay and be hard to find. He had not found anybody he could identify as her family yet. Looking for Anna Kepka had been fruitless. There were also thousands of Pooles all over the country, and he had no reason to connect any of them with her either. She was probably too sensible to go and hide with family anyway, because staying with them would ultimately make finding her easier, and make killing them necessary. Killing Benjamin Spengler had bought Sealy some time, but it almost certainly had alerted Justine Poole to the fact that a professional was coming for her next. He was fairly sure she would stay in LA, but try to be invisible.

If she had been working at Spengler-Nash she must know Los Angeles well, and that meant she knew places she could go where she wouldn't be easy to spot or to get close to. Her profession also made her potentially challenging in other ways. The personal security business was mostly about keeping drunken fans away from celebrities and about smoothing the way for businessmen whose time was worth a lot of money, but sometimes clients were people with real enemies, so she would be in the habit of keeping her eyes open and recognizing who was harmless and who wasn't.

He guessed that she would be skittish tonight, and very watchful. If he were Justine Poole, he would stay where he had a feel for things and knew people. A benefit of her job was that many of the people she knew carried guns. She would probably be staying with a friend from work or a group of them. When it was late enough, he finished his dinner, paid for his food, and went to get his car. He put on his baseball cap and KN95 mask, drove down the ramp onto Broxton, and headed downtown.

He was going to watch the changing of the shifts at Spengler-Nash. The eight P.M.-to-five A.M. had to be her regular shift if she had been on duty the night of the attempted robbery. He still had not seen a picture of Justine Poole, but he thought he probably could pick her out. He expected she might be good at sneaking out of the place at the end of her shift, but he would find her because the others would show her to him by trying to protect her.

Sealy followed his rule of not driving past the place where he intended to commit a crime, even when he was driving a car with stolen plates. Security cameras were everywhere. He parked one street away, walked between two buildings, and waited in the dark space across the street from Spengler-Nash.

He watched the eight o'clock shift arriving. They drove into the entrance to an underground parking lot, then disappeared down a ramp. It was hard to see drivers well, but some of them were women.

At eight he knew she was probably inside. The people in her specialty, the ones who went out to guard clients, would be leaving on assignments soon. He couldn't be sure that she would be going out on assignments so soon after Spengler had gotten himself killed. She might be stuck at a desk while she waited for things to cool down or get worse. He needed to get a different angle to watch the bodyguards leaving. He walked down the sidewalk from the building and stopped just around the first corner near the traffic signal so he could study each car that passed. Four of the cars that went by were nearly identical black SUVs with the Bentley logo on them. The drivers, male and female, wore the same black outfit. He couldn't see who else was in the cars, but he guessed that they were all on their way to an event or events where the security was supposed to be visible and substantial, but still upscale. There were other cars that seemed chosen to go unnoticed. The bodyguards were alone or in pairs, driving cars that seemed to be personal and ordinary, practically invisible in a city with three million cars. His attempt to spot someone who had to be Justine Poole failed. He headed back toward the building.

As he walked, he studied the buildings near the Spengler-Nash office. The headquarters space was on the fifth floor, so he needed a higher vantage to look down into the fifth-floor windows. There were three buildings that were tall enough, but he saw problems that would preclude his using any of the three. One was a bank, so it would have all of the best technology installed to keep out people like him. The second was a fancy apartment building, so the only entrance to the elevators and stairs was through a single lobby with twenty-four-hour security guards and doormen, also there to keep out people like him. The third was too far away from the Spengler-Nash building, and the apartment building blocked the view from there. A single clean kill with a rifle shot through her office window was not practical this time.

Sealy returned to his car and drove back toward his apartment to wait for Justine Poole's shift to end, so he could watch her and her colleagues emerge from the parking garage and head home. He hoped to pick her out immediately, but he knew now that spotting her wouldn't be that easy. He would have to look for a twenty-nine-year-old woman who left with another person, and follow them to a house or apartment. If it was two women, he would see which one used a key to open the door, and kill the other one. If it was more than two people, he would ignore the one with the key and shoot as many of the others as he could before they could scatter.

At four A.M. he returned downtown to the Spengler-Nash building. His parking space on the next street was still empty when he arrived. After a few minutes watching he began to see morning shift people arriving. Each time a car arrived, the iron gate on the entrance rose to admit it. Spengler-Nash was obviously on a twenty-four-hour schedule, and it made sense that shifts overlapped, so if a bodyguard on a job needed help there would be plenty of people to send. But this increased the number of people and cars in the garage during the overlap, and it gave him his chance. He watched for a few more seconds, then got out of his car and walked toward Broadway, the street where Spengler-Nash was. He crossed the street half a block away so he could approach the entrance near the left side while the morning shift cars entered on the right side. He walked to the entrance, pivoted to the left and walked along the inner wall to an aisle where every space was taken, and knelt down to tie his shoe beside a car. The people arriving who might have noticed a man on foot on the other end of the garage parked their cars and disappeared into the elevators.

He saw the first members of the night shift come out of an elevator. They were both middle-aged men, one of them a tall, athletic-looking Black man with short gray hair. He wore a gray sport coat that was slightly looser than the current style, and Sealy supposed it was to conceal the gun in his shoulder holster. The other man looked to Sealy like the type of prey he had at first assumed he'd be after. This one had dark, thinning hair and a mustache. He leaned from side to side as he maneuvered his paunchy body from the elevator to his car. Everything about him said he was a retired cop, probably one with a leg injury.

Sealy ducked into the emergency stairwell and climbed. He ran up the stairs two at a time, and arrived at a door marked "5" quickly. He was breathing hard, but he controlled this, taking deep breaths in through his nose and out through his mouth for only about thirty seconds before his breathing was silent. He opened the door a crack and looked toward the elevators.

Both elevators were stopped on the fifth floor filling up with another load of night-shift people going home. What he was doing was risky, but if he got even a brief look at Justine Poole's face and followed her to the address where she was staying, she was as good as dead. And taking risks was what Mr. Conger was paying him for.

People came through the hallway and into the elevators. Some wore clothes that Sealy could only think of as disguises—garments designed to help them fill a role. One man wore a tuxedo, another wore a sweatsuit that said "University of Pennsylvania" on it. Four men wore black synthetic jackets and pants with a lot of zippered pockets, and two women in cocktail dresses clutched small purses as they headed for the elevator on high heels. Both of them were older than twenty-nine, he judged—too old to be Justine Poole. The elevator doors closed, and while the next bunch gathered to wait for it to come back up, he had more time to study them in full, bright light and listen to their talk.

Sealy kept watching and evaluating. He rejected the males and, one by one, the women wearing costumes. After a few minutes he began to feel the urgency of picking one. He couldn't wait until they were all gone to find her. Already the stream of people was starting to thin out. He began to think he might have missed her. Then he realized he might have misinterpreted their tactic.

If they really wanted to protect her, they might be waiting until everyone was gone instead of bringing her out early. Maybe all of the first people out were, in a sense, decoys. Somewhere behind the darkened windows on the ground floor one of the staff could be watching for somebody like him to make a move and reveal himself. Maybe his best countertactic now was to outwait them.

It took a great deal of self-discipline to stand in the stairwell watching through a half-inch open space in a nearly closed door. Several times he tried to guess which of the people who had already left had been the one. He had also guessed that Justine Poole and her friend would get into the same car. Maybe that had been his mistake.

Then he saw three women, all wearing the black uniforms, emerge from a doorway and head to the elevators. They talked to each other in quiet, friendly tones, but he couldn't make out what they were saying, except for an occasional phrase or single word. It was like eavesdropping on a conversation in a foreign language. Then one of them, a woman about forty, said, "Justine."

At first he wasn't sure, but then all three of them looked behind them as though to see if anyone else had overheard. Just then the elevator arrived, and one of them tugged the one who had spoken into it while the third pushed a button in the elevator and the door closed.

Sealy spun and descended the stairs as quickly as he could, grasping both railings to hoist himself up and vault down four or five steps at a time. When he reached the garage level, he saw the three women walking away from the elevator. He took out his cell phone, steadied it by leaning on a pillar and began taking pictures, about three a second.

They walked to the same gray car. He memorized the shape, height, and walk of the woman heading for the driver's side, and when she opened her door and the dome light went on, her face. She had just eliminated herself in his guessing game. Justine Poole would not be the one to do the driving. The second woman got into the passenger seat. She looked about the right age, but she was the one who had said "Justine" upstairs. If it was her own name, she wouldn't say it. The third got into the back seat, and she looked as though she could be more or less the right age too. She bent down and picked up something from the floor, put it on her lap and looked inside. It was about the size of a gym bag, but he couldn't see it for long because she shut the door and the dome light went out. She was the one, he decided. The one who would need an overnight bag was the one who was staying with friends to be out of sight.

The car started and the driver pulled out of the entrance and turned right. Sealy hurried to get out before the iron gate could close and kept going across the street and down the alley, got into his car, and drove to the next corner, and then made the turn onto the street where the gray car had gone.

11

Sealy followed the car with the three women in it from a distance of about two hundred yards. At 5:15 in the morning the traffic was not heavy enough to hide in. It was still early enough so cars had their headlights on, and that would keep the women from getting a good view of the shape and color of his car, and his lights gave him a better view of theirs. There was a round decal in the lower center of the back window and another reflective one on the left rear bumper. Those would help him distinguish their car from any other small gray cars if he lost sight of it briefly.

He studied the back of the car with a vague notion of pulling up into the blind spot in the right rearside with his window open and firing a shot or two through the head of the woman in the back seat. This stretch of road wasn't wide enough to make that maneuver, and he couldn't see far enough ahead to predict a wider stretch.

He watched their car pass under a traffic signal just as it turned red. He slowed down and watched their car diminishing ahead as he completed his stop. He looked to both sides and didn't see any approaching cars near enough to hit him, so he accelerated after them, and kept accelerating to get the women's car in sight again. He didn't see it, so he stepped harder on the gas pedal and watched for the gray car to separate itself from the stream of cars while it turned to the left or right. As long as it didn't turn, he would catch it.

When the next traffic signal turned red ahead of him, he simply went through the intersection. His luck held, and a minute later he saw the women's car veer into the left turn lane, its left taillight blinking. He slowed to keep from catching up. As soon as the woman made the left turn, he made a quick left at the corner before theirs where there was no traffic signal, sped to the first intersection, made a right turn there, pulled over, and waited on that short block with his headlights off until he saw the small gray car go past, and then followed.

It was only a few blocks later that the gray car swung into the parking lot behind an apartment building. He stopped a distance away, got into the back seat of his car, reached down, pulled his AR-15 rifle from under the black mat on the floor, lowered his window, rested the rifle on the door, and looked through the scope. He watched while the car parked. He leveled the crosshairs on the car. The driver passed through his crosshairs as she got out, but he knew she couldn't be Justine Poole. The other two got out on the far side of the car. The woman in the front passenger seat stepped out from behind the car first, and he could have killed her too, but the woman he had come for wasn't visible yet. He heard a sound through his open window: another car was approaching. He pulled the rifle back and lay on the back seat while he pressed the button to shut the window. He heard the car pass by, and raised his head just enough to see it going on down the street.

He sat up and saw the three women just entering the door of the apartment building. He reached for the rifle, then saw the door swing shut. He hid the rifle, put on his medical mask and his baseball cap, and walked up the sidewalk. It was 5:20 and the windows of the apartment building were all still dark. After about forty seconds he saw the windows of an apartment on the second floor light up. He took a picture of the side of the building so he would remember which apartment it was, and then went back to his car and drove off. He knew where she was staying, and he was sure he would remember her face, her walk, her blond hair.

⇌

It was barely seven in the morning when Justine Poole approached the last turn and could see her condominium building in Santa Monica. She saw a white van parked nearby with "NEWS 7" painted on the side, and this one had its mast raised. There was a man with a television camera aimed at a woman with a microphone. She was talking to someone, and after a moment Justine recognized it was her neighbor, Ally Grosvenor, because of her familiar black-and-turquoise jogging outfit. Justine supposed the reporters must have cornered her as she emerged from the building for her early morning run. Justine kept going around the block and parked her car on the street behind the building to keep out of their sight, used her key to get in the back gate near the dumpster, and went up the back stairs to get to her condo.

On the stairs it occurred to her that when the mast on one of those vans was up, it usually meant they were transmitting to their station. She opened her door and hurried across her living room to pick up the television remote control, press the power button, and push "7." There was Ally Grosvenor. Justine turned up the sound to hear what she was saying.

"The sliding door on our balcony was open, and the weirdest thing was that leaning on the balcony railing was the pole for the pool skimmer." Justine was puzzled.

"For cleaning a swimming pool?" the reporter asked.

"Yes. You know—for getting leaves and things out. I woke up and saw it, and I asked my husband why he'd put it there. I mean, we didn't have one of our own. The building pays a pool man for that."

"And you think it had to do with somebody breaking into the building to come after your neighbor and choosing the wrong condominium?"

"What else could it be? Some criminal murdered her boss at the security company two nights ago. I understand Mr. Spengler joined her the other night after she saved Jerry Pinsky and his wife, but she was the heroine, the one who did it. I believe in coincidences like two people having the same birthday. I don't believe this was just by chance."

"And what did the police say when they came?"

"The manager let them in to do a welfare check, but Justine wasn't home. I just hope she's all right."

The camera focus narrowed to stay on the reporter's head and torso. "And that's the way we all feel about Justine Poole. We hope she's all right. Back to you, Martha."

Justine turned off the television set and walked through her condominium, looking closely at everything. The living room was the way she'd left it. She always kept it neat because a small living space felt roomier if there was no clutter. The bathroom looked the same. Her office space seemed about as usual, with its surfaces clear of clutter and dust. She opened the drawers of her desk and her filing cabinet. They were less uniformly orderly than usual. When she had opened them to get her important documents the day after the Pinsky shoot-out, she had pawed through them in a hurry. She had known she shouldn't leave things like her passport, checkbook, and IDs if she wasn't going to be staying here in her condo for a while, and she had taken bills with her so she wouldn't be late paying them. She'd packed her overnight bag, thrown papers and some other things inside, slammed drawers shut, and gone. It was impossible to tell if anybody else had opened the drawers after she had. She looked through the drawers now to see if she'd missed anything, and noticed in the back the empty blue tax folders from the past three years. Then she saw the copies she'd made of some credit cards and other papers, pulled them out, and put them through the shredder, then closed the file drawer.

She went to the sliding door of her balcony and checked the latch. It was locked, but she couldn't be sure whether it had always been locked, or if the police had locked it as a courtesy.

Her other rooms didn't seem to have been disturbed—the furniture, coat closet, kitchen cabinets and drawers all seemed as usual. She went into her bedroom. The clothes closet looked the same. The clothes in the dresser were still neatly folded and in their places. She opened the drawer of the nightstand.

The flashlight was wrong. She always had it aimed at the back of the drawer, not the front, and as close to the bed as possible so she could roll over, open the drawer, and turn it on with her left thumb without fumbling around for it. She wanted it in her left hand, to keep her right, the dominant hand, free to defend herself.

She felt a chill. The flashlight had been taken out and put back. She was beginning to think about asking the cops to fingerprint it, but then realized that she couldn't even be sure its rough, knurled surface would hold a print. And could one of the cops have picked it up? A cop looking around to see if a woman had been taken might use a flashlight to see if there were signs of a struggle—marks on a wall, tiny spots of blood, strands of long hair pulled out. But cops carried their own flashlights, so why would they open the drawer at all? She had to get out of here.

She emptied her overnight bag into the laundry basket and then repacked it, putting an envelope at the bottom with the important papers she'd taken with her when she'd packed to sleep at the office.

She went into the kitchen, put the perishables from her refrigerator that wouldn't fit in the freezer into her trash bag, and added the shredded papers. She took a quarter cup of flour from the canister, returned to her bedroom, and tossed two pinches of the flour into the air to create a thin layer on the hardwood floor that would show footprints, and did the same for the floor just inside the sliding door from the balcony.

She went down the back stairs and out past the dumpster, where she left the trash bag, and kept going to her car. She started it and drove.

The killer had been in her condo. She needed to find another place where she would be out of sight for a while. She couldn't stay with any of her friends from work. That would make finding her too easy for the killer. Even if he couldn't get a list, he could follow each of them home and make his own list. When she was two miles from her condo she pulled over and called a hotel near the airport for a reservation. She had been inside it a couple of times with business clients who needed to meet with a foreign counterpart and had found it safe. That was all that mattered now.

12

Sealy woke up feeling eager. He made his breakfast, did some exercises, and then sent the digital images of the three women from his phone to his computer so he could enlarge and study them. He saw right away that the shots were as good as he had hoped.

He had been up all night, but he had remained alert and determined. He enlarged the image of the blond woman with the overnight bag so it took up the full screen, and then zoomed in until her face was about half the picture and saved it that way. He had clear shots of her from the back and side, so he enlarged those too. It seemed likely that he would need to spot her from the side or back. There was no advantage to walking right up to her and staring her in the eyes. She should be dead before she looked in his direction.

He took up his phone again and used his fingerprint to sign into his bank account to check his balance. It was healthy. He didn't need to deposit any of the money Mr. Conger had given him. He might not need money to get this job done anyway, but if he needed it, he had it.

He went back to the computer and looked at the rest of the pictures he had taken. He had accidentally turned on the video near the end, and he pressed the arrow and watched the women finish the walk into the building. He concentrated on the blonde. He watched her closely, concentrating on the differences between her and her friends. He didn't want to shoot the wrong one.

The main difference between a professional like him and the amateurs was in the planning. No matter how much thought and effort he put into the kill, he put just as much into what would happen afterward, and how he would navigate the transformed environment—the noise, confusion, people in motion to run or hide—and disappear unidentified or, better, unnoticed.

When he was confident that he would recognize the blonde, even from a distance or in dim light, he decided to prepare himself with a fallback strategy. He printed ten copies of the best picture of her. He didn't think he was going to need them, but he liked to anticipate needs before they occurred. If he needed to, he would show people the photo and say she was his sister, who had mental troubles and had wandered off a few times before, but this time she had left her medicine behind, so he was very worried. He would give a fake name and the number of whatever burner phone he was using at the time.

In midafternoon he prepared his equipment. He chose to bring his 5.56-millimeter AR-15 in case he had a chance to get her the easy way, from cover at a distance. The rifle was small, light, and easy to break down, and no pistol had remotely comparable range and velocity. With the night scope, he would see clearly and she would see nothing but shadows and shapes.

He knew what usually happened the instant when the deafening clap of a gun's report shattered the silence. Most people nearby jumped or jerked and then swiveled their heads, looking for the place where the shot had come from. Often one of the people nearest to the dying person knelt by the body to provide help while others ran for cover. The biggest group would be paralyzed, apparently able to see everything, but unable to move.

The exceptions were the quick reactors, the few who could think clearly right away. They would instantly have a phone out, dialing 911 or trying to get a picture of him. Others would be trying to chase after him to see his license plate, or would even try to attack him. A couple of times he'd had to kill one or two of them to escape, and he was always prepared for more.

He knew how bystanders were going to behave, but almost none of them knew because they had never been to a murder before.

Sealy charged his night scope's battery, his phone's battery, and the battery of his bright tactical flashlight. He made sure his two pistols and rifle were fully loaded with rounds that he had never touched without gloves. This time his plan included a few defensive measures. He had seldom had any need to wear his bulletproof vest, but he planned to wear it tonight. The time to take out Justine Poole was in the hour before first light, when she and her friends had just ended a shift. He would choose a position that would give him the best view of the door they had used when he'd followed them home.

By early evening, he had his clothes and equipment prepared and laid out on the living room floor, and his mind was calm and resolved. He set his alarm for 3:45 A.M.

At eleven he turned on the television news. He was excited to see the newswoman standing in front of Justine Poole's condominium. "This morning I was at this condominium building, where Justine Poole lives. She's the heroic young woman who foiled the armed robbery of the beloved Hollywood couple Jerry and Estelle Pinsky two nights ago. I spoke with her next-door neighbor Ally Grosvenor. And just this evening I spoke with her again. Here's what she said."

The lighting of the next picture seemed to be evening. The woman Sealy had seen on an earlier broadcast wearing a running outfit said, "It was chilling. My husband and I knew what she did for a living, but we never expected that the job would ever be so violent."

"What about Justine herself?" the reporter said. "What can you tell us about her?"

"She's a quiet, respectable young woman—very kind and soft-spoken, and pretty as they come, but bright too. One of those girls whose smile can light up a room."

Sealy smiled. For some reason that was the cliché that somebody was sure to say about every murdered woman. This time it had come early. He hadn't even killed her yet.

The newswoman said, "And you have a picture to show us?"

"Yes."

Leo Sealy leaned forward in his seat and looked at the DVR to be sure the recording light was on.

⚜

In her hotel room near the airport, Justine was watching the interview with Ally Grosvenor. She heard herself whisper, "No, Ally. Don't!"

But there it was. In the editing they had made the picture fill the screen. It was Ally and Justine smiling at the camera, both of them in bathing suits and cover-up tops holding plates of food from the barbecue grill on the building patio. Justine's dark brown hair was wet and hanging very straight and stringy, because she had just pulled a comb through it after getting out of the pool. That picture was fresh, taken during the recent Fourth of July weekend. It was probably going to get her killed. Now the shooter would know her face.

⁂

Sealy stared, open-mouthed, at the television screen as he watched the news report scrolling rapidly backward. He stopped the image and pushed the arrow to play the segment forward, his thumb resting lightly on the pause button. When the photograph of the two women at the pool party reappeared, he stopped it, lifted his cell phone, framed the younger woman, rested his elbow on the arm of the couch, and took the picture. He took three more to be sure he had the best, steadiest version of it.

This was not the woman he had seen leaving the Spengler-Nash building. This was not any woman he had ever seen. He had been completely prepared to go out in a few hours and kill her, or all three of the women, if necessary, and none of them was Justine Poole.

13

Justine's cell phone buzzed. She stiffened as though a high-voltage shock had gone up her spine, and opened her eyes, ready to fight. She recognized the sound and rolled over in bed to reach in the direction the sound had come from, and at the same moment remembered why she was in this strange room. She had been crying about the death of Ben Spengler for most of the night until she was too tired to be able to think clearly, and she must have dozed off with her clothes on. On her phone was a text message from Janice Fortner, night shift supervisor of communications at Spengler-Nash.

Justine was pretty sure she knew what this was going to be. Janice was undoubtedly getting in touch to say she was sorry that Justine had been fired.

There had already been about a dozen of those. All had included compliments, and some had offered to serve as references. Since some of the older ones had titles like shift commander or director of international operations, the offers were not worthless, but she was not thinking about her next job. She was thinking about staying alive until the end of the week.

She noticed her phone screen said 8:21 A.M., which meant it was too late to go back to sleep anyway. She had a vague memory of noises in the hallway hours earlier, which hadn't been annoying enough to bring her to full consciousness, but now she was awake. She touched the screen to read the text. "Justine, the security cameras in the garage picked this man up watching at shift change the night after Ben was killed. Maybe trying to find you? We're not supposed to communicate with you, but you need to see these."

Justine touched the symbol of the attachment and saw the first picture appear. It showed a man trying to stay in the shadows behind the last row of parked cars. The garage was dimly lit, but the security cameras made him clear and sharp. There were other pictures, but she wanted to answer right away. She typed, "Got them. I owe you. Take no more chances. Love, etc." Janice was the last person in the world to make a mistake like using a Spengler-Nash account or a piece of company equipment for personal calls, but her job gave her legitimate access to the security recordings.

Justine looked at the first picture. She remembered that when Ben had ordered the newer cameras installed, he had said that they were to protect company clients. If someone was planning to stalk a client, one way to do it would be to track the car of the client's bodyguard to wherever the client was. Ben would never admit he was also trying to protect the bodyguards, but he was still protecting her now.

Justine looked at the next few pictures. The man was white. His hair was light, but not light enough to be blond. It was straight and short. His face had a chiseled look, maybe partly because he was straining to see something in the parking garage. His eyebrows were drawn together and jaw muscles tight. He seemed to be in his midthirties to early forties, not a kid waiting to break a car window in a lot to steal something. He was too well dressed to be down on his luck and sleeping rough—creases in his pants' legs, a dark, well-fitted jacket, a baseball cap with no logo. She realized she might very well be looking at the man who had shot Ben Spengler to death two nights ago.

She wished Janice had sent the shots to the police too. They might recognize him or have his car on a license plate reader near Ben's house. She was almost positive Janice hadn't sent them, though. Sending them would bring the police back to Spengler-Nash asking more questions, and if Ben's siblings learned she'd been in touch with Justine, she might be considered disloyal, and she'd lose her job too.

Justine looked at the pictures again to try to discern anything she could. One of the shots showed the man standing by the stairwell door. She knew that the doorway was seven feet, and he seemed to be about a foot shorter, but he was ducking his head, so he could be slightly taller than six feet when he stood up straight. He was trim, but not thin, with a flat belly and upper arms that looked thick.

In the end, what she could tell about him was all bad. He was ordinary looking for Los Angeles. He was mature but not old. He was in good physical condition and patient enough to stand for at least an hour or two doing reconnaissance. She kept thinking about him, looking at each of his pictures again and again, but there was a block between her and what she wanted to know. He might as well be a statue of a man. Nothing about who he was or what he was thinking could be gleaned from any of the pictures. She had a panicky feeling that she was letting herself waste time sitting in this hotel room while the day went by. She needed to put her phone down and get ready to use these pictures to start trying to find Ben's killer. She went into the bathroom to take a shower.

She turned on the water, let it run long enough to adjust it so she wouldn't get scalded, and stepped in to let the water soothe her. She found herself thinking about Justine Poole.

The name had happened near the beginning of her second summer at Spengler-Nash. Ben had begun her training for the part of the business that wasn't done in an office. He had come to her desk and said, "I want you to think up a nom de guerre. Everybody here has to have one."

"Why?"

"A bunch of reasons. It's like an actor's name, the right name for the image you want to project. Good ones are simple and comforting. They make clients remember you. If somebody wants to bitch about you, they only know a fake name. They'll complain about Lisa La De Da or whoever. If the complaint sticks, we make up a new name for you. Sometimes female agents get noticed in the wrong way. You're young and not as ugly as you could be, so you might get stalkers. You're not completely incompetent so you'll make an enemy or two. They want to come after Lisa La De Da? Let them. She's gone, moved on."

"I'm kind of used to being Anna Kepka."

"Oh, and the other reason is that I told you to. Bring me a good name before end of shift. Write it down so we both spell it the same."

The name she had invented was Justine Poole. It sounded like the name of a woman whose family had come from a place along the Thames, not the Volga or the Danube. It was short and easy to remember. When she had handed him the name he had nodded and typed it on a form in his computer.

Two days later he brought her the plastic identification card that said she was Justine Poole and showed a picture of her like the others all had. Eventually she had one that carried all of her professional information on it—the number of her concealed carry permit and the firearms she was authorized to carry—9 millimeter, .40 caliber, .45 caliber. It noted that she had completed a defensive driving certification, CPR and lifesaving certification, and martial arts training. That was all for the benefit of clients, an easy way to reassure them that she was qualified. It also said she was a level 4 protection agent. There was no level 1, 2 or 3. After that he never called her anything but Justine Poole, and nobody else did either. Anna Kepka faded and became a bit of private history. Over the years she had used "Justine Poole" more and more often, so her real name got to be like an alias.

As she stood in the shower she thought about Anna Kepka. The surname was already a shortened version of her family's name, an abridgment her grandmother had done so it would be easy for Americans to say and accept. Her grandmother had told her that Americans were impatient people who resented having to memorize long or difficult names from other languages, so she had decided not to irritate them. When Anna had asked her what the long version of the name had been, she'd said, "You're an American too. Use your America name and be grateful. You'll only need this one until you're married and he gives you his nice new one anyway."

14

Justine Poole's filing cabinet had held the temporary white printout copy of the ownership papers for her car and a copy of its registration the night when Sealy had broken in. He had taken a picture of each. The car was a gray Honda Civic, and the license number was seven letters and numbers strung together, not a vanity plate or a tag that spelled a word or anything. He spent hours checking and rechecking Justine Poole's condo building, but her car never appeared, and now it was so late he was sure she wasn't coming. He was beginning to wonder if she had left town after all.

Sealy decided to use a skip tracer. He had also taken pictures of the copies she had made of both sides of two credit cards, so he had what he needed. Using skip tracers was tricky. They collected information about not only the people they traced, but also about the clients who hired them. Their fees were high, and presumably some clients skipped out on them, or tried to.

A few years ago, after he'd been told about the skip tracers, Sealy had used a false identity to incorporate a company, listed the business as an employment service, and begun paying a monthly fee to be a regular client of a skip tracer. Since then, he had used their services only a few times for his real business, but more often just had them locate random strangers so a survey of the subjects of his searches didn't all lead to people who were now dead. He also wanted to keep the volume of searches high enough to justify the fees he was paying. Nothing would make the skip tracers curious faster than noticing that a client was wasting his money on their services.

He typed his account number into the rectangle over the screen and waited. The site recognized it and bloomed into its full-color home page. He clicked on "New Search" and filled in all of the things he knew about Justine Poole. She was a woman who lived a neat, orderly life, so he wasn't surprised that she only had one card in each category. She wasn't the kind who applied for every credit card that had a new come-on offer.

He supplied the information he had gotten from Justine Poole's Visa and Mastercard backup copies the night he had been in her condo. This was the part that had always made the high fees worth paying. Skip tracers had twenty-four-hour instant access to information that ordinary people simply couldn't get. They could get purchase histories for the people they were tracing, and because credit transactions occurred in seconds, the information was fresh.

He kept the site open while he made a cup of coffee. A few seconds later the tracer site produced an entry on her Mastercard. This was one for a Mobil gas station on La Cienega Boulevard, forty-six dollars and seventy-two cents—about half a tank. It figured that she was a person who never let her tank get below half full.

The next charge was for the Aero-Won Hotel on Century Boulevard. It was a hundred dollars even. He began to feel excited. That was the charge that hotels put on a card at check-in to be sure the card was real, current, and had unused credit. When a person checked out, they deleted the hundred and put in the actual cost, which was almost never a round number. If the skip-tracing site was up to the minute—and why shouldn't a computerized system be?—then she had not checked out yet.

He typed in the name "Aero-Won Hotel" and looked at the web site. The hotel was right near the airport, which explained the name. She could practically walk to the terminal. Sealy had not put away the equipment he had laid out for his canceled early-morning trip to the three women's apartment building. It took him only a few minutes to put it all into big black trash bags and carry it to his car.

⚶

After seeing the photographs of the man in the garage, Justine knew she could be in trouble, and she suspected her situation was deteriorating. It had taken about ten minutes after Ally Grosvenor's first interview for her condo building to be recognized and the address to appear on the internet. Now her photograph was out there too. She looked in her wallet and found the business card from the police officer who had been the main interviewer when she and Ben were taken to the police station after the shooting. His name was Sergeant Rodriguez. She considered calling him to ask if she could get some help, but she already knew that would backfire.

The police department was understaffed and too busy to be even marginally useful for protection. The profession she'd been in since college was based on the common knowledge that the department's motto "To Serve and Protect" was mostly aspirational. The most the cops could do for her was send a car past her condominium building a couple of times a day. And asking the police for help would be giving them permission to keep checking that she was in one place and not moving around, which was the opposite of what she would have to do if she wanted to stay alive.

Justine put away her two phones and began to pack. Whatever she was going to do, she had better get started. In minutes she had collected her belongings, packed them in practical order in her suitcase, and checked out of the hotel. She was in the lobby on her way to the parking lot when she saw him.

She was looking at him through the thick and reflective surface of a glass door, so she wondered if she had imagined this was the same man. She decided that she had not made a mistake. She had stared at his picture too many times, and he was close, just driving past the main entrance toward the parking lot beyond.

He had a BMW—black, like most of them were—and he pulled into the small strip of spaces reserved for the cars of people who were just checking in, then got out and started walking toward the front entrance.

Justine clutched her bag and hurried to the elevator, rode it to the second floor, then hurried along the hallway to descend the next staircase to the first-floor hallway and slip out the side door to the large rear parking lot. She had parked her car near the back of the building when she'd arrived because she hadn't wanted it or herself to be visible from the street. She got into her gray Honda, drove along the rear of the lot to the exit, and headed away from the airport.

She drove to the new economy parking garage on 94th Street, took a ticket from the dispenser, and parked on the third level. She locked her bag in the trunk, went down the stairs, and walked quickly to the shuttle pickup spot at the southeast corner of the first level, where she boarded a shuttle bus that was just filling up with travelers.

When Justine had traveled by air with a client, most of the time Spengler-Nash assigned a second bodyguard to drive them to the right terminal, but she had occasionally driven the client to one of the terminals herself, dropped them at the curb, parked in the economy parking garage, taken the shuttle back to the same terminal, and rejoined them in one of the airlines' VIP lounges to wait to board their flight. She had judged that this complicated route—driving to the airport, then doubling back, disappearing into a garage that held four thousand cars, and returning in a crowded bus identical to every other bus—would be very difficult for an enemy to follow. That difficulty was what she needed now.

She knew the ride to the airport's loop of terminals only took about five minutes. She sat back in her seat so the bigger bodies of the male travelers would block her from view. She took a few pictures of the road behind the bus by aiming her phone over her shoulder at the back window. Then she looked down at the screen to see if the black BMW had followed. She had learned the habit of using her phone to take pictures of what was behind her when she was guiding a client through public places, and had occasionally detected unexpected threats.

There were nine terminals at LAX, but the one she wanted was Terminal 1, because just north of it was LAXit, the pick-up spot for the rideshare services and the loading zone for taxi cabs. The shuttle took an elevated lane to the departure level to begin its long horseshoe-shaped counterclockwise route. When the shuttle stopped and the doors huffed open, Justine joined the file of passengers shuffling up the aisle and stepped down onto the sidewalk. She went inside the terminal immediately and rode down the escalator to the arrival level, walked across the baggage claim between the carousels, and went out the automatic door to the street. She joined the straggling stream of people pulling their wheeled suitcases along the pavement toward the LAXit.

When Justine got there, she found the crowd was large. She could see that the line for Uber and Lyft rides was long and looked disorganized. It wasn't a surprise, because the rideshare services were cheaper than taxis. But she saw people going to the wrong cars and being turned away, families or travel companions who were too numerous or had too much luggage to fit in one car, people frowning at their phones, seeing their drivers had canceled, and starting the process over.

She went to join the taxi cab line. Most of the rideshare line was English-speaking Americans, but the taxi line held lots of tourists from the rest of the world, some of whom spoke no English. The confusion was the right kind for Justine, because foreign tourists knew enough to stand in line, and taxi drivers knew enough to wait for the cab ahead to load and leave, pull up to the loading zone, load and leave. There was no matching of passenger to car.

After Justine was in line, she could see one problem. There were too many people with too much luggage and too many children, and not enough cabs.

She stayed in the line, but looked around to see whether it would be practical to walk back to the Uber and Lyft area. As soon as she turned, she saw the black BMW again. It was in the LAXit, moving a few feet whenever the cars ahead did, and then stopping, another few feet and then stopping. How could he have followed her so closely? Had he seen her drive out of the hotel lot? Speculating about it was just a distraction. Whatever she had done wrong was already done.

She knelt on the pavement, pretending to tie her shoe so she could crouch beside a big suitcase belonging to the family ahead. The suitcase stood upright on its wheels with its handle extended. She didn't dare look straight in the direction of the BMW, only peering out from behind the suitcase with one eye and then looking down again. She was sure the driver was the same man, but now he had two signs on his dashboard saying Uber and Lyft. The car seemed out of place to her. Who would use a high-end BMW to drive for a rideshare company? Nobody else seemed to even see him. The car was moving so slowly that the killer could look at all the people standing in the ride lines. His slow advance would bring him within fifty feet of her. She slipped her phone out of her pocket and held it down near her foot to take several more pictures in the direction of the BMW, then put it away and pretended to finish tying her shoe.

She kept her face turned away from him, but that brought on the excruciating feeling that he would be approaching with a pistol on his lap, and at any moment he could be right behind her pressing the button to roll down his window and shoot her in the back. How close was he now? How close now?

Then the man who owned the upright suitcase grasped the handle and moved it ahead in the taxi line. He came back to the rest of his family's suitcases, grasped the handles and moved them ahead two at a time until they were all collected ten feet closer to the cab loading zone. Justine moved to catch up more slowly than she could have because she wanted the murderer to get past her and drive on. He must be almost beside her now, and she couldn't kneel here any longer, because the people ahead of her had moved forward and taken her hiding place with them.

As she stood, she saw a young blond woman about twenty feet ahead of her who had a hoodie on that said "Sorbonne." It seemed like something only an American tourist would wear. She stepped to the left of the line away from the curb and advanced to where the young woman stood. She said, "Hi. Do you speak English?"

The young woman said, "Yep. In Encino most of us do."

Justine said, "If you'll let me share your cab, I'll pay for both of us."

The woman smiled. "You know it's at least a hundred bucks, right?"

"I'll pay for the trip, the tip, and give you an extra fifty for your trouble."

"Why would you be in such a big hurry?"

Justine snatched a lie out of the air and began to tell it. "I'm divorced, and in an hour my child custody days start. If my ex comes to drop them off and I'm not there to take them, he gets to make a big thing out of it. I'm the unreliable parent and all that."

The young woman craned her neck to look down the long line behind them. "Some of those people are not going to be happy, but okay."

Justine stood with her in line, agreeing that the people behind her were probably resenting her, but hoping they'd think she was just joining a traveling companion after getting separated in the terminal and then searching for her. Justine's need to stay alive was more likely to be urgent than other people's need to get to their hotels, but she still felt guilty.

Justine took the dangerous move of glancing toward the rideshare lane where she had seen the killer. She didn't see the black BMW, but couldn't risk looking harder and longer. Losing sight of him didn't make her feel safer. It didn't mean he was gone. He could have pulled out, left his car at the white curb in front of Terminal 1, and be making his way back to her on foot.

She needed to stop staring in all directions and looking tense and uncomfortable or she was going to spook this girl and lose her ride. She forced herself to look into her eyes. She said to her, "Are you just getting back from France?"

"The Maldives," the girl said.

Starting a conversation with this person was an effort, like trying to get a fire started in the wilderness. Justine had just struck a spark, but it had not gotten the tinder to burn. She had to keep the conversation alive, and she sensed that the young woman distrusted strangers who asked questions, so she stopped asking. She tried another lie. "Before I got married I always wanted to go there, but it never worked out. I had a boyfriend who actually thought of it himself and asked me to go with him. We set everything up months in advance, but by the time the date came we had reached that awful stage where you know the relation-ship is not getting any better, and being stuck for a month in a foreign country together will not help. Other times I was set on going alone, but that didn't work either."

The young woman said, "Why not?"

"Whenever I had that much extra money it was because I had a good job and didn't have enough time off. When I had the time, it was because I was laid off and it didn't seem smart to spend my sav-ings having fun until I had another job. And then I got one and the cycle began again. Then I got married, and since then all my travel is about meetings."

The couple ahead of them stepped into a cab and a moment later it pulled away toward the exit lanes. Then they were first in line. Even the wait while the next cab nosed up to them and stopped seemed an eternity, and she spent most of it trying to spot the man who had been driving the BMW. The next cab driver popped the trunk and came around to take the young woman's bag and put it inside, then looked at Justine, shrugged, and got back in. The young woman got into the back seat and Justine quickly slid in beside her so she wouldn't be visible for an extra second.

The driver said, "Where to?"

The young woman said, "Encino. 46001 Blossom Court."

The driver entered the address on his phone, then looked at Justine, so she said, "You should take her first. After that, I'll tell you where to let me off." She had not chosen a destination, and this would give her time to select one.

"You don't need to do that, Miss. I just put it in the phone and the GPS will take us to it."

"Studio City. The cross streets are Laurel Canyon and Ventura." She had chosen it because it was in the Valley at least a couple of miles from Encino, but was several miles and over the hills from her condominium and the Spengler-Nash building. It also formed a picture in her memory that was pleasant and included pedestrians. The driver typed it in and pulled ahead.

She buckled her seat belt and let herself scan the cars and the people walking on the sidewalk outside the baggage claims of the terminals. She didn't see the man or his car, and she felt her heart beginning to slow and her muscles relax. The cab's backseat side windows were tinted, so it was unlikely that anyone outside could even see her face. The cab pulled onto Sepulveda and took the entrance to the 405 freeway.

The northbound freeway this morning was a sluggish stream as tens of thousands of cars competed for an extra car-length of progress while the pavement narrowed and shed lanes to pass through the central part of the city. As time went by, Justine's one-sided conversation began to run thin without the young woman contributing more than grunts and nods and the occasional half-hearted chuckles, and eventually it died.

When the cab reached the young woman's address, it was a vast green space with a huge brick house on it. The young woman got out, accepted her suitcase, and walked into the house without saying anything. As the young woman disappeared, it occurred to Justine that neither of them had remembered that she'd offered the young woman fifty dollars plus the cab ride.

The driver said, "Okay. Now for Studio City."

Justine thought of asking him to wait while she ran to the front door with the fifty dollars, but she realized that maybe the girl had felt uncomfortable accepting fifty bucks in front of her parents' eight-million-dollar house. She hesitated, and the driver pulled away.

The drive back along the freeway seemed faster to Justine, and as the cab came closer to the destination, she began to dread the end. She'd had no plan except to get out of immediate danger. She seemed to have slipped the noose, but now she needed to make a plan that would last more than a few minutes. She had not proven to herself yet how the man had found her hotel, but the most likely way she knew of was to pay a company that had access to credit card purchases. Everything that had happened in the past couple of days had seemed to come from some unexpected place, some other reality, but she had to react to what she saw and heard, not what she'd expected. Using the credit card that she'd used to pay for the hotel was now a risk. Any card in the name Justine Poole would be a risk.

While the cab veered onto the exit ramp at Laurel Canyon and kept going south for the next two blocks, she looked at the meter. The ride was going to be over a hundred dollars without the tip, and she didn't have enough cash with her. She had stopped carrying much money during the pandemic, when clerks became reluctant to touch anything that had been passed around from one person to another. She opened her purse, felt for the secret pocket opening and took out the Visa card that said "Anna S. Kepka."

The corner of Ventura Boulevard and Laurel Canyon was too busy for a cab to stop and let a customer off, so the driver pulled forward fifty feet into the entrance to the free parking lot behind a row of stores beside the CVS pharmacy. She paid with her Anna Kepka credit card, got out of the cab, and stood still for a few seconds fiddling with her purse by the open door while she scanned for any sign that they'd been followed by the BMW. There was no sign of it, so she said, "Thanks," closed the door, and hurried into the pharmacy.

She walked through the pharmacy and out to Ventura Boulevard. There was a lot of traffic going east and west on the street, and the broad sidewalks held a steady stream of people walking among the stores, restaurants, and banks. Ventura Boulevard was essentially the main street of the San Fernando Valley.

She'd had a few long-term assignments during her time at Spengler-Nash, and one was running interference for Melisandre LeVos, a young Canadian singer who lived nearby and liked to stop at a coffee shop near here. Justine had enjoyed some parts of the assignment—being awake in the sunlit hours, staying on one assignment for more than a night at a time, working with a client her own age. She had been able to relax a bit during rehearsals and taping sessions, where studio security departments were already providing most of the protection. She began to look for the coffee shop.

She walked west at a quick pace, past the art deco Studio City Theater, which had been converted to a giant bookstore long before she'd ever seen it, then past an antique furniture store and a hairdresser's salon. She wanted to get indoors, to a place where she could be safely off the street while she figured out what to do next. Finally, she recognized the coffee shop she used to go to with Melisandre. She stepped inside and joined the short line of people waiting to order. The line moved quickly, and she ordered and paid in cash for an iced black tea and a muffin and gave the name Terry for it. Terry was called in about two minutes and she picked up her order, went to the end of the counter, and added the cream her grandmother had always put in the tea but omitted the sugar. She sat at a small table near the back of the shop so she wouldn't be easy to see from the street.

As she nibbled at the muffin and sipped the tea, she thought about how the killer had found her. The fact that her name had been released so quickly was a by-product of reporters' eagerness rather than an intent to endanger her. Her name had led him to her address, and her photograph came to him courtesy of Ally Grosvenor via Channel 7 news. He had broken into the Grosvenors' apartment and hers. That must have given him access to her credit card number—maybe all of her Justine card numbers.

She studied the other people in the coffee shop. There was nobody who seemed even remotely threatening. She'd had a difficult morning, but for the moment she was in a calm, sheltered place, and she had apparently bought some time. The people around her definitely didn't include the man who had come for her in the BMW. Most of them were young and sitting with other people. She liked the fact that about half were female, because the kinds of erratic behavior that were dangerous were almost exclusively male.

She had become expert at these assessments and it had helped her steer her clients away from trouble. Her gaze drifted upward over the heads of the coffee drinkers and caught an image that made her breath stop and her lungs stay inflated for two seconds. It looked like the same black BMW, sitting at the traffic light outside. She watched it nose into the intersection and turn right. As it did, the car showed its left side to the coffee shop window, and she saw the face of the driver. It was the killer's face. He was scanning the side street for parking spaces.

15

Joe Alston glanced over the rim of his cup at the woman who had just taken the table in the back of the shop. He had noticed her because she was attractive, about the right age—maybe five years older than the youngest group in the shop—and alone. He realized he would have sounded like a stalker to a person who could read his mind, but he was just looking and wondering. Her long, thick, dark brown hair made him want her to brush it aside with her hand so he could see her face better. She was drinking something in a transparent plastic cup through a straw, probably iced coffee.

Alston allowed himself one look and then turned away toward the big front window, where he watched the activity on the busy corner. There were crosswalks and a traffic signal, so some cars were gliding past while others were waiting to go the other way, as were a few pedestrians. He kept the lid on his coffee and sipped through the little hole on top because once the lid was removed, the paper cup couldn't be trusted to remain rigid. He watched the people going past and wondered about each of them—who they were and why they weren't at work somewhere. In this part of Los Angeles, looking at people was irresistible and hypnotic. There were always so many of them out, and they were all moving, and anyone could be anything.

He was good at remembering faces, but not at remembering the context. If he saw one that looked familiar, he might have seen it at a movie theater or on a movie screen or both. To complicate this kind of people-watching, he could walk a block and see the CBS Radford lot. Universal Studios was within half a mile, and a ten-minute drive past that were Warner Brothers, Disney, and several music studios.

He subscribed to the theory that in the past century, the best-looking young people born in the benighted, hopeless, and sunless places east of the Mississippi had come here, drawn by the belief that regular features, abundant hair, and a faultless complexion could make them rich. Even when that magic didn't happen, other magic did and they married and produced offspring like the people on Ventura Boulevard.

Joe Alston had been born in Upstate New York and educated in Connecticut and drifted here like the rest. Although he was in good shape, six feet tall with reasonably pleasant features and a full head of light brown hair, he had never been tempted by the entertainment business. He had been hired by eastern newspapers as a reporter and then a feature and opinion writer. After he'd made a respectable name for himself, he turned to freelance writing, mostly for magazines. He'd come to Los Angeles one February tracking a story about dark web profiteers and decided it would be insane not to make LA his home base.

He'd incorporated his business in California and the way he found out about jobs was his phone. Early morning was the time for communication from London, New York, and Boston, and from ten on, Chicago, and then Los Angeles, San Francisco, and Seattle. He took out his phone to look at his email.

He felt a shadow move over him and looked up. It was that woman, standing beside him. She seemed to be looking at his phone screen, an act that was unthinkable, but he hadn't actually caught her, so he simply set the phone face down and looked up into her eyes, his eyebrows raised.

She said, "Hi. Are you, like, honest?"

"Like honest?" he said. "No. I'm actually honest."

She set her drink on his table and said, "I thought so. Please watch my jacket." She slung it onto his lap by the collar, then walked to the teak door of the ladies' restroom to the left of the counter, opened the door, and went in.

He looked after her in astonishment and then was distracted by his surprise that she could walk right into a restroom during a busy time like this. Usually there were women in line waiting for a turn. She was obviously one of those people who was lucky in small things.

He picked up his phone from the table and returned to the business of scrolling down the entries on the screen looking for work. He kept the jacket on his lap and pulled his chair closer to the table so his solar plexus was touching it and the jacket couldn't be easily snatched and wasn't sitting on the table getting stained by old spills or the condensation from her cold drink.

One of the emails he had been hoping for was there. It was a note from a magazine editor to let him know he had been paid electronically for a long article. This was good, because it had only been printed a week ago. Usually, magazine editors talked as though the accounting office was located on the far side of a mountain range that could only be crossed on a narrow footpath above a chasm. Once there, the editor had to persuade an argumentative legislative body to discuss the payment until they had unanimously agreed to it and then make the trip back with the money. Alston did a quick check on his mobile banking app to verify the deposit and then wrote back, "Thank you, Donald. It's been a pleasure. Best, Joe." SEND.

He looked at other emails while he waited for the woman to come back for her jacket. A reader had liked an article. "I'm pleased that you liked it. Thanks for taking the time to let me know. Joseph Alston." SEND. Someone believed she had found a mistake in another article. She was wrong, but he wrote, "Thank you for giving the article such a close reading. It's good to know somebody is paying attention." He decided he couldn't let the misunderstanding stand. "I think you'll find that in the third section, though, I share my reasons for suspecting that Mr. Harrow's 'informed source' is Colonel Maijiti himself, and not an outside supporter. We know the mysterious memo originated from the colonel's IP address and was sent to one of his cousins, then to Mr. Harrow." SEND.

Joe Alston sipped his coffee, found that it had cooled enough to drink, and looked at the time on the upper right corner of his phone screen. He wished he had looked at it when she had gone into the restroom. It could have been seven or eight minutes and only seemed longer. He felt stupid. Timing someone when they were in the restroom was an infringement of their privacy and a useless waste of his consciousness.

Still, his discomfort was increasing. He had never seen her before. A suspicion was forming that he was being fooled somehow. He lifted his eyes and surveyed the coffee shop. The people looked like the same segment of the population that had filled the place since he had first seen it a few years ago—nearly all in their twenties or early thirties, most of them fit and attractive in the seemingly effortless way that such people were. None of the others seemed to be aware of him. He knew he couldn't trust that impression because being fully involved with one's companions or with one's own phone was the norm, but he welcomed their inattention right now.

And what was now? He looked at his phone screen. Over ten minutes had passed. She was apparently just another of those women who used restrooms as their personal salons for redoing their hair, makeup, and so on. He noticed the sweat from her iced drink was slowly spreading toward her jacket. He lifted the jacket to set it on the chair next to his. It felt heavier than he had expected and he wondered what was in the pocket.

He sat there and determined not to look impatient. He assumed a studied expression of thoughtful calm.

A telephone rang and after a moment he realized that must be what had made her jacket feel heavier. She'd left her phone in the pocket. It rang again. What should he do? He looked down at the jacket and saw there was a zipper on the side pocket. He touched the pocket and felt the vibration as the phone rang a third time. He unzipped the pocket and slid the phone out, planning to simply shut off the ringer so the caller would run out of rings and leave her a message.

He looked at the screen and pressed the minus sign to make the symbol of the bell and the sound bar appear, but staring back at him was the face of the woman, apparently aiming another phone at her face. He hit the answer icon and she said, "Thank you, love. Can you please come around to the back of the building and bring my jacket?"

"Sure," he said, silently congratulating himself for ending the call with one syllable. He slid the phone back into her jacket and walked out the side door around to the back. He was in the coffee shop's patch of the parking lot, a short strip of asphalt that was occupied by a dumpster and two cars that probably belonged to the baristas who came to get the place ready to open by six A.M. He didn't see the woman.

⚔

Justine saw him. While she had waited by the dumpster for him to come out, she had wondered what to say to him. She couldn't say who she was or why she was acting strangely. He probably wouldn't believe her and if he did, he would mess everything up and get himself killed, or at least think it was his duty to call the police and get her into more trouble, or leave her here in the place where her killer would find her.

She was scared and she was out of time. She needed to be cheerful to keep him on her side and she had to show herself now. Maybe she could be funny. Her memory search for how to do that brought back a role she had sometimes assumed to amuse friends. She would become Anna Kepkasovanovich, a girl with a Balkan accent who thought of herself as a captivating beauty with sophisticated tastes and a world-weary demeanor. If anyone mentioned a popular boy, she would say "He's just like all the others. He calls me every night to flatter me. I get no sleep." She needed to be someone like that now.

She stepped out from the other side of the dumpster, gave him a quick wave and an engaging smile. He stepped to her and held out her jacket. She looked deep into his eyes as she said, "Thank you so much," which made her accidentally touch his hand as she reached for the jacket, but because clumsiness seemed worse than flirtatiousness, she gave the hand a quick squeeze, slung her jacket over her shoulder and set off. After two steps she stopped and looked back at him. She said with a slight accent, "Are you staying here? In an empty parking lot? Why?"

"I hadn't made a plan."

"Then you can follow mine. Come on." She hurried away along the lot. In a few steps he caught up with her, not sure why, except that she was more appealing than he had thought. Seeing her in the bright sunlight had made him curious. He also had to acknowledge that he had no reason to remain standing in the parking lot alone.

He said, "Why did you do that?"

"I saw a guy take the turn up the street to look for a parking space. I didn't want him to see me."

"A boyfriend?"

"A possibility. Not for a long time."

"Not for a long duration or a long time ago?'

"More like a stalker," she said.

"So you went out the back way?"

"There is no back way. I went out the restroom window. The only other door is next to the counter. You can see it even from the street."

"Did you leave the restroom door locked?"

"No. Do you think I'm a monster?" she said.

"What's in your jacket that I was holding for you? Drugs?"

She looked at him with exaggerated surprise, her eyes and mouth wide open. "I would never do that to you—leave you holding the bag. And look at my skin. My teeth. Do I use drugs?"

"Probably not."

"Do you?"

"No."

"How old are you, anyway?"

"Thirty-two."

"I'm twenty-five, but I'm smarter than you are."

"That's evident."

"So we're well matched."

"Is that what we're doing—sizing each other up for a date?"

"What else?" she said, and held up her hands. "No rings on either of us. I saw you looking at me before, so don't pretend you didn't like me."

"I look at everybody."

"You certainly do. And everything. I was getting embarrassed."

"So embarrassed that you brought your drink and your jacket to my table."

"I didn't say I wanted you to stop looking. Just not enough right then to make other people look too."

"It was curiosity. It's always been my weakness."

"Mine too. Something else in common."

"What's your name?"

She said in a thick accent, "Ajkuna."

"No, it's not."

"Besjana."

He looked at her closely. "Could be."

"It's Anna."

"I'll buy that. I'm Joe." They reached the end of the alley and he could see his car parked on the side street under a sycamore tree. He felt an instant of relief to see that the tree hadn't dropped any branches on his car, as they sometimes did in the summer. He took a step to the sidewalk in that direction. She was still at his side. He had expected her to step in another direction. He stopped.

"What?" she said.

"I guess this is the end of the line. That's my car over there." He paused. "I'm planning on going to work now."

"What do you do?"

"I'm an assistant district attorney for Los Angeles County."

"No, you're not," she said.

"Nope. But that reminds me. You should take a look in your jacket, and verify that everything is still there. I don't want to be accused later of taking your dowry or your plans for a cold fusion reactor."

"No need. I don't bring those things when I go to a coffee shop. And you said before that you were honest."

"That's also what a crook would say."

"But I have my jacket and I can feel my phone is in it. I told you I have a stalker. Aren't you going to offer to take me home? Is chivalry dead?"

"Where do you live?"

"I didn't mean to my house. I meant to yours. It's after ten. I can see your hair is damp and smell your soap. You just had a shower but you're dressed like a twelve-year-old. You're not going to an office."

"I work at home, but it's still work and I have to get it done." It felt hollow to him as though he'd lied, even though it was true.

"I get it. You've already decided you don't like me. It's fine. Maybe we'll see each other around sometime, but if we do, don't say hi." She started to walk toward the back door of an Urban Outfitters.

"It isn't that I don't like you," he said. "It's that I'm a little afraid of you. Nobody behaves this way. How can this be anything but a scam?"

She stopped. "You should have more confidence in yourself. Women sometimes talk to men just because they look interesting or seem smart, and women love confidence. All women. If you learn to have confidence, then next time somebody talks to you, you won't think she must be a criminal."

"I'll try to remember that. Thank you," he said. "Look, let's not just stand here. I'll take you where you want. I don't want to leave you stranded."

"No, thanks," she said. "I have some errands and then I'll call somebody." She started back down the alley. She heard no sound of him moving. Was he watching her walk? Then she realized that her steps had left him far enough behind so his proximity wouldn't keep her killer from shooting her in front of a witness. This "Joe" person was over and now she had to get out of this neighborhood. She heard rapid steps behind her and spun around, ready to put up whatever fight she could to prolong her last morning alive. She said, "Hi, Joe." Had the words sounded calm? No. But maybe he would attribute that to the fact that nobody wanted anybody running up behind them.

"Look, Anna, I'm sorry. Please come with me. I'll get some work done and you can tell me where you want to go later."

She tried to think of the right response, and it came to her—nothing. She took a step in his direction, he turned, and they walked toward his car in silence.

⚶

Leo Sealy had left the BMW in the Bank of America parking structure, and now he was striding along Ventura Boulevard looking in the window of each business to search for Justine Poole. He had taken a few minutes to find a place to leave the car where she couldn't see it, but then he'd realized that if he parked at the bank he didn't need to walk through the building to get out to the street. He was always leery of banks, because they had the best, clearest surveillance footage. Today he was being extra careful because he had his customary two pistols on him. He didn't have any reason to believe there was a metal detector at the bank, but he knew one had been installed in a Chase branch in the Chicago area at least eight years ago. He'd always been sure not to be armed in banks even before then. If somebody bumped into him and felt a gun under his shirt, it would probably be in a crowded place like that and banks had reason to be on edge and expecting trouble.

He went into a Mexican restaurant, a pharmacy, a fancy bakery. When he saw a coffee shop across the street, he picked up his speed and headed straight for it. If she was anywhere around here, that would be it.

16

Joe's place was a separate building behind a big house in the Hollywood Hills—what real estate people used to call a "mother-in-law unit." Justine had always hated that name. The current jargon term "accessory dwelling unit" was no more elegant and less human. She liked the term "guesthouse." Both buildings were painted the same creamy off-white.

The guesthouse was about sixty feet from the main house and about forty from the five-car garage, which was cloaked in magenta bougainvillea vines. Two mature California oaks shaded the guesthouse and the back part of the main house. As Joe's car reached the upper end of the driveway, she could see that the backyard was a garden full of well-tended greenery.

He opened one of the garage doors with a remote control, coasted into the empty space, and pressed the remote to close the door behind them. She liked that, because if Ben's killer had seen Joe's car, he didn't see it now. She happened to be looking at Joe in profile as he turned off the engine. He noticed and said, "It keeps the car from getting hot. The midday sun can be brutal."

"I live in LA," she said. "I like shade too."

"I meant that I'm not putting the car away, really. I can take you wherever and whenever you want."

"I wasn't worried," she said. "I believed you before. What's your last name, by the way?"

"Alston." He didn't ask hers.

She followed him out a side door of the garage to a flagstone path that led to the guesthouse, which he used a key on his keychain to open. It was one of a dozen tiny indications that he was who he said he was and had a right to be here. She stepped in and looked around. There was a rectangular sunlit living room that evolved into an office as she moved down the length of it, past some nice gray furniture arranged in a conversational grouping to a space with a large desk and matching filing cabinet with a printer on it.

She could see a short hallway with one door on either side that had to be a bedroom. Across the living room was a rudimentary kitchen that consisted of a wall of counter space and cabinets interrupted by a refrigerator, a small electric stove top with a ventilation hood above it, a dishwasher, and a single sink. She said, "It's a pretty, cheerful space."

"Thank you."

"Who lives in the big house?"

"A friend who rents me this pretty, cheerful space."

"What's her name?"

"His name is James. The reason he has the big house is that he's the executive producer of *Sacajawea*. The reason he's seldom in it is that he's the executive producer of *Sacajawea*, which is shot in Canada. Before that it was *Doctor Frank*, which was shot in an old decommissioned hospital and soundstages in LA. Even then he wasn't hanging around much because he worked such long hours."

She said, "So you just keep an eye on his place, walk his dog, and make sure nobody but you sleeps with his wife?"

"No dog," he said. "And no wife right now either, probably because he worked too much to spend time with her."

"Too bad. And this is the place where you work?"

"I do the real writing here, but part of the time I'm out doing research, taking pictures, and doing interviews."

"Articles, then. And who buys them?"

"You sound like my mother."

"You're evading her question."

"Magazines, newspapers, and syndicates, some of them online. And anything I don't sell I publish on my blog."

"Can you earn a living that way?"

"I get by."

"How?"

"You know the ant and the grasshopper?"

"Not personally."

"Aesop's fables. The grasshopper fools around all summer and dies when the winter comes. The ant works hard, saves part of whatever ants get paid by their editors, and thrives."

"He's still an ant, though."

"True."

"Well, I'll stop bothering you and let you get to work. I need to check my phones."

"I wondered about that. Why do you have two phones?"

It seemed fair to her that he was retaliating for her prying questions, but she tried to end it. "One work and one life." It was not quite a lie. The police had held the work phone she'd had the night of the shooting, but when she'd gone home to collect her things, she'd reactivated an older work phone because the numbers and information it held were still valid.

Joe Alston recognized that she had accidentally given him an invitation to ask about her work, but he made a decision not to use it. He sat at his desk and took a laptop computer out of the deep drawer on the right and opened it. She was relieved that he really did have work to do. She had bought herself some time in a place where her killer would never look for her. She could stop and think of a way to help get Ben's killer caught.

She walked to the conversation area where the furniture was, took her charger out of her purse, plugged it into the wall to charge her main phone, and sat on a couch nearby. It had occurred to her that she had little reason anymore to have two phones, but the old work phone had possibly crucial information on it and she had to keep its battery charged. She went to the wall and exchanged the phones.

She took another look at the pictures of the man who had been standing in the garage at Spengler-Nash. Then she looked at the pictures she had taken of the man driving the BMW. She was sure she had been right that they were the same man. She decided to see if he had turned up in any other pictures without her recognizing him.

This morning she had taken a few shots while she rode the shuttle bus, while she waited in line for the taxi, and then a few through the rear window of the cab. She had taken a few more in the coffee shop while she had been pretending to read her email. And there, among the people at tables, was Joe Alston, surreptitiously looking in her direction.

Justine wasn't sure why she was doing what she was about to do. She wasn't afraid of him or anything, but she had decided to look him up. She found he wrote under his own name, Joseph Alston, which made him seem more adult and legitimate to her, so she tapped a link.

The first article she found was from a month ago. It seemed at first to be just another of the innumerable articles about depressing failures of the city government. A group of local business owners and CEOs had begun trying to make a practical plan to build water storage systems and make possible reuse of water. Since they, together, employed a large number of engineers and architects and owned heavy equipment, they had made a good start. It was a good article.

She scanned another one. It was about unions and the recent attempts to organize fields that had never had unions before. She had begun to read with skepticism. Spengler-Nash had never had a union and for all of her time there she had received constant training, steadily rising pay, and friendly working conditions among people prepared to risk their lives for her. But as she read some of Joseph Alston's interviews with employees in other specialized industries, she began to recognize some of the complaints. While Ben was alive everyone loved and trusted him and he treated them well. But before his body was cold, his brother and sister had come in and obliterated Justine's working life and made her more vulnerable to Ben's killer and to criminal charges. A union might have been able to help her in a number of ways. It was another good article.

She began to feel guilty about Joe Alston. She had correctly assessed him in several ways—a heterosexual on his own and therefore susceptible to manipulation by a young woman; a decent guy, and therefore not likely to refuse a favor, steal her jacket, or make a scene. She'd guessed he was some kind of freelancer and therefore someone with time for her to waste. She had used him to make sure that when her killer looked in the coffee shop windows, he wouldn't find her.

She regretted that she had put him in danger—or really, drawn him into her danger. It was an unfair thing to do even in a moment of extreme need. Still, thanks to her selfish moves, they were both here in this secret place. He seemed to be doing his work, which was all he'd wanted. And every minute she wasn't out on the street showing her face was a minute when her killer was wasting his time and energy, getting tired and frustrated and learning nothing.

⋯✦⋯

About fifteen feet away Joe Alston was looking at his computer screen. On it was a photograph of Justine Poole, the professional bodyguard who had won a shoot-out against five armed robbers, killed one—no, now it was two because the surgery hadn't saved the wounded one—and blocked the escape of the others and gotten them arrested.

He had just written the last lines of a draft of his article about a group of unscrupulous real estate lawyers. They had been using some recent well-meaning but foolish legislation that had outlawed local zoning. His article followed several projects sure to transform residential neighborhoods into overcrowded, overheated slums with great profits to developers. His first draft had most of what he needed, but the evidence he had collected wasn't going to disappear. If anything, it would grow fuller and stronger in the time it would take him to explore another topic.

This Justine Poole story was impossible to ignore. Reporters were already calling her a hero. Every journalist in the city was looking for her, hoping for an interview, even some small part of her story that would rate a byline or a one-minute report in front of a camera. And Justine Poole was sitting on his couch, no more than fifteen feet away.

17

Leo Sealy had turned in the BMW and was driving a white Toyota, his third rental car since he'd begun this job. He was changing everything he could, in case Justine Poole had seen him at the airport or afterward. He would keep changing things until he got her. This afternoon he was wearing a tan baseball cap with no insignia on the crown and a pair of wraparound sunglasses. These small transformations mattered. He had to fool not only Justine Poole, but random people too. Anyone who saw him twice was a potential witness.

A different car made it possible to make any sight of him a onetime thing. He was just one driver in the endless stream of cars going past. A second sight of him could raise curiosity. He tried to rent his cars in the most common colors—black, white, or silver—and never the same make or model as the last one.

Since he had succeeded in finding her hotel, guessing she would be at the airport, and following her cab from the airport way the hell out to Encino, he had temporarily lost sight of her when she'd doubled back. He had sped up and realized the cab must have turned off around the Studio City exit, so he'd gone back, found a parking space and searched

Ventura Boulevard. He had walked in and out of about ten stores, four restaurants, and a coffee shop, stared into many windows, and not seen her. He had gotten back into the car and driven up and down Ventura Boulevard and its cross streets for another hour. She was on foot, so she should have been visible on the sidewalk at some point. "Should have been" meant nothing. She had probably gotten a Lyft or Uber out of there right away.

Leo Sealy usually had more success at stalking female targets and finding them quickly. They were smaller and slower and they didn't have his physical stamina. The vast majority wore shoes that hurt them and about half were used to wearing clothes that made them stand out—bright colors, very tight or very loose, and, in this weather, short.

This one was different. She had worked in a job that involved getting clients in and out of public places without attracting attention, glancing at spaces ahead and instantly judging their risk potential and the directions trouble might come from. He was beginning to wonder whether she had seen his face at some point and could see him coming. It would also not be out of the question for her to turn serious about getting on an airplane. Los Angeles wasn't the world. She had not done it this morning but it might have been because he had been too close behind her. She would know he'd buy a ticket, follow her in past the metal detectors, and see which plane she took.

For the moment he had to keep trying the standard methods in the hope that he would see her in one of her usual places—her home, her employer's building, and the streets between them. If that didn't work sometime this afternoon, his skip-tracing company might find more activity on one of her credit cards. If she was determined not to go home, she would probably need another hotel. If she kept moving with a small bag, she would need to buy clothes. If she had no place to cook, she'd need to pay to eat somewhere. Almost anything she did would bring him straight to her. He was also always thinking, trying to invent another way. That was what made Leo Sealy one of the best.

⚓︎

It took Joe Alston five minutes to decide to set aside everything else and write the story of Justine Poole. He liked to think of himself as a man dedicated to finding and revealing the truth. He used this view to make himself get out of bed each morning and get to work. Not all truths were lofty or useful or made him like human beings better, but he had to write stories that were likely to strike editors as worth pursuing because people would read them.

This story seemed to have everything—a very attractive woman who had a career protecting celebrities and powerful people. That didn't necessarily make her a sympathetic figure. It was pretty much what the Praetorian Guard had done for a living in ancient Rome. She was already shaping up to be the latest one to be canonized by the media as a hero, something they often did just before they tied the hero to a stake and set them on fire. For the moment he had to set these bits of knowledge aside and get to work.

Joe had to concentrate on taking practical steps right now, before everybody started moving again and it was too late to guide the situation in the direction he wanted it to go. At the moment, he had exclusive access to the heroine of an adventure story. He hoped he could keep it that way.

She was behaving as though she was desperate to stay hidden. She had gotten herself home with him by taking on a false identity—Anna—and acting flirtatious in a way that women almost never were with strange men. He made a mental note to see if he could get her to spell the false surname when he was ready to write, since she hadn't even said it aloud yet. The main thing was to keep her here.

She had pretended to be attracted to him, which was almost insulting because she would never have acted that way unless she thought he was stupid. She had probably really been avoiding somebody and maybe it was really a rejected suitor, as she'd said, but it could also have been a reporter, or even someone she thought might harm her—friends of the robbers she'd shot, maybe? His internet introduction to her had mentioned that the supervisor who had been with her at the shooting scene had been murdered the next night. That would be enough to scare anybody.

He had to keep her here, but behave in a way that would avoid alarming her. He had to lie to her in a way that meshed with her lies to him. She would be Anna, and only Anna, for now. He had to let her believe he was fooled by her lies, but at the same time, not fear he expected an instant sexual relationship with her. That would make her bolt for the next hiding place, one that would hide her from him as well as everyone else.

He looked up from the computer search he had been performing on Justine Poole as though staring at the wall for the right unwritten word, and took the chance of giving her a sideward look. She had fallen asleep on his couch. He was relieved. He would have more time to think through what he would say to her.

⚬

Justine had seen him look up at the wall and then at her and then go back to work. She felt relieved that his reaction had been to leave her alone and let her sleep. She knew it wasn't going to last, but the truth was that she really had fallen asleep until she'd heard his movement across the room. She was used to working at night and the change in schedule and the hide-and-seek of this morning had left her tired. She hoped she hadn't snored, as exhausted people sometimes did, and she knew that some also drooled. She moved her face on the pillow no more than an inch and moved it back, and found that she hadn't been drooling. She didn't want to be gross and disgusting—to anybody, not just Joe Alston, whom she barely knew and would probably never see again.

Joe was a victim. She had seen the killer through the coffee shop window and the easiest way to evade him was to use the man she'd caught noticing her. She had not been exactly lying when she'd pretended she'd felt some attraction to Joe. The qualities she'd thought might make him easy to manipulate, if viewed another way, were compliments, but she couldn't think in those terms at the time. He was there, someone she could use as a way out. He had turned out to be a good choice, but depending on a stranger had created new problems and maybe even new dangers. As soon as she let him know she was awake she could be dealing with unwanted advances.

She moved ever so slightly to restore her circulation and waited to see if he had noticed. For a moment she thought about the articles she had read. He wasn't stupid. He was also not a jerk. She had to hope that he was—what? Trusting, maybe. That trust might buy her a little more time in invisibility.

What she realized was going to interfere with her plan was that she had drunk most of that stupid large iced tea. More than large. What did they call it? Venti. And she had not gone to the restroom to pee, but to sneak out the window. She felt that now she had used up the time her body would allow her before she had to get up from the couch.

As she stood, Joe looked up from his computer. "Good morning," he said.

"Sorry to fall asleep." She had dropped the Anna accent. "Is your bathroom through there?"

"Yes," he said. "The door on the right."

She got past him and was inside with the door locked at last. After she had relieved herself she fixed her hair with his hairbrush and used some Kleenex to blot her lipstick and make its borders conform better to her lips. She was mainly concerned about what her next few steps should be. She was safe until Joe kicked her out, but she'd thought of nothing that would help catch Ben's killer, or even decided on her next refuge. She returned to the main room.

He was still at his desk frowning at the laptop screen, the keys clacking as he worked. She glided by behind him and walked along looking at the pictures on the walls as though she were in a gallery. There were only four of what she thought of as trophy photographs, pictures of Joe in exotic places with one or more politicians or other well-known people. One that she lingered at showed him without a shirt on a sailboat tilting in a strong wind and gripping a rope with one hand beside Lars Helgerson, the composer and conductor of the Oslo Symphony Orchestra. She only recognized him because she had seen him at a performance in LA where she had been assigned to accompany an Italian opera singer. If the pictures were intended to impress women Joe brought here, he must have courted only smart ones. Maybe he displayed these as a test.

There were also a few good paintings. There was an autumn landscape that could be from one of the nineteenth-century Hudson River clique; a big sailing ship on a level course on a blue sea, so minutely detailed that she could feel the painter's pride in the ship as the latest and best; and a couple of naked women, probably turn of the century

French, by somebody who liked women. She didn't think Joe's essays were the sort that would make him able to afford these, but plenty of people who did the sort of work he did were born into rich families and got sent to the best universities, then felt they had to do something to justify all that luck.

As her browsing brought her closer to him, he closed his laptop, turned to look up at her, and said, "Do you need to get someplace this afternoon? I've done enough on this project for now, so I can take you anytime."

"That's really sweet, Joe," she said, "but I was just about to call a Lyft." She walked past the cluster of furniture and unplugged the phone she'd been charging. She had blown an opportunity to stay out of sight for a few more hours, but maybe there never had been an opportunity after her odd behavior in the morning.

"Or we could talk," he said. "I mean, as you pointed out before, we both noticed each other in a place that was full of people this morning. It seems as though that might be worth looking into."

She smiled and shrugged. "I was mostly trying to be funny. But okay." He wasn't so smart after all. But he must think that she was attractive—not unpleasant looking, anyway—and she might be able to use that. She could still stretch this for at least an hour or two and maybe even stay invisible until dark. Maybe right now the best she could do was to stay alive and let the piece of human scum who had killed Ben Spengler wear himself out looking for her.

18

Leo Sealy was watching the Spengler-Nash building through the rearview mirror of the parked white Toyota he'd rented when his phone buzzed. He wasn't expecting a text message, so he looked at it, guessing it would be a wrong number. The screen said it was from a woman named Tania Marsh, and all it said was "Same place, now."

The only person who had this number was Mr. Conger, so Sealy didn't bother to think about it much, just started the engine, took a last look in the mirrors to be sure it was safe, and drove. Sealy had to expect this kind of thing. Clients were all reluctant to speak to him on any electronic device, so certain things had to be said in person. He would have ignored most of them, but Mr. Conger wasn't somebody he could ignore. Sealy headed for the Griffith Park golf course.

When he arrived at the parking lot, he saw Mr. Conger walking toward him from the direction of the eighteenth green pulling a two-wheel cart with a bag of clubs. Sealy easily recognized the three men following him pulling golf bags on carts. Mick Noore was a very tall Black man, Vaughn Pineda had tattoo-sleeved arms and a shaved head, and Ducky Sanders had an unusually muscular torso and arms he'd built lifting weights in prison, but noticeably short legs. It didn't seem possible to Sealy that any of these men played golf.

They were all crew bosses with ties to Mr. Conger, whose operations included fencing stolen jewelry and other items. The golf bags were the perfect carrying place for a long gun, and the thought gave Sealy a tight feeling in his chest for a few seconds. He had hidden rifles that way himself. He gained control of the feeling by reminding himself he was in Mr. Conger's good graces. The three men couldn't be there to harm Sealy. They were just the rest of a foursome.

The other men went to three different cars and busied themselves folding carts, putting bags in their trunks, and changing their shoes. Mr. Conger walked to his own car, opened the door, and sat on the seat to remove his spikes. Sealy approached and Conger looked up and smiled. "Hello, Leo. Thanks for coming."

"Happy to." Sealy tried to make it sound true.

"Well, unless you got her today and hid the body, I'd say you're stuck."

Leo Sealy shrugged. "It's taking a little longer than I wanted. I almost caught up with her this morning at a hotel near the airport, but by the time I made the rounds of the parking lot she was gone. I was pretty sure she was just trying to make it look like she was flying somewhere, because I figured she'd want to stay in LA until the police gave her the okay to leave. I saw her getting into a cab at the airport and followed her, but ended up losing her in the Valley. I was about to check for other leads when I got your message."

"If you'd gotten her at the airport, you would never have made it to the freeway anyway. You don't see many cops there, but they see you. You're always on a bunch of cameras."

"Probably, but I was hoping to follow her to a safe place to do it. What can I say? I lost the cab, and so far, I haven't found her again."

"I figured it was worse than that. You were a genius to get that close in two days. Don't be embarrassed. You bought us both time by getting Benjamin Spengler right away. All of the amateurs will be thinking it's over. Want to know why I texted you to meet?"

Sealy said, "You've got me curious."

"Well," Mr. Conger said, "the parents of the two guys she shot have been complaining to me. These two were regular employees with balls and loyalty who had brought me money over time, not just part of a pickup team for one night."

Sealy said, "I don't know what I can do except get her for them."

"No, this isn't about doing anything for them," Mr. Conger said. "The bitching about it was starting to annoy me, but then it gave me a brilliant idea. A beautiful, elegant idea."

"Really?"

"Yes. It's not like there was any doubt about what happened. They got into a gun fight with somebody who was better at it. There isn't going to be a lawyer saying they were miles away at the time of the robbery. They were found with guns that they had fired at her. Both mothers are heartbroken. Both of them have told me that part of the hurt is who killed them."

"I don't understand."

"This was a girl, outnumbered and defending an elderly couple. It's humiliating. Their young sons are being made to look like punks. The least they wanted for their sons was to be remembered as serious badass men who were shot down in an ambush. I want that too, for my own reasons."

Leo Sealy wasn't sure why Mr. Conger thought he could change what had already happened and been reported, but he knew it was always best to wait and listen while Mr. Conger talked.

"It occurred to me," Mr. Conger said, "that I could build the shooting into something better. I could get these two families to demand to know why Justine Poole hasn't been arrested and brought in. She'd been lying in wait and shot two boys who didn't actually get far enough to commit a crime. If the roles had been reversed, they'd certainly both have been locked up that night. That much is true."

"Reversed? You mean if she and the Pinskys had tried to rob them?"

"No. If they'd been the ones who had seen her first and won the shootout. Why isn't she being interrogated and investigated by the police?"

Leo Sealy widened his eyes and said, "It's genius. If they can get under the police department's skin, the cops might make her stay in one place."

"Not the cops. The DA is the one I want to get to. He's a politician, so he'll do anything to help himself win his next election. If you know she's coming, you can be waiting near police headquarters. Bang, it's over. But you don't even have to get her right away."

"That's a relief."

"Right. If the cops bring her in, some assistant DA will be there to tell her not to leave town. They might make her turn over her passport and call in every day. If not, they can get a judge to order it."

Leo Sealy felt uncomfortable. He had been in her condominium and could have searched for her passport but hadn't because he'd been trying to kill her quickly and hadn't expected her to live long enough to leave the country. He said, "If she has to stay around and be available to the cops, it might give me good chances to trace her to where she's staying."

Mr. Conger smiled. "I think we can keep her available to be dragged in and questioned again and again. The families can prolong this stuff for months, or for as long as it takes."

"The one thing I wonder about, though—isn't it dangerous for you to deal with the parents directly?"

"I won't," Mr. Conger said. "I've already retained a couple of my favorite lawyers to represent these two families. They've been paid cash in advance, but they're going to say they're doing this pro bono, so there won't be any money to trace."

Leo Sealy said, "I don't want to be presumptuous, but if you've already protected your reputation by getting Spengler, why do this?"

Mr. Conger looked down and shook his head, then brought his head up and stared at him, the pupils of his eyes like pinpricks in the afternoon sun. "Don't think of reputation like popularity. It's more like the opposite. What I want is that when somebody hears my name, they start to feel a little shaky and sick to their stomach. So far, you've brought a boost to my name, and that's better than money. But what kind of fool ever gets half of what's on the table and then says, 'That's enough. I'll leave the rest in case somebody else needs it'? I can see the way to have more, another boost to my name, and killing her is it. Over the next day or two, watch a lot of local news on television."

19

Justine Poole and Joe Alston had trapped themselves into having a conversation about their prospects of a relationship and both had been more willing to listen than talk. After establishing that both were only interested in the opposite sex, that neither of them had been married, that neither had a lover at the moment, neither had made any overtures or invitations, and the discussion died of neglect.

She never hinted that her name was anything but Anna, and he never hinted that he knew it wasn't. They agreed to the lie that they had given each other a lot to think about. Joe said the most important thing would be learning more about each other and Justine pretended to agree.

Joe Alston waited until the woman who was still calling herself Anna had gone outside to the shady area in the backyard where he had left the lawn chairs. When she began to look at her phone, he went out toward the garage. He had decided that the best strategy for dealing with her was to give her the impression that he at least tentatively accepted her lies but had just met her and it was too soon to think further than that. He was sure Justine Poole would not want any complications or distractions and if any appeared she would leave. He didn't want to lose his exclusive story.

He started his car and she got up and hurried to his side window. "Where are you going?"

He didn't roll down the window, just smiled and waved and said loudly, "I'll be back in a little while," and backed down the driveway. He could see that she had bare feet, and as he reached the street and moved forward, he saw her nimbly retreat off the sun-heated pavement onto the grass.

He could tell she was disconcerted and mildly annoyed, but he had already thought through this. He had offered repeatedly to drive her wherever she wanted and she had refused. She wanted to be at his place. What he was doing would give her at least two hours to be irritated and then realize he was doing her a favor—two hours when she didn't have to talk with him and risk making mistakes while she tried to keep her story straight, and more important, two hours when the enemies she was hiding from could look for her all they wanted and get nowhere.

Alston pulled the car over in a shady spot beneath a row of California sycamore trees with smooth light gray bark and used his phone to look up Justine Poole's address. There it was, available to anyone. His first thought was that it was no wonder she was behaving oddly. Somebody had just murdered her boss. If there were people connected with the robbery who would kill him for revenge, why not her too?

Alston put her address in his navigation app and let the robotic woman's voice give him the GPS's chosen route to the place. If he was going to write her story it should be her whole story. He was fairly sure he was not going to learn much about her at her place, because she was staying away from home, but if he didn't, at least he could get some pictures to show one of the three skeptical editors he was considering that he had gone after the story like a pro.

⚹

At that moment Justine Poole was looking at a collection of the pictures Joe Alston had already taken. She had found the yellow sticky note he had stuck to the back page of his desk calendar with his password on it. He obviously changed his passwords frequently and protected his story files with their own passwords. She'd thought he was probably that sort of person. Like all great ideas, having dozens of passwords had a built-in flaw, which was that he had to write them down.

She had found what he'd been writing all morning. It was about her. She could hardly believe it. He had shown no hint that he had recognized her at the coffee shop. Had he looked inside her purse when she'd dozed off and found her driver's license or something? Everybody's purse had about ten plastic cards with their name embossed on them. How had she been so careless? She was angry with him, and then with herself for wasting time thinking about it. It didn't matter how he knew. He'd found out. He knew.

She read the notes he had typed. "She saw me in the coffee shop in Studio City and, for reasons of her own, decided to use me as her decoy [need better word], allowing her to slip out, but reassure the person she was eluding that she hadn't gone anywhere. She came to my table, put her drink down and left her jacket with me while she used the restroom. A few minutes later she called the cell phone in the jacket pocket from a second phone she had with her to tell me she'd gone out the back window.

"When I met her outside, she had seemingly acquired some kind of Eastern European accent, openly declared she had selected me based on my potential as a dating partner, and asked me to take her home to avoid a male acquaintance she had spotted nearby. It turned out she didn't mean her house, but my house. She struck me as a mixture of shrewd premeditation and insanity."

Justine jumped from that part to the next and then found a file that held cell phone photographs of her. There were a few taken while she was asleep, a few taken while she was reading articles on her own phone, some taken while she had been walking around in the guesthouse, and some taken through the living room windows while she was in the garden reading. There were several that made her reluctantly admit that he had talent for photography. The natural light from the windows and skylights on her face and hair seemed to have been composed rather than noticed. He had also not neglected her body, which in her opinion was barely average and certainly nothing special in Los Angeles, but men were men at all times and in every situation.

He'd written in the same file, "Her appearance is the most obvious reason she has been in demand in her work. She can go unnoticed among the rich and privileged. An observer might assume she was an actress he couldn't quite place, but clearly somebody who belonged there. If she was not next season's celebrity, then maybe a girlfriend or daughter of an important insider."

Justine couldn't help feeling slightly less angry at him after reading those notes. They also gave her a better idea of what he had been thinking and feeling, and maybe she could find a way to use that to her advantage.

She looked at the time in the upper right corner of his laptop's screen and then closed the files. She didn't want the history of when they'd last been open to be too long after he had left.

She also wanted to use the time before he came back to search for things that would help her stay alive. The next priority was to search for a gun.

✳✳✳

Joe Alston drove toward the address he had found for Justine Poole. He was not quite sure what he was likely to be stepping into, so he took some precautions. He looked at the phone navigation app map a step before the destination, ended the robot instructions, parked a block from the address, and proceeded on foot.

The neighborhood was like many on the west side, full of little houses with white stucco walls and red tile roofs with old-LA details like doors and windows with rounded tops or late Craftsman–style places with porches and wooden beams. The trees on the lawns and parkways were big and the electrical wires threaded through them about midway up. He had the pessimistic feeling that they were soon to be torn down and the replacements then sold at high prices to buyers who should have been smart enough to see that they were losing vanished craftsmanship and irreplaceable materials and getting giant barns built fast and cheap.

Justine's condominium building was another phenomenon, built right where the R-1 zoning stopped. It wasn't bad. The facing was brick with horizontal strips of reinforced concrete at each floor and balconies on the second and third. There was an underground garage beneath the building with an iron gate across its opening.

When he came closer to the corner, he could see three news vans parked on the street near the front entrance with their transmission masts in the air and about twenty people on the sidewalks and driveway walking back and forth in front of the television cameras carrying signs. The first sign he could make out said, "Mourn for Darryl and Kyle." The next had the word "Justine" in a red circle crossed out and "Justice!" below it. The third just said, "Killer!" Alston took out his phone and recorded a video of the scene, then ventured closer.

There was a middle-aged man in a light gray summer suit standing close to a newswoman Joe recognized, the tall, skinny blond one they usually sent out to report floods and fires. The man was telling her, "It's been almost seventy-two hours since Darryl and his friend Kyle were shot to death by the woman who lives in this building. That is not in question, and it's the only thing about this incident that isn't. Justine Poole was working as a private bodyguard, a person whose right to discharge a firearm in any circumstance is extremely limited. She was not part of law enforcement sworn to serve and protect. She was a civilian employee of a very expensive service paid to stand between the very rich and the common people."

"And whom do you represent, Mr. Waltham?"

"I represent the family of Darryl Stimson," he said, "one of the two young men who were shot down in cold blood near the gate of Miss Poole's clients. The parents of Kyle Davis have their own attorney. If this shooting had been done by a police officer, there would already be at least an internal investigation. Why isn't there one this time? What are the police chief and the district attorney waiting for?"

The newswoman said, "The police department has said the incident is being investigated."

Waltham smirked. "We'll believe that when there's evidence of it. So far, the parents have not been contacted. And the only three surviving witnesses to the shooting, the other young men present, all say she opened fire on them in an ambush."

"Thank you, Mr. Waltham," the reporter said. She looked into the camera and said, "This is Nancy Faye Kirschner, live at the home of Justine Poole. Back to you, Kate."

Joe Alston knew instantly that he was seeing something crucial to his story. He reached for his phone again and realized it had still been recording in video mode from his shirt pocket. He kept it there and walked in the direction of another set of protesters and newspeople. There was another lawyer with this reporter, and he seemed to be making the same sort of protest. Alston heard him say, "I think the people of this city have become sick and tired of the incredible gap between rich and poor that we see on display every day. We haven't been able to do anything about the huge disparity, just learned to tolerate the different lives the rich live here—private schools for their children, restaurants and clubs so exclusive there are no signs on the buildings, huge houses on acres of land hidden behind high hedges and walls when there aren't enough parks for our kids to play in, private jets on special airstrips polluting our air with thirty-mile flights. But the people are not going to put up with the rich being allowed to hire private assassins empowered to shoot to kill on their own say-so."

Joe Alston kept walking at a leisurely pace, listening and recording as he went. The newspeople had their reports pretty quickly and began to pack up, return to their vans, and pull away. The demonstrators continued until all the cameras were gone, then the two lawyers called them into a circle and said something to them, which seemed to be a dismissal. A moment later they dispersed and walked off to get into cars.

Alston turned at the first corner so he could go around the long block to get to his car. He didn't want to become a familiar face to the demonstrators, since they were a faction who might play a big part in later phases of his story. He might need to approach them in the future under circumstances that made them essential and appearing to spy on them now would not make them want to talk to him.

When he got to his car, he looked at the clock on the dashboard and realized that it was later than he had thought. In a couple of hours it would be time for dinner and he had nothing in his refrigerator that he could make into a meal to serve to a guest. He was not going to have much chance of keeping Justine Poole around if he didn't feed her, and he was positive she would refuse to go to a restaurant, where she might be recognized. He drove to his favorite Szechuan restaurant, placed a take-out order that consisted of six different dishes—one containing beef, one chicken, one shrimp, one scallops, and two vegetarian—and waited for it to be packed up while he thought about Justine.

There was no question that most of the city was thinking of her as the hero she had been made out to be, but public opinion came from news sources and news media needed something new to feed the customers every day. Now that Justine was a hero, people calling her a murderer would be a delicious new story. That was how the ritual destruction usually began. He picked up the bags containing the food order and got them into the trunk of his car, keeping them upright by putting them inside an empty cardboard box he hadn't remembered he had, and then he drove home. He parked in the garage and carried the box of take-out bags to the guesthouse.

20

Joe felt a growing tension as he stepped inside the guesthouse, not sure whether he had already caused Justine Poole to leave, losing his exclusive story. His departure had been intentionally casual and indifferent to keep the relationship friendly rather than romantic. As soon as he had learned who she was, he had known her interest in him was only an act to make him want to keep her around, and he wanted to take the pressure off. The fact that she was trying to make herself safe from whoever had killed Benjamin Spengler was hard to resent. He hoped he hadn't been too indifferent.

All she undoubtedly wanted was for him not to find her annoying or troublesome enough to throw her out. At least for the moment, that suited him too. Had he made a mistake? He heard the noise of his hair dryer coming from the bathroom. He was relieved. She was still here.

He set the food bags on the counter to be sure she would smell them and then see them when she came out. He walked deeper into the house to the doorway of his bedroom and saw her clothes laid out on his bed. He stopped there. In a moment he heard the hairdryer stop and she came to the door of the bathroom wrapped in a beach towel tucked under her arms and retreated back in. She called out, "Is that you?"

He started back up the short hall. "Yes."

"Are you alone?"

"Yes."

She stuck her head out. "Sorry. I didn't think you'd be back so soon."

He smiled. That had been masterful. She seemed convincingly unconcerned that he had been gone and pretended not to have noticed it had been over three hours. "It's fine. Make yourself comfortable."

"I left my clothes in your room."

"Do you want me to bring them to you?"

"No," she said. "I'll go in there. Okay?"

"Be my guest." He sat on the couch at the far end of the living room and watched her come out, her hair longer and straighter than he remembered it, then go into his bedroom and shut the door.

About ten minutes later she came out to the living room. "What's that smell?"

"Dinner."

"Ooh," she said. "That was so sweet, Joe. I didn't really feel like going out. I went for a swim in your pool, and it got me all relaxed and tired."

"Really? You had a bathing suit with you?"

"You didn't look in my purse while I was out of the room?"

"I didn't look in your purse at any time."

"There wasn't one," she said. "I went skinny-dipping. You said your landlord was away, and I saw you leave, so I knew I was alone." She pushed back a tress of her hair. "It was so nice." She watched him to see if her words, the clothes he'd seen on his bed, and the carefully choreographed glimpse of her wrapped in his towel had produced the desired effect. After a few seconds she was sure it had. Men, even sophisticated men, were so easy that she was sure part of his mind was thinking about her right now, forming images that were making him wish that he had been here.

She knew that any interest he might have had in her had probably been crowded out of his mind by the wish to write about her, but keeping up the fake flirtation allowed her to stay here and maintain control of the situation without telling him anything that she might not want published. It was as though they were both in a play about two people who weren't them, but were a bit like them.

She looked at the big bags on the kitchen counter with the Chinese ideograms. "Mister Fong," she said. "That's a great place. No wonder it smells so good. Should I put it in the refrigerator for later?"

"I don't think so," he said. "It's already after six, which is early for dinner, but we never had lunch. And refrigerating it can kind of thicken the sauce and diminish the flavors." He thought about the tease she had been perpetrating and added, "Besides, we may want to turn in early anyway."

She kept her expression unreadable. "I'm hungry. I'll sign on to any excuse."

They carried the food bags to the table and went back for serving spoons and plates. Without asking her he opened a bottle of Malbec and filled two wine glasses.

She didn't react, simply opened white cartons and spooned food out onto their plates. "I love Mister Fong," she said. "I actually heard that there are rich families from Taipei who plan their flights to be sure they can eat there before they fly home."

"I'll bet that's at his original restaurant in Monterey Park. It's supposed to be less Americanized."

She squinted. "I don't know. This is pretty darned good."

"I'm glad I guessed right," he said. He took a sip of wine and went back to eating. He was trying to remind her that her glass was there when she wanted it.

After a minute she did the same. She had in that time decided the wine was useful. She could let it relax her even more and nod off before he began to get too friendly. She could stay the night, extend her period of invisibility for eight or ten more hours, and not have to deal with the hopes her teasing might have aroused.

After dinner she insisted on clearing the table, storing the large stock of extra food in plastic containers and refrigerating them, recycling the packaging, and washing the dishes, to which she added his breakfast dishes.

They both sipped their wine as this was going on, and she noticed that he had half-filled her glass, but replaced the cork and didn't pour again. She decided that he had learned from experience that this was the amount that a 130-pound woman with a full stomach would take to be pleasantly relaxed, but not impaired. She had an unpleasant thought and scrutinized his face. No, he wasn't somebody who would ever put something in a woman's drink. The thought had only come because everything in her life seemed to have been ruined and obliterated in two days, and being drugged would be the next shock in the worsening series.

She followed him to the couch and sat close while he used the remote control to turn on the big television set that dominated the wall. He set it to the Channel 9 local news, which was the one that showed an eight o'clock report. He said, "I write about current issues, and I like to get an early hint of what's up every night, in case something happens that makes one of my analyses stupid."

"Checking sounds like a good idea," she said. "If it is stupid, do you leave town or wear a disguise for a week?"

"If I can, I correct it. If I can't, I kill it."

And then the news came on. There was the anchor couple—a woman, Darla Stevens, and her partner, Sean Kepler. "Demonstrations today at City Hall and at the home of the young woman who shot the two alleged home invasion robbers, right after this." Joe Alston waited through a couple of commercials, but saw that Justine was beginning to get agitated. He stood up, said, "Excuse me," and walked to the bathroom before the report began.

He urinated, washed his hands, combed his hair, turned on his electric toothbrush and brushed his teeth, then decided he had killed all the time he could there, came out and went into his bedroom to straighten the bedspread, and listened to the voices. He wondered if the report would scare her off, but he had felt it was necessary to be sure she knew what had been going on. He went back out and saw that she was still there, transfixed. For the first time she seemed unaware of him.

He waited for a few more seconds and then said, "It's obviously been a slow news day. Unless you're interested in this local stuff, I can find a movie."

She managed a smile. "Good idea."

He switched the television set from cable to streaming, found the category "Romantic Comedies," and framed one that had a picture of two actors whose faces were familiar. "Have you seen this one?"

She said, "I don't think so, but have you ever seen one where they didn't hate each other but end up together anyway? I don't see anything better, though. We may as well try it."

He clicked the remote control on it. He had anticipated that Justine Poole might not necessarily be a fan of romantic comedies, but it was likely that the woman she was playing—Anna—would be. He had done the fair and responsible thing, and let Justine Poole see the report of what was happening in her case without revealing that he knew anything. Whatever she did next was up to her.

What she did was watch almost all of the movie and then pretend to fall asleep and listen to the happy ending, which was actually more realistic and sophisticated than usual, and therefore not entirely unpleasant. He gently shook her as though to wake her up. "Come on," he said. "You know where the bedroom is. Go there and sleep."

"What about you?"

"The main house has seven bedroom suites. I'll be over there."

She stood up. "Wow. I'm sorry to be such a bore. That movie hypnotized me. Were they still together at the end?"

"More like together again at last," he said. "I guess the studio probably tested it both ways and the audience didn't like the one where she turns on him, stabs him to death, and eats his liver."

"The wisdom of crowds," she said. "Are you sure you want to sleep in the main house? I can easily sleep out here on the couch."

"No. It's really not a problem. Good night." He picked his keys up from the desk and locked the front door, then went out the side door and locked that behind him.

Justine stood there for a few seconds, moved closer to the big window, and watched him walk to the big house and disappear inside. A few seconds later she saw the light go on over what was probably the staircase. After a few more seconds she saw a light go on in an upper window.

She went into Joe's bedroom and undressed, then lay down. The bed had been made this morning, but the sheets had not been changed. She didn't care. She had what she'd needed so badly, a place to stay hidden for a whole night and give the killer a chance to make mistakes and get caught by the police. She hoped the rest and good food would also make her stronger and more clearheaded, but the main thing was being alive.

As she drifted toward the emptiness of sleep, she realized she was smelling Joe's scent, his skin, and she caught herself being drawn into thinking about him. What if circumstances had been different? She had studied him for most of a long day. He was a smart, decent man who had at first decided to be helpful to her without feeling entitled to anything, in spite of the fact that she'd been lying to him. After he had noticed she was delaying her departure, sometime before noon, he had not acted worse. Now she regretted having taken the naked swim in the pool. She had done it partly as a way of manipulating him into being less indifferent, and partly just to get back at him for snubbing her, pretending she hadn't noticed the sneaky keyhole cameras in the yard and making him see who he had just rejected.

What if things had been different, and she hadn't been in fear for her life when they'd met? Would she be here, sleeping in his bed alone? She brushed away the thought. If she hadn't been desperate and running, they never would have met, because she would never have approached him.

She felt anxiety about the people who had been picketing her condo building. She had been concentrating on the man who had been hired to kill her. It had not been wasted effort, because studying his picture and recognizing him a couple of times had kept her alive, but the news report about the demonstration had given her ideas that might help her find out who had ordered Ben's killing and hers. The two lawyers had been pretty effective, so they were probably expensive. Who was paying them to defend the robbers who were in jail? Had anybody begun the process of bailing them out? Where had the Mercedes the robbers had been driving come from? Was it stolen? If so, who had stolen it from whom, and how had it gotten to these young robbers?

She felt sorry for the families of the two men she had shot. To have a child who was pulling armed robberies was terrible. To have him killed at it was pure horror. She felt something worse than regret that the attempted robbery had ever happened. They had lost their boys—babies they had borne and loved and raised, and she had lost everything—Ben Spengler, her job, and more—her place in the world. She had the realization that she had never fully understood what she had been doing all this time. If a person's profession was to carry a gun to protect people from violence, how could something like this not happen sometime?

She had spent the night of the shooting in the police station answering questions. The first night after that she had slept in Ben Spengler's office while Ben had been murdered. The second night was in the hotel by the airport, and that made this one, borrowing a stranger's bed, the third. And then she realized that she had lost her train of thought some time ago and was too exhausted to sort through the threads again. She slept.

⚜

Joe Alston slid the false wall panel to the side and unlocked the door to James Peter Turpin's combination office and panic room in the architectural center of the big house. The hidden room had no windows, of course, and even the entry panel was off a large, sparsely furnished second-floor common room that could be fully surveyed by an intruder from the doorway on the upstairs landing and dismissed. It seemed designed to accommodate groups, possibly cocktail parties or even dancing. The last owner of the house had been a music executive who had needed a safe place because he had tax, drug, and hatred problems, so this innovation had probably been his.

Joe went inside the office, closed the door, and turned on the large surveillance monitor with the remote control on the desk. He looked at each of the twenty sections for a few seconds and satisfied himself that nobody was lurking on the property at the moment, then ran the recording in reverse until the time was three P.M. and restarted it.

He ran the recording in fast forward until he saw movement, then ran it at normal speed. There she was, coming out of his guesthouse carrying his bath towel. She stopped on the pool deck, looked around her in every direction, looked back a second time at a few things he could not see on the screen, and then stepped out of her clothes and walked down the steps into the pool until she was completely immersed. She came up, the water streaming from her hair, and began to swim.

She was a strong, graceful swimmer with a good, correct freestyle stroke. When she reached the end of the pool she completed a quick flip turn, pushed off the wall, and remained submerged while she swam breaststroke back to the wall beside the steps and pushed off to swim backstroke for a length. She swam easily and unhurriedly for about twenty minutes, smoothed her hair with her fingers, then sat on the steps for a few minutes. She ducked herself under again for a few seconds and then stood, went up the steps, and lay on the nearest chaise longue while the sun dried her skin.

She was very pretty—beautiful was the only appropriate word in spite of how liberally people bestowed it—much more attractive than he had allowed himself to admit, because it had seemed to him to be a distraction, and therefore a probable source of manipulation and clouded judgments. He had already taken a much more leisurely view of her swimming session than would have been necessary to identify what had been going on. He ran the file back to the moment before she had stepped out of the house, erased all of it up to the present, and then turned to the security camera focused on the desk and said, "Hi, James. I just came in to see if there had been a prowler poking around in the yard while I was gone today, and I accidentally erased part of this afternoon's security recording. It was all birds and squirrels, so if you see this, don't worry." He shut off the monitor, turned off the light, and stepped out. He relocked the door, slid the panel over it, walked down the hall toward the guest rooms, and thought about Justine.

She had been overconfident, probably because security was part of her profession. She might have assumed she would see any security cameras, which would have normally been mounted along the eaves of the house. She hadn't known about the previous owner before James, who'd had twelve keyhole cameras mounted in places like false drainpipes and circuit boxes and even woven into a coaxial cable on the guesthouse.

Joe stopped at the door to the first guest room. He remembered that James had told him once that when he'd moved in, the old owner had left some of his belongings in addition to the fixtures and wiring. James had not said what they had been, but now Joe wondered if at least one of them might have been a gun. Maybe he should go back inside the office and open the safe to see. James had shown him where the combination was hidden, but he had never had any reason to use it.

The old owner had apparently exhibited that familiar combination of paranoia and malice that made it unlikely that he hadn't had guns somewhere. It didn't matter where they had been; if James had them, they would be locked in the safe and had probably not been touched since then. But now Justine was here and she was in real danger. Joe decided against the guns. He had seen no indication that anyone knew she was here, and getting caught with an unregistered pistol that might easily have been used in some old crime was not going to make her safer.

As Joe pulled back the covers of the bed, he had a difficult time forgetting what he had seen on the recording. Sleep would be welcome, maybe to blur the bright, sunlit clarity of the memory image, at least.

21

Justine woke at five in the morning, probably because she had finally gotten a night of quiet, comfortable sleep. Justine had not spoken with anybody at Spengler-Nash since she had gotten the pictures of Ben's killer lurking in the company garage. She texted another friend, Linda Fry, "It's me—JP—can you call me when you get home?"

Five minutes later her phone buzzed. She said, "Hi."

"Hi, Justine. I'm in my car, and I'm out of sight a half-mile from the building, pulled over, so it's safe to talk."

"I'm a half-mile poisonous?"

"More than that—radioactive. We can't see it or how potent it is, but it's bad. They both came in at the start of all three shifts to say a lot of crap about moving the business into a new era, which only showed how little they know about the business. They also mentioned that you had made some unprofessional choices and were no longer associated with the company. Any communication with you from now on could make the company and us, individually, share legal jeopardy for your actions. Mostly us, since management—meaning Ben—could no longer be charged."

Justine said, "I kind of knew that was going on. I just wondered if there was anything new."

"Yes," Linda said. "When we were all getting back from the night shift a few minutes ago the cops were here waiting for us. They thought you would be working your usual night shift with us, I guess, and they wanted to talk to you."

"Oh, crap," Justine said. "Who did they talk to?"

"They went straight for Bailey, like most strangers do."

Bailey was tall, straight, and gray haired. He was about fifty, and he looked like a Black Marine general. "What did he tell them?"

"What we all agreed among ourselves to say—that you're taking personal time off to get over what happened. Anybody would, and if they didn't, Ben would have made them."

"Thank you, Linda. And please thank Bailey when you see him. If I keep getting in touch with people directly, I'm afraid I'll get somebody fired."

"The cops asked for your address and phone numbers again, like they thought they must have copied them wrong the first time or something. They want to talk to you, and that doesn't go away. They said a detective has been assigned to your case. I have his card. His name is Sergeant Kunkel." She spelled it and said, "I'm sending you his phone number."

"Thanks, Linda. I'll give him a call today and get them off all of your backs."

"I'm so sorry it all hit the fan, Justine."

"Me too."

"Don't let it keep you from calling our personal numbers. The nightmare twins aren't going to be hanging around when our shift lets off."

"Thanks. I appreciate all of you. Go home and get some sleep now."

"Will do."

They both hung up. Justine put away the backup work phone she had been using since her work phone had been taken into evidence and called the number of the police detective on her personal phone. "May I please speak with Detective Kunkel?"

"Speaking."

"Hi," she said. "This is Justine Poole. I just heard you wanted to talk to me."

"That was quick," he said. "We do. What time is good for you?"

"You mean today?"

"Yes, I do."

She tried to calculate how long it would take to get to the airport, case the parking area and surrounding roads to be sure it was safe to pick up her car, and then drive it to the LAPD headquarters building at 100 West First Street, get inside, and find him in Homicide Central. "I think I can be there at ten, depending on this morning's traffic."

"All right," he said. "We'll be expecting you."

⚔

Leo Sealy had been delighted with the television coverage of the people picketing Justine Poole's building. The lawyers that Mr. Conger had hired had made it sound crazy that the authorities hadn't already arrested her. He knew nothing about the parents and relatives Mr. Conger had recruited, or if they were even real, but they made good victims. They acted like anybody who had ever lost a kid. He guessed that the lawyers had persuaded them that they might even get some money from a lawsuit against Spengler-Nash, its liability insurance company, maybe even the city. Anything would do—that the police didn't let the ambulance team onto the property fast enough, or that they'd concentrated on the three healthy robbers instead of the two shot ones. The city would do anything to settle instead of going to court, because so many people hated the police.

Sealy looked at his watch. It was about the time of day when Justine Poole must be used to getting home, so he figured she must be up by now. Whatever she was going to do next, she was going to be running out of clothes. That meant her first stop would be the place nobody else expected her to return to now, her condo.

⚜

Justine decided to sign onto the Lyft app with her old work phone instead of waiting for Joe to wake up and asking him for a ride to the police station. He already knew who she was, but that didn't mean he had to know that she knew he knew. She didn't want to have the Lyft driver pick her up at his place, because then there would be a record of the exact spot where they had picked her up, identified by her name and photograph.

She put Joe's sheets and pillowcases into the washing machine and started it, and then wrote him a quick note. "Dear Joe, thank you for your hospitality and generosity." She considered signing it "Justine," to show him she knew, but she couldn't think of a good reason for the impulse. What would she gain by letting him know she had caught him? She signed it "Anna."

She hurried out and walked two long blocks down the hill to Mulholland, picked the place where the street sign for the next side street between canyons was, and summoned her Lyft car. When the driver's face and vehicle came onto her phone, he was already three minutes away.

When the car arrived, she got in quickly and told the driver what he knew already, that she wanted to go to the airport. The driver was Eastern European and had skin about the shade of her grandmother's, with a similar accent. It occurred to Justine that he could be a distant relative. The driver made his way onto the 405 freeway and headed south. He didn't talk much during the trip, so she sensed she shouldn't either. It was still very early, and she wondered if it was good for her because she could move quickly, or bad because she had no crowds to hide her. She knew that she was an innocent person who was thinking and behaving like a criminal, but she reminded herself that what the police were investigating her for was murder.

When they reached the Century Boulevard exit, she said, "Please turn right. I need to go to economy parking."

He pulled up outside the lot entrance and let her off, so she said, "Thank you," and as she walked away, gave him a twenty percent tip on her phone screen. The lot was filling up already and people there for morning flights were dragging rolling suitcases toward the shuttle bus pickup. She told herself that her car was close and she was not encumbered by luggage, but it took her longer to find it than she had expected. She got in at last and started the engine, drove to the exit kiosk, paid for her time with the Anna Kepka card, and headed toward her condominium. She needed clothes. She needed a plan for her upcoming police interrogation. She needed a lawyer.

Ben Spengler had hired various kinds of experts to give his agents basic instruction on various specialties every year—the capabilities of new weaponry that an assailant might use to attack a client; new scams they might use to track or record phone conversations or emails to learn locations, routes, or schedules; new devices for tracking cars without being seen; and real nut stuff like ways of blowing up a car.

It had already occurred to her that the person hired or assigned to murder her might be capable of using an explosive. Explosives were rarer and more vivid than gunshots and made a frightening noise that was capable of knocking bystanders off their feet or killing them with concussion. If the purpose was to obliterate her and scare other potential enemies, it was hard to beat a well-made antipersonnel bomb.

She had not thought of giving her car the sort of examination she had been trained to give it, and now she was speeding north on the 405 freeway. If she had missed something, it hadn't been connected to the ignition circuit. She supposed there could still be a chance of an initiator that only fired after a wheel or fan had turned a set number of times, or of an accelerant ignited by the heat of the exhaust manifold, but neither seemed likely. She needed to think about things that were likely.

She needed a lawyer, but what lawyer was in his office at 6:22 A.M.? She had been foolish to say she could be in police headquarters before ten. It made everything she had to do harder to fit in. She took the Olympic Boulevard exit and pulled into the parking lot of a supermarket, then used her phone to look up law firms. There was one named Ralph Zaragoza, who had a bunch of television commercials about car accidents and the wiles of insurance companies who didn't want to "give you what you deserve." There were a couple of guys she'd seen wearing ties and white shirts under leather biker jackets who specialized in motorcycle cases. Most of the other names might as well have been random lines of letters ending with either "& Assoc." or "Esq."

She thought about the cost of lawyers. She had heard they started around six hundred dollars an hour, so the kind she would need must be at least twelve hundred. She didn't have serious savings or a job. As she was thinking about all of the obstacles that were lining up against her, she thought about the television news coverage. It had blown her identity, revealed the building where she lived, and shown her photograph while she had needed to stay out of sight.

The publicity had also done something else. It had made her problem into news. Maybe a big lawyer of the sort that appeared on television every third case would like to be on television again. She found the name of a law firm she remembered—Smallwood, De Kuyper & Fein. They had represented some clients of Spengler-Nash, and when the clients had talked, it had sounded to her as though they handled all kinds of legal issues.

She called the number. There was a recorded woman's voice. "Law Offices." Justine had forgotten that: they never seemed to say which law offices. "Business hours are nine A.M. to five P.M. Pacific time, Monday through Friday. If you would like to leave a message, wait for the tone." Justine noticed that there had not been a promise to call back, but when she heard the tone, she spoke. "Hello. My name is Justine Poole. I've been asked to go to an interview at police headquarters at 100 Main this morning at ten A.M., and I need to find a defense attorney. The detective in charge is Sergeant Raymond Kunkel. My phone number is . . ." and she read it off the screen and ended with "Thank you."

She pulled onto Olympic Boulevard and then back onto the 405. Talking about the interview had reminded her that she was still wearing two-day-old jeans, a tank top, and running shoes. There were no clothing stores she knew about that opened before ten. She thought her situation through again. There might very well be a plan to arrest her this morning, complete with a perp walk in handcuffs. In any case, they would be planning to intimidate and overwhelm her with their questions, trying to get her to say something stupid or get her locked into a story that included misleading statements. She knew that was the way the game was played whether they knew she was innocent or thought she was guilty, because it put her in their power.

It was foolish to be in this predicament. If she'd thought clearly about this day, which she'd known must be coming, she should have started looking for a lawyer right away. Clothes were a lesser issue, but they made an impression. She had a really nice blue pantsuit that had been bought for her by Spengler-Nash so she could appear to be one of the accountants and executives accompanying Giancarlo Scrimante, the head of the Scrimante Milano fashion company, while he was in LA on business. It was hanging in her closet in a suit bag right now.

She had decided it would be worth taking the chance of going there if she was careful and efficient, but her decision had been made in the absence of other options. She drove into her neighborhood at 7:20. It was no longer very early, and each second things could get worse in many ways. She had to meet Kunkel in Homicide Special, which probably wasn't a place she could just walk right into, and before that she would have to get ready here and face the serious and unpredictable downtown morning traffic. It was also late enough now so that many people in her building would already be up and about, so sneaking in and out unseen might be hard to do.

Justine couldn't ignore everything she knew about moving in safety. She cruised the neighborhood searching for signs of trouble—the man who had been stalking her, the car he had been driving, any sort of parked vehicle that kept its driver shielded from view, like a car with too-dark tinted windows. She didn't see any, so she parked her car a block away from the back of her building and walked toward it.

She kept her eyes up, scanning, the way she had while she was working. This was the same, only today the life she was trying to preserve was hers.

✦✦✦

Leo Sealy was afraid that it might be too late in the morning to catch her. If she had been planning on coming to her condo, she should have been here by now. In the past hour he had seen at least a half dozen people from her building emerging to go to work or whatever else they did in the morning. Maybe she had come in the night, gotten what she wanted, and left before he'd arrived.

He was ready to get back into his car and drive toward the police station. Today was almost certain to be the first day of her interrogation, given the public pressure Mr. Conger had been manufacturing. His best move was probably to see if he could get a space on an upper floor of a parking structure near the station so he could be ready when she walked out of the station later.

He decided that before he moved on, he should first drive past the underground parking entrance of her condo building and see if she had somehow driven in past him and was still inside.

Mr. Conger had called Sealy late last night to make sure he had seen the convincing stink his lawyers had raised on television, making the police look as though they'd been coddling a pretty girl who protected the rich. Sealy had been effusive. He had said Mr. Conger was a genius. Of course, he'd had to say that. Mr. Conger had already paid him a lot of money and intended to pay him more. The truth was that Mr. Conger really was a shrewd man and his idea had been a reasonably good one, probably because he knew that the people who ran the city were susceptible to that kind of pressure. The elected officials—the DA, the mayor, the city council—would have the police chief, their hireling, order his cops to get the investigation of Justine Poole started.

Still, he'd learned that Justine Poole was smart too. She had spent a lot of her working life with people who had thrived by making ordinary people like them. She had to know that she was pretty and appealing, and she was probably expert at seeming small and unoffending. Anywhere she went in front of a lens was going to be good for her, if she had a chance to present herself well. He was puzzled, though. He really had expected her to show up this morning. The place for her to get the right clothes, makeup, and everything to look the way she wanted to had to be at home.

He conceded that he must have missed her move, which he had hoped would be the one that killed her. He walked toward his car, clicked the key fob to unlock the driver's side door, turned his head to be sure he wasn't about to swing the door open just as some noiseless car was about to pass by him, and saw Justine Poole.

She was walking on the lawn skirting the side wall of her building. She looked as though she had come around the back and was taking the shortest route to the front entrance. Sealy reached behind his back to move the pistol he had in his belt under the front of his shirt so he could keep his hand on it, and began to run.

He knew he had at most a few steps before she would see him, because motion was what the human eye had evolved to notice first. He loped with long steps, hoping to fool her for a few seconds into assuming he was just someone jogging for exercise, but as soon as her eyes flicked to him, they didn't leave him, and she didn't hesitate. She pushed off and dashed for the front door.

Sealy sprinted to get to the door ahead of her. She was much closer to it, and he hated himself for having turned away from the building to walk to his car. If he had waited a little longer, he would have seen her sooner and had a few extra steps on her. He could see that she was much faster than he had assumed, and she was going to win the foot-race unless he stopped her. He tightened his grip on the pistol as he ran, tugged it out of his belt, and ran the next few steps with it in sight. He couldn't assume he would be able to hit her from eighty feet away while she was running across his field of vision, but he was ready now and in seconds she would have to stop and turn her back to unlock the front door and slip inside.

He had to get as close to her as he could, so he ran hard with his head up and his airway straight, pumping his arms and making his fastest strides. He saw her take the last two strides with her arm stretched toward the door. She grabbed the door handle to stop her momentum and poked four numbers into the keypad quickly, hitting them with all four fingers of her free hand. She was already swinging the door open when Sealy stopped and fired.

The bullet pounded the glass and left a milky impact scar like a frozen explosion above her head. His second shot went to the opening doorway but passed without touching her body. She was pivoting into the lobby and tugging the door after her, so he ran toward her again, this time firing a triple tap at the diminishing space, aware that his aim was bouncing with his steps. The door shut. Would the door's electronic lock relay stay disengaged for a couple of seconds?

Sealy reached the door and tried to tug it open, then tried to duplicate her hand gesture in the hope that his fingers would hit the right four keys in the same order. He looked in the glass doors and saw nothing, but she must be crouching nearby. He spun and looked behind him in desperation.

There was a tall, thin man scurrying along the side of the building away from the door, trying to get out of the line of fire. Sealy made a quick decision. He sprinted after the man, pressed the muzzle of the pistol against his head so he would stop, and said, "Open the door to the building."

The man's mouth gaped. "I—I can't. I don't know the—"

Sealy swung the pistol down onto his head hard enough to start the blood flowing from his scalp, then held the muzzle against his forehead so he could see Sealy's index finger on the trigger five inches from his eye as the trickle of blood reached his cheek. "One more chance."

The man went limp and let himself be dragged to the door, punched the four numbers into the keypad, and pulled the door open. Sealy pushed him inside, shot him through the back of the head, and saw the blood spray appear on the upper wall as he ran past the falling body.

He knew the way to her condominium, so he threw open the door to the staircase and ran up the stairs toward the second floor. The door to the stairwell slammed shut behind him as he ran.

⚜

Justine heard the slam. She was crouching against the wall inside the elevator holding the "Close Door" button because a 9-millimeter pistol probably couldn't penetrate the stainless steel doors, and if it did, she made a tiny target.

She heard the second floor stairwell door slam shut, pressed the "Open Door" button, ran out of the elevator and out the front door of the building. As she ran along the side of the building, she dialed 911. She said, "I'm at five-seven-nine-four Ashburton Street and a man is inside the building shooting people. He's killed one man already, right inside the front door."

"Your name, please."

"Justine Poole. Got to go." She ended the call and ran as hard as she could toward the place where she had left her car on the next street. Her killer might not have seen her car, but she wasn't going to bet her life on it. She started it and drove. When she was about a mile away, she pulled the car to the curb, picked up her phone off the passenger seat, looked back at her recent calls, and pushed the icon to call Detective Raymond Kunkel.

She heard his voice. "Kunkel, Homicide."

"Hello. This is Justine Poole. A man just tried to ambush me at my home and killed one of my neighbors."

"You sure he was killed?"

"He was shot through the head. A lot of blood spatter. I called 911."

"I'll be there in a few minutes."

"I'm not there anymore."

"Just stay put and keep your phone on. I'll come to you."

22

Justine sat in the car, looking in her rearview and side mirrors, then staring ahead through the windshield every few seconds in a repeated sequence, trying to look in every direction at once but also to breathe slowly and deeply to get her heart to stop pounding. She kept experiencing the light-headed feeling that came after a big scare and the rush of adrenaline and then feeling the weight of the exhaustion coming on. She kept seeing the body of the man who had been on the floor when she had dashed from the elevator to the front door.

He had been face down with an entrance wound in the back of his head. He had light brown hair, darkened because the wound on his head had bled so much. She tried to figure out which of the men in the building he had been. He'd been wearing a sport coat, something nobody in the building did very often, and blue jeans, which men did to say, "Don't take the coat too seriously." The shirt had been dark blue. The outfit seemed to be the kind of thing men in their forties wore, because the kinds of jobs they had tended to fit that look. Art Grosvenor was too old; Dave Campbell was about that height and shape, but his hair was dark brown. So was Sam Melendez's, and Charles Tucker was Black. They were all decent guys who didn't deserve to have anything bad happen to them, so there was some relief, but then who was it? This was terrible. Whoever had gotten killed was dead because Justine had run inside and locked the door.

Just as she felt herself sliding into the guilt, she saw the cop cars. The first was a plain blue sedan. That stopped beside her car. Was it to shield her from the shooter or to keep her from opening her door? The second pulled up behind her car, and the third came around the next corner and stopped right in front of her grille.

She couldn't tell if they thought she was still in imminent danger or thought she was the danger. It took only a few seconds before she knew. The two cops from the patrol cars got out and stood on the grass parkway above the curb with their right hands resting comfortably near their belts, not looking at her, but not looking at anything else either. Detective Kunkel finished saying whatever he had been saying into his car radio, got out, and stepped to her window.

She rolled the window down. "Hi," she said. "Thanks for coming."

"Can you please step out and come with us? Leave your keys in the car."

He sidestepped out of the way so she could open her door and get out.

She said, "Is somebody going to my building?"

"A SWAT team was dispatched before you called me."

"Good. Great. Did they—"

"We'll have plenty of time to get to everything. Don't forget your purse."

She turned, snagged the strap and pulled it off the passenger seat, backed out, and closed the door. "Are we going to the station? I'd be happy to drive myself."

"It's not procedure in a case like this."

"You have somebody to drive my car to the station?"

"That's not procedure either. There's a tow truck on its way. Don't worry, one of the officers will wait for it so your car is safe."

She went with him to his car and stood aside while he opened the backseat door. She had been expecting the back seat because of his tone. This was all going to be by the book. She extended her hand toward the seat belt, but then imagined the menagerie of microbes that were likely to be on the belt in the back of a police car and thought better of it.

Detective Kunkel said, "Seat belt, please."

She tugged it across her body and clicked it in place. The tow truck was just coming up the street as they pulled away. She was fairly certain that this towing stuff was really about wanting to search her car without asking permission. There was nothing compromising in it, but this was another of several warnings that any of her dealings with the police could be adversarial from now on, and they were very good at making everything move fast and keeping people from objecting or even thinking clearly until things were accomplished.

She said, "Have your colleagues caught the shooter in my building?"

"Not yet."

Justine knew that this meant they weren't going to. He had been in the building, had fired his pistol about four times—no, five—and probably would have even broken down her door to get to her. If he had gotten out and eluded all the cops after that, how could they even recognize him if they saw him? She said, "Do they know the name of the victim?"

Detective Kunkel said, "I'm sorry to say it was your next-door neighbor, Mr. Grosvenor. That's got to be kept quiet for now, because Mrs. Grosvenor isn't home and doesn't know yet."

Justine admitted to herself that she had guessed it was him, but that her mind had not allowed him as a possibility because she wasn't ready for it to be him. She was not going to allow that again. All she had was her brain, and there could be no delusions or she was not going to survive.

It was Art Grosvenor. Her killer had made Art open the door to get to Justine and then shot him through the skull. The Grosvenors were the benevolent older couple who had bought their unit at least a decade ago and knew everybody and could show her how to make things work. They invited any newcomer to dinners and barbecues so they could be introduced and feel welcome. That had been why Ally Grosvenor had been able to give a reporter her picture. In a way it had been the same impulse: Justine is such a nice young woman that you should know her too. Justine felt sorry for Art Grosvenor, and now she was also beginning to be heartbroken about Ally.

"Does that hit you hard?" Kunkel said.

"I liked him, and I like his wife. This is going to ruin her life."

Kunkel paused, then said, "Look, I know you didn't murder anybody. You were protecting the Pinskys. But we still have to ask you all the logical questions. It's the way the system works. It's intrusive and sometimes unpleasant, but it protects the rights of everybody equally. The only advice I can give you is that your answers have to be serious and, above all, complete and true."

"Thank you," she said. "But I wouldn't have lied anyway."

"I didn't think so. It's just that some perfectly fine people get nervous when the police ask questions, and then they make mistakes."

"I guess I am nervous," she said. "There are people hunting me. A man just ambushed me at my condo building, shot at me when I was running to get inside, forced my kind neighbor to unlock the door for him, and then shot him to death anyway. I guess I'm not at my best. Do you think we should do this at another time?"

"I'm sorry, but I have orders to get this investigation going right away. And now it's even more urgent. This is a new murder, and the killer is still loose and armed. We have to try to stop him while we still can. That's to your advantage, the Pinskys', Spengler-Nash's, and the victims'."

"What victims?"

"All the people who have been shot. It's just a common term in a shooting investigation."

"Ben Spengler was a victim. Art Grosvenor was a victim. The two men I shot weren't victims. They were attackers. The common police term might be suspects. Something like that."

Detective Kunkel nodded, but said nothing. That confirmed for her that he was recording their conversation.

For the rest of the ride to the police station she volunteered nothing. Whenever Kunkel made an attempt to get her to say something she would give him an answer that was as much for his recording as his question was.

"You know, you're lucky I came in early enough to get your call," he said. "What were you doing up so early?"

"I like the early morning sunshine."

When they reached the station, she followed him into an elevator and up to the floor where he worked. The interrogation room was approximately what she had expected it to be—small, a table, cameras mounted in the upper corners, no windows. She supposed the idea was to use the sense of confinement to make the civilian want to get out, at first mildly and later desperately.

Kunkel, in a fair imitation of politeness, pulled out a chair for her, presumably to place her in the spot where she would be best seen in the video. He sat in the chair to her left. A large man came in wearing a pale blue shirt and a tie that he wore without buttoning the top button of his shirt.

"This is Detective Wright."

The man nodded and mumbled, "Miss Poole." He sat across from her, making her feel hemmed in left and center.

Justine had been thinking since she'd learned that Kunkel wanted to talk to her about what this moment would be like. So far, she had been right. Next, she thought they would say, "Could you please tell us about the night when you went to the Pinskys' house?"

The answer she wanted to give was, "I know what you're doing. You're supposed to lock me into telling the story to record my exact words and then compare those words with the words I used on the night of the attempted home invasion right after it happened, and then if there is the tiniest difference you can say I'm lying now, or that I was then, depending on which words are worse for me. Let's skip that and just play over the first recording." She would not say that. It would change their crafty, subtle manipulation into open hostility in an instant, and the next sixteen hours would be as hellish as they could make them in front of the cameras.

Wright said, "I'm pleased to meet you. The average person never gets into a situation where he has to take on the biggest risk to protect somebody else, so they don't know what it's like." He studied her face. "What happened today?"

She said, "I guess you both know that the night after the thing at the Pinskys', my boss Ben Spengler got murdered. I'm pretty sure the one they were looking for was me."

"Why do you think that?"

"Because since then, a man has been stalking me. He was at the Spengler-Nash building when the night shift—my shift—ended one morning, broke into my condo and the one belonging to my next-door neighbors the Grosvenors, and turned up at the hotel where I was staying because I was afraid to sleep at home and he tried to follow me. This morning when I went to my condominium building to get some fresh clothes and things, he shot at me. I made it into the lobby and shut the door, so this man forced Art Grosvenor to open the lock so he could get at me and then killed him, probably because he was a witness."

Kunkel said, "Do you know who this man is?"

"No," she said. "But I have a picture of him from a surveillance camera mounted in the Spengler-Nash garage. It's a light-enhanced camera, so it's a little odd, but I recognized him right away when I saw him."

The cops looked at each other. Wright said, "Were you planning to show it to us?"

"Of course."

"When?"

"This morning is my first chance. Until a few minutes ago I was busy trying to live through his latest attempt on my life, so it wasn't the first thing I thought of. It's on my computer."

"Where is your computer now?"

"I don't need it. I can send the picture to you on my phone." She reached into her purse.

Kunkel held out his hand. "I'll take it."

She sat still.

"What?" he said.

She said, "Since this started, the police have asked for and I've given them everything I had to protect myself. They took my firearm—okay, you needed it for the ballistic tests. That was legit. They took my work phone, which not only had all my work information but also lots of other things, including the numbers of people who might be willing to help me stay safe—work friends, clients, and so on. Now you're working up to taking my personal phone. That will put me in even more danger and you know it. That's the part that disturbs me—that you know it. Without my phone, I could die today."

"Send me the picture," Kunkel said. He sat back in his chair with his arms folded.

Justine found the email with the photographs attached. "What's the number you want to receive it?"

He recited the same number that was in her phone. After a moment she said, "There. You should have the pictures."

He took out his cell phone, looked at the first image, scrolled to the next and the next, stood up, and went out of the room, still looking at it.

Justine sat with her purse on her lap for a minute, then dropped the phone into it and set it on the floor by her feet.

Wright said, "Just to be clear, that picture is the same man who shot Mr. Grosvenor this morning?"

"Yes. Absolutely."

"And the one who has turned up at other places and followed you."

"Yes."

Kunkel seemed to be taking a long time. She glanced at her phone again, then put it back in her purse. She had noticed that the screen said it was twenty-eight minutes after ten. She wondered what could be keeping Kunkel, and then she supposed that could be another police tactic too. It didn't matter what time it was. Time was theirs, not hers.

The door opened and Detective Kunkel came back in holding a folder, but he did not come to the table or sit down. He kept the door ajar. He said to Justine, "Your attorney just showed up. He's waiting outside."

He looked down at his folder, as though there were something written on it, but there wasn't. "What are you waiting for? You're free to leave. This interview is over."

Justine stood and said, "I was wondering, is my car in the lot down-stairs, or what? Are the keys in it, and how do I find it?"

"You don't."

"Why not?"

"We'll have to hold it for the forensics people. It might have the answers to questions about this morning's incident."

"The killer was never in it or near it. How can that be necessary or even useful?"

"We'll have to let you know after it's been examined for evidence. You were at a murder this morning."

"The killer never even saw my car."

"He found you somehow."

"Is this because I called a lawyer?"

He shrugged. "Every choice costs something."

She looked at him for a moment, then walked to the door. He stepped aside and opened it wider for her and she went out into the broad, open space of the office.

There was a man standing in front of her looking at the watch on his wrist. It wasn't one of those heavy ones with little extra circles that were tachometers and timers. It was a slice of white gold, thin as a coin with a plain white face and a brown leather band, like the ones she'd seen on some of her clients. He was wearing a light gray suit that seemed to complement the gray hair he wore slightly long that she thought of as prematurely gray but probably wasn't. He looked up and said, "Justine." It wasn't a question. "I'm Aaron de Kuyper."

Of course he would have looked up her picture. She said, "Hello. Thank you for coming."

"Happy to help. Shall we go?"

She went with him for a few steps, but a voice came from behind them. "Miss Poole!"

She turned. Detective Wright hurried to her. "We'll still need your phone."

She looked at Aaron de Kuyper. He shrugged, pantomiming that it was something to be endured, but said to Wright, "You'll send me the inventory of the belongings you've collected, right?"

"Right," Detective Wright said. His hand was still out, so Justine placed the phone in it, and he walked off.

De Kuyper glanced at her, and she could tell it was a diagnosis. "We're going to the office. The car is out front."

23

They stepped out the door of the police headquarters and a black Mercedes sedan appeared a half block away and glided up to the curb at the spot where they stood. De Kuyper opened the door to let her into the back seat and then slid in after her. "Office," he said, and the driver pulled away. The whole maneuver reminded Justine of the way a Spengler-Nash getaway team spirited wildly popular performers away from concerts.

For the first time all morning, Justine felt the muscles in her back starting to release their tension.

De Kuyper said, "You must have told them things."

"A few."

"Didn't you know you weren't supposed to talk to them?"

"I had a couple of things I wanted them to know."

"What things?"

"This morning when I was walking up to my building to pick up some things, I saw a man running toward me to keep me from getting inside. When he realized he wasn't going to get there ahead of me he took four shots at me, one of which left an impact mark on the safety glass right above my head. After I was inside, he saw one of my neighbors nearby and made him open the door at gunpoint. I was already in the elevator so I hit the 'Close Door' button and held it. I figured the steel doors might stop a bullet or at least make me hard to hit. He shot my neighbor to death, and then I heard him run up the stairway toward my condo. I slipped out and ran to my car. I also sent Detective Kunkel some pictures of the man taken by a security camera at Spengler-Nash."

De Kuyper's tone changed. "Okay. You had to tell him that. Anything else?"

"Since they've done nothing to protect me, I complained that they had held onto my pistol, my work phone, and as of this morning, my car and my personal cell phone."

De Kuyper shook his head. "Those things are lost causes. Police are entitled to collect evidence. They certainly had probable cause once they saw the two bodies at the Pinsky's. And your car could be full of incriminating stuff. It isn't, is it?"

"No."

"Any drugs, stolen merchandise, pornography, large amounts of currency?"

"No. The only things I even care about getting back are in an over-night bag in the trunk on the wheel of the spare tire."

"What's in it?"

"Some clothes I packed when I left home a couple of days ago. I also took some papers—my deed, licenses, bank statements, passport and stuff."

"Why would you need those? Were you planning to go on the run?"

"So the killer couldn't find them and use them. I wouldn't go on the run and expect to have access to my bank records and credit cards, so no."

"I know that, but I didn't know you did. Is there anything else you should tell me?"

"Yes," she said. "I can sum it up quickly. There is a man or men who are trying to kill me because I shot those two home-invasion robbers at the Pinskys' house. The night after it happened, they killed my boss, Ben Spengler, while they were looking for me, and now one has killed my neighbor Art Grosvenor, also trying to get at me. The police are behaving as though they want to charge me with something, and they don't seem to want to protect me or let me protect myself. They both said they knew I was innocent, but I know they're allowed to lie."

"You definitely need legal help."

"Can you fix this?"

"We'll try."

The driver pulled up in front of a tall building on Wilshire Boulevard and de Kuyper looked out the window. "Good. We're here."

"Am I about to go broke and never get out of debt?"

"Forget money. You don't have much, and in a couple of days you won't have any, but we'll still help you long after that. We don't take cases like yours for the fees. We're taking you on so we can turn you into Joan of Arc. People—especially women—with real money will learn about it and stand in line to get in our door."

Justine said, "Even the guilty ones?"

"If they're our clients, they're not guilty." He got out of the car and held the door open for her, then took her arm and conducted her toward the front door. She noticed that the driver had gotten out of the front seat and was looking up and down the street, his right hand near his open coat. It was a stance she had taken many times, so she knew what it meant.

She didn't know if the driver knew who she was or not, but she knew that bodyguards knew far more than their clients thought. She smiled at him. "Thanks for the ride." He smiled back and made a small gesture like the tipping of an imaginary hat. He knew.

De Kuyper walked past a security desk where a pair of tall men in suits were on duty and entered a larger-than-normal elevator without features except for a single button, which de Kuyper pressed. It rose and opened so quickly that there was a sensation that the building was what had moved.

The office was ultra-modern with featureless surfaces but ostentatious at the same time. The lobby was round and three young receptionists sat at desks so many feet apart that each seemed alone. All were carrying on conversations with invisible people and looking at screens.

Justine was still wearing the same clothes she had worn since she'd put them on to check out of the airport hotel yesterday. She felt that the three sleek young women must be pitying her, but she never caught them looking at her at all, which at this moment seemed worse. She followed de Kuyper into a too-large conference room where they both sat near the end of a long table. Through some unseen preparation, he was sitting in front of a blue folder. He said, "We can sit anywhere you're comfortable," although she couldn't detect any difference among the twenty chairs.

"I'll start with a ladies' room."

He pointed. "That way, third door on the right or left. Unisex."

She found two doors which each had a triangle with a circle super-imposed on it. Everything she saw was lit by skylights and every fixture conveyed the message, "This is the best, not just the most expensive."

When she returned, de Kuyper had placed several short stacks of paper along the table in front of her with the print facing her. "This one appoints us as your attorneys. This one allows us access to your financial, personal, and business histories in the defense against any criminal or civil charges." He went down the table telling her what each was for. He stopped halfway through. "These are duplicates." He held out a black Montblanc pen. "If you want to read them, I can come back later."

"No point," she said. "It's like inspecting the only lifeboat."

"Okay. I'll follow along and scoop them up as you sign."

The process took no more than five minutes, and the papers all ended up in the blue folder. He said, "Okay. Here comes the important part."

"What's that?"

"I'm going to turn on the recording equipment now. We need to know everything that has happened to you since you went to work on the evening of August 1. I'm going to stop you from time to time to ask questions, but otherwise this is your show. It's all protected by the attorney-client privilege you just acquired." He used his cell phone to trigger some remote switch in the room's electronics and held up his phone to show her a red indicator was on. "Start by telling us your name."

She hesitated for a second. Should she go into the whole Anna Kepka business now? "Justine Poole is a work name. The one I was born with is Anna Kepka." She began to tell the story. It took her about an hour. She included every detail that she could remember, and she had been training herself to notice details for at least nine years, so there were many. She told the truth about everything, and although she told only part of the truth about a few things, at least she kept out the lies that kept offering themselves to her unexpectedly.

When she talked vaguely about leaving the coffee shop and staying the night with a friend, she added, "Someone I met at the coffee shop."

"That morning?"

"Yes."

De Kuyper said, "I'm not prying now, but is this friend male or female?"

"Male."

"Again, I'm not trying to pry, but if this comes up, and it will, we've got to have answers. Is this relationship intimate?"

"This will come up? Why?"

"It's an opportunity for the other side to prejudice a certain kind of juror."

"It's not intimate. I just met him."

"Why did you stay with him?"

"I didn't feel I could go home, because the killer had already broken into my condominium once, the same night he murdered Ben Spengler. And of course, he knew where I worked. He knew or could find out who else worked there. I didn't want to put any of them in danger by staying with them. If I went off with a perfect stranger, there was no connection that the killer could find. He couldn't trick anybody I know into telling him about this guy. Neither of us could be identified on each other's Facebook accounts or anything else. He was safe, and I was safe. I left his place early this morning while he was asleep."

"What's his name?"

"Joe—Joseph—Alston. He's a freelance writer—news investigations, research essays, that sort of thing."

"I think I may have heard of him. It's possible we may have sued him, or thought about it. And you picked him because?"

"He seemed like a nice guy. It turned out he is."

"Good," de Kuyper said. "Last question. What made you choose our law firm?"

"Because a couple of the clients I worked with at Spengler-Nash had mentioned the name, and they were the sort of people who could be choosy."

24

Leo Sealy's phone rang. He'd left it charging on the kitchen counter, so he had to trot across the apartment to get it. He was hoping it was going to be a friend, maybe Bobby Danziger. Before this job had been offered to him, he and Bobby had told each other they should meet for a drink soon. They were both in the same line of work and they had known each other for a few years, since the time when they had both been hired by an old guy in Palm Springs to kill the same list of eleven people. Neither of them had known before they'd driven out there to meet him exactly what the job was or that anybody else was on it. The first they knew about it was when he arrived and the old guy let him into this sprawling one-story house. Sealy and the man crossed a vast living room with a view of Mount San Jacinto but kept walking and talking. "There's somebody else I need you to meet."

When he had given them both copies of the list of names and addresses, they both realized that this was a very big job. The targets were all over the country, were of both sexes and a range of ages. Leo and Bobby had let their resentment of the old man go after they realized that he wasn't expecting to get a bargain. He was willing to pay very well for each killing. Leo and Bobby worked out a system, dividing the country so each took five names in a geographic area, and began scouting the targets. On the seventh of the next month at midnight, each would start the slaughter, trying to get through the five names as quickly as possible so the later ones would be less likely to hear of the earlier ones. Whoever got his five first could take, and be paid for, the eleventh. Leo got that one.

He reached the counter and looked down at the phone. It wasn't Bobby, and it wasn't a friend. It was Mr. Conger. He picked it up. "Hello." He listened to Mr. Conger's question. "Yes, sir. That was me, but I wasn't just being random and stupid. Thanks to you, I knew that once the mayor's office and DA saw the families picketing and listened to their lawyers' interviews, the cops would make a show of getting her in right away. She'd been hiding from me for two days, but I thought she might drop in to shower and change her clothes before she turned herself in. She would have to come early in the morning before people were expecting her. I saw her walking to the building, but she saw me right away too. She sprinted for the door and beat me to it. The door automatically locked behind her. This guy was coming along the building, so I made him open the door for me, brought him inside and shot him. I went upstairs to her condo, but she wasn't there. Somehow, she got out of sight. I don't know how. Maybe another neighbor let her in because they'd heard the shot. I heard sirens just then, and I had to get out. Your strategy to flush her out of hiding worked, and my strategy of watching her building worked. But this time the dog didn't get the rabbit. I'm frustrated and disappointed, but it happens. Luck doesn't last forever, or rabbits would be running the world."

Mr. Conger said, "So this guy you killed this morning, you don't even know who he is. He's not a friend of hers from Spengler-Nash, or a boyfriend, or anything. He's just a guy?"

"A guy who lived in the building. When I was locked out, I turned away from the door, and he was there."

"I don't know about this," Mr. Conger said. "When it was Benjamin Spengler, it was great for me, but you and I know it was still a mistake. Nobody asked you to go after him, you stumbled on him in the dark. This guy is different. The first one seemed like when Spengler-Nash offended me, I came right back at them and had somebody take out their leader. This looks like you panicked and executed some random retiree."

"I didn't panic. In a split second I knew I was locked out and saw a way in. I couldn't let him go after that. He'd seen me."

Mr. Conger's voice was colder when he replied. "I'm not talking about the nuts and bolts of your job. I've already helped you too much with that. I'm talking about optics. You know I don't give a shit about those two little bastards who couldn't even rob a husband and wife with a combined age over a hundred and fifty. And I care even less about the three who are still alive and got themselves captured running away. What I have to care about is my reputation on all sides. I want anybody who considers giving me trouble to see that it's fatal. I want the guys who work for me to get proof that what people have said about me is true. Mr. Conger is one scary guy, who always avenges the men he loses. I want the three in county jail to think that I'm a powerful friend but that betraying me would be suicidal. Your shooting some harmless bystander doesn't contribute to making either of us look ice-cold and efficient."

"But you do look ice-cold and efficient. You'll destroy your enemies, no matter who has to be cut down to get to them."

Mr. Conger's breathing became heavy, like the breath of a man so enraged that his body was unconsciously oxygenating its blood before a fight. He said with a careful, mock-patient tone, "I guess I have to explain history to you. Years and years ago, people—all people—believed in

God—a god, anyway. They did what they thought God wanted them to do. Even the bad ones believed. They just thought they were better than other people because they were kings or something, so God had given them a pass at birth. They all thought if they broke the wrong rules God would quick-fry them with lightning or something. They even reversed it, so if somebody got hit by lighting, they must have pissed God off.

"Then, gradually, people realized that these punishments—from lightning, plagues, wars, and all that—weren't God's justice accurately and precisely taking out the people who pissed God off. They weren't targeted at all, they were random. Some of the worst people alive got every good thing. That was the beginning of the end of God-fearing. Since then, religion has dwindled down to making up excuses for why God doesn't do what he was supposed to do. Now, with this in mind, what I want is to have people stay Conger-fearing. You see? If I'm just having people killed randomly, whether they've offended me or not, why should anybody bother to please me?"

Leo Sealy was speechless. Every reply that came to him seemed likely to be dangerous. Finally, he said, "I'll do my best to get this done, Mr. Conger. It shouldn't take much longer."

Mr. Conger hung up.

Leo Sealy had been recording the local news channels on their daily schedules and fast-forwarding through them so he wouldn't miss any tidbits that made it to the screen. He had also spent a couple of hours a day searching the internet sites. It was hard to be out hunting a target in likely parts of Justine Poole's habitat without risking being photographed or leaving trace amounts of DNA or simply becoming familiar, so he relied even more heavily on electronic sources today. Two hours later he saw an internet mention of a news conference about Justine Poole.

He clicked on the link and was sent to the front of a building with a lectern bristling with microphones but no human being, so he assumed he must be waiting for a live statement.

Then there was a man standing behind the lectern without walking there, so he knew it had been pre-recorded. There was a set of white letters identifying him as Attorney Aaron de Kuyper. He looked right for the job—expensive, well-fitted suit, sculpted haircut, slight tan that made his blue eyes stand out.

De Kuyper seemed utterly relaxed, as though he were welcoming guests he knew at a party. He listened to someone off camera for a moment and then said, "The police interviewed her today, and I understand it went according to protocol. The police have a highly legitimate need to investigate every violent fatality as fully as possible, so that justice will be served."

"Is she cooperating with the police?"

"Of course she is," he said. "She has been recognized by the media since the incident occurred for saving at least two lives in preventing a violent crime and for calling the police immediately. She also—and this hasn't been said enough—stopped using deadly force immediately instead of applying it to three other suspects who were not a clear threat. The fact that she's a heroine does not mean she has no responsibility to help further. I might also mention that her employer Benjamin Spengler has been murdered in an apparent reprisal for her incredibly brave act, and she has been the target of at least two separate attempts on her life, one of them just this morning. Since then she has shared some leads that the homicide detectives will be following up right now."

"You don't think there will be any charges against her?"

"I can't imagine that police officers, who spend their careers risking their lives to save others in jeopardy, just as Justine Poole has, would be unable to interpret the facts in this case. She single-handedly saved two beloved and blameless citizens from five armed attackers."

"We were told that you have a request for the press."

"Yes. I'm here to ask that the press and the public be patient and give the police a chance to do their job without undue pressure. And also, that news organizations take into account the fact that Ms. Poole is still in grave danger. Any help you can give us in keeping her whereabouts and movements confidential will be essential and greatly appreciated." He nodded and said, "Thank you," and walked out of the view of the camera.

Sealy resumed his search. First, he looked for any sign that a news organization had reacted by releasing her location just because they resented the implication that they put her in danger and should stop reporting everything they knew. After a few minutes he saw that they hadn't, but he kept open the possibility that they would and planned to keep checking.

The lawyer could be a lead—Aaron de Kuyper. The name seemed familiar. His Google entry identified him as a partner in Smallwood, de Kuyper & Fein. That was where Sealy had heard it before. He turned his attention to the firm. The search engine picked up dozens of mentions in connection with court cases involving well-known names in Los Angeles and New York. The clients seemed to be roughly the sort of people that Spengler-Nash protected, and the cases tended to be rich people problems—big divorces and custody fights; contract disputes with music companies, studios, agents, producers, magazines, and publishers; and slander and abuse cases against ex-lovers. The overlap in clients had to be the connection that had given somebody like Justine Poole access to a firm like Smallwood, de Kuyper & Fein. He supposed it was even possible that Spengler-Nash had a standing relationship with them.

What mattered was whether he could use the firm to find Justine Poole. A company like that would be smart enough to know that she needed to be hidden someplace. Where would they hide her?

He clicked on the first mention of the firm, looked at the article, then the second, the third, and on down the list. There were articles that stretched over about thirty years. He began to notice right away that often there would be a photograph of a client, or the client and a lawyer from the firm, in similar formats.

There were a number of pictures he recognized as taken in the corridors of the Superior Court building right outside the courtroom doors and a few in the sunken patio outside the front entrance of the Foltz Criminal Courts building. A few had been taken in front of a large building with double glass doors. It wasn't any of the court buildings he'd seen in Los Angeles. Around the double doors was a façade that looked like mirror-polished black marble, and courthouses didn't look like that. The later photographs were in color, so he could see that the door handles and frames were polished brass. He assumed it must be the building where Smallwood, de Kuyper & Fein had its offices. He kept looking, moving to the next and the next, trying to find a caption or identifying feature. There were old photographs, but there were also ones from no more than a year ago, some apparently stills clipped from the footage of some celebrity show.

Finally, he reached a differently angled photograph about fifteen years old showing the actress Sally Walstrop coming out of the brass-framed doors with a man in a suit. The caption said, "Sally Walstrop, shown yesterday with her attorney Davis Fein, makes her first appearance since she left Sumpter Ricks five weeks ago. Moments later, Mr. Fein announced her record divorce settlement." About six feet above the door and to the right were five numerals, 22764.

That was a very high number. Even Los Angeles didn't have an unlimited number of streets with 22,764 lots. That was roughly 227 blocks. He thought of Parthenia in Northridge; Sunset; Hollywood Boulevard; Wilshire, which ran all the way to the ocean; Ventura Boulevard, which ran the length of the San Fernando Valley; La Cienega, which ran from Sunset south to the airport; San Fernando, which ran from the old mission to beyond Pasadena; and maybe Vermont and Normandie. He would start with those. He used Google Maps to take a look at what was located at number 22,764 on each of those streets. As he thought of other long streets he inserted those into the list.

Sealy found it. What he found was 22764 Sixth Street, Le Chateau d'Or.

Sealy had to pause and think. He knew that he had made errors on this job. He had relied too much on Mr. Conger's delight at the death of Benjamin Spengler to keep him content for a long time. He had been too confident in his own abilities and the woman's lack of them. He had been sure he could go about his job by putting himself in the vicinity of Justine Poole and assuming he'd be able to kill her. Those errors had caused him to diminish his options. He couldn't afford to kill any more bystanders. He couldn't afford to act on impulse, taking off after the woman like a dog after a rabbit. But most importantly, he could no longer afford to keep Mr. Conger waiting.

Every bit of new information he was able to tease out of the random bits of trivia in the air was a precious thing. It was also ephemeral. It was true right at this moment, but it would change, which meant it was already on the way to changing. This particular bit was tantalizing, because Justine Poole would have no way of guessing what he already knew. What Sealy now knew was that in the past, when Smallwood, de Kuyper & Fein had a client who needed to be kept out of sight, they put her in the Chateau d'Or.

25

Justine was asleep and in her dream she was in her grandmother's house in Eastern Europe. Her grandmother had never said where it was, and somehow young Anna had accepted her dismissal of the question—that it didn't matter because there had been several countries, all about the same—dark, poor, cold, muddy, and dangerous, and all of those houses had stopped existing long ago. Her grandmother never spoke about how she'd made her way across fortified borders, mountains, forests, and oceans, but she had. When Anna asked if she'd ever wished to fly back for a visit, she gave a bitter laugh, like a snort. The Anna in the dream knew all of this because Anna the dreamer did.

There had been one place that Anna had constructed in her mind from details in her grandmother's stories. She was there now—the big leather chair stuffed with horsehair, the Persian rug, the paintings on the wall that had been hanging so long that the men and women in them looked like they lived in a shadow.

Her grandmother was speaking. "Don't let yourself be sent to prison."

The little girl who was Anna, not yet Justine, didn't reply because patience and attention were respectful and keeping her grandmother talking was like not startling a bird that landed on her shoulder.

"The people who guard you are in prison too. They're only free at night when they sleep. And they get worse and worse locked up, just like you do. You get through a day and you think, 'That wasn't so bad. I can get through it again.' Then it's worse, but you do."

Anna didn't know how she knew that her grandmother had been imprisoned. She knew it, though. It was just a fact, like the scratch on the table, there before Anna was born.

Grandmother said, "You do one thing and it bothers you for a while, but then you don't think about it very often, and then not at all. Life is more powerful than any of the living."

A telephone rang, and her grandmother turned her head quickly, as though the noise had been a shot, and then she and her parlor were gone. The room was dark. Justine rolled over in the big bed and fumbled with the hotel phone receiver. "Yes?"

"Hi, Justine. This is Marina Obermaier. I'm one of your lawyers from SDF. I'm in the lobby. Can I come up?"

"Sure. Yes," Justine said, flustered but awake. "Come up. It's room four-something. Just a second and I'll tell you."

"Four-eighty-seven," the woman said. "See you soon."

Justine hung up the phone. She saw the horizontal line of light coming from under the door and used it to find her way to the light switch. She pushed her hair out of her face, squinting to fight the glare as she oriented herself. Her phone screen said it was after nine P.M. She had locked the door, taken a long, hot bath, and then slid under the covers to keep warm and fallen asleep. She couldn't stand the thought of putting the same clothes on again, so she didn't. She put on the big, fluffy white bathrobe and cinched the belt around her waist. The robe seemed to have been made for a man, so it went around her almost twice and hung down to her ankles.

She listened for the sound of the elevator arriving. When she heard the faint *ding,* she stood at the door and looked out the fish-eye lens. The woman who came into her field of vision looked about thirty and had amber hair that hung straight, with bangs cut just above her eyebrows. Her sharp brown eyes were staring into the lens.

Justine opened the door, let her in, quickly closed it again, and reset the locks and chain. Justine had not met this woman, but she had expected there would be one. Marina Obermaier was confident and relaxed. She crossed the room gripping the loop handles of some large shopping bags with each hand, not waiting timidly near the door to be beckoned ahead. She stopped at the foot of the bed and placed some of the shopping bags there and one on the desk. "I had the girls watch our office recordings of you so they could guess your sizes, colors, and tastes. They didn't have much to go on, so I hope you like what they picked out."

Justine peeked into the three big bags while Marina Obermaier continued. "There's a court outfit, a kind of brown-gray twill, with a silk blouse, some shoes with a moderate heel. And there are three outfits for surviving in this hotel. Also underwear, bras, and so on."

Justine pulled the four outfits from the bags and stretched them out on the bed. "They're lovely. Great estimate of sizes, too. Who are the girls?"

"You didn't see them when Aaron brought you in? They sit at the desks in the reception area. I thought you'd remember once you'd seen them. They're all improbably gorgeous. If I wanted to, I could make a really good case of a sexist and hostile workplace just by bringing them into court together."

"I did notice, to tell you the truth," Justine said. "You're not serious about the lawsuit, right?"

"Of course not. I would have moved to a different planet when I found out at puberty what this one was like, except that all my friends and relatives were here."

"Well, thank you and them. I really like the clothes, and it's late for you to be working, so this trip was above and beyond anything I would have wished for."

"You haven't even seen this bag," Marina said. "It's food. It occurred to me that you probably haven't eaten since morning, so I picked this up. I could tell by looking at you that you're high protein and never saw a vegetable that you didn't like. The salmon is probably cooled off a bit, but there's a little microwave mounted in the cupboard above the mini-bar in these rooms."

"Wow. That was thoughtful."

"More like premeditated. You're probably going to get found here. The reporters are looking for you, and now that Aaron did his little press conference to feed them free footage that says you're a hero, it will probably get worse. So for now, eat what I brought you. Don't go into the hotel restaurants or any other restaurants. After this, order room service. There's a menu on the desk. I've got to go back to the office, so you can eat in peace."

"Go back? Why?"

"Strategy and tactics. We'll be putting in a lot of hours to keep you above suspicion and immune from arrest."

"I'm sorry. I feel awful. And your firm is going to end up eating the cost, because I can't possibly pay for it."

Marina laughed. "Is that what Aaron told you? He may not have known when he talked to you, but Jerry and Estelle Pinsky have already volunteered to pick up whatever your defense costs." She went to the door and said, "Got to go," and she was out.

Justine went to the door to reset the locks. She was already thinking about the food, since Marina had mentioned it. She took the bag to the small table at the side of the room near the big windows and unpacked it. Everything was tightly wrapped so there was a layer of plastic sealing each container. On the containers, napkins, and plastic were seals with the logo of Ample, one of the best restaurants in Los Angeles. Justine had been there a few times with Spengler-Nash clients, often working with a male bodyguard about her age, sitting with him at the next table. They had always gone in just ahead of the clients and done a quick inspection, scanning the dining area and bar, making a trip to the men's and ladies' rooms, and taking a quick look in the kitchen to be sure that if the worst happened, they could bring the clients out that way. It had never escaped her notice that Ample was a wonderful place.

When she thought of it that way, she realized that someday, if she lived through this, she would probably feel depressed about those losses too—not just the big, heartbreaking losses like the death of Ben Spengler or the frightening things like the serious chance that she was going to die too. There was also the certainty of the end of her access to the special places. She had been with clients in establishments that were practically unknown outside of certain circles. She had been living—not living, visiting—a fantasy life.

It wasn't fantasy for her clients. Being in public was work for them. She had been watching over performers who would come off a stage, their fancy outfits soaked with sweat and their hair plastered to their necks, their faces showing traces of the slack muscles and wrinkles that were one day going to end their careers. The light, almost weight-less steps onstage a minute ago were now stiff limps of strain and exhaustion. She had been with comedians going over their material before stepping toward the curtains, their eyes looking panicky, as though they were already on the roof of a high building listening for the cue to step off.

Most of the time Justine had ignored that part of it. She was being paid to see everything that was going on everywhere but the stage, to notice every person in sight, and to be ready to move when one of them stood up, slipped a hand into a pocket or inside a coat, looked nervous, or changed in any other way.

When they came off the stage, the performers would be revealed as what they really were, people risking everything and struggling to be good enough. Afterward the pretty masks would return, and everything was easy, natural, and relaxed. She had gone with them on their wonderful vacations, been to parties in beautiful homes, and listened to the conversations of people who had been brilliant and funny and full of knowledge. And most of the time she had been presented as though she were an actual guest. The male bodyguards with the huge muscles and serious faces were a few paces back except in the bad moments when they went to work, stepping between a client and a possible assailant, or guiding an aggressive, drunken fan into an adjoining hallway that led to an exit.

Justine's disguise had been to be just another pretty woman in a room full of pretty women. A hostile person might speculate on what she was—girlfriend or wife or daughter of somebody, a studio executive, an agent—but bodyguard should never come to mind. She had done a few interventions herself, but they were rare and mostly subtle and quick, and the rest of those evenings were wonderful.

That was over. As she ate the dinner that Marina had brought, she remembered the rooms of Ample in perfect detail. She had studied the place, knew the entrances and exits, even the ones some of the restaurant staff didn't. She would never be in that place again. She couldn't even imagine wanting to go again. The idea would just remind her that she didn't belong, couldn't afford it, couldn't even call for a reservation because requests without a big name attached would be placed on a waiting list that never got much shorter.

As she ate, she thought about how useless most of the skills she'd worked to develop were, now that she had lost her job at Spengler-Nash. She wondered how she would be able to make a living—if she wasn't killed or sent to prison. Maybe she could get a job driving an armored car for one of the big companies, like Garda or Brinks. At the moment she was still an experienced security professional with a clean record, so she was bondable. She had even taken courses in defensive driving, although she couldn't imagine spinning one of those fat-ass steel boxes without tipping it over.

There were other kinds of trust-dependent jobs. She would make a good messenger. She could deliver documents, precious stones, even small artworks. Maybe not. There would be too much trust required from her. A messenger could easily find herself at an airport search discovering that her briefcase was full of some kind of contraband. She kept thinking. She had protected and guided some important business people, including some who would probably remember her. Maybe one of them would hire her for their company.

She closed all of the food containers, tied the bag around them, and thought about putting it in the hallway, so the room service waiters would collect it with the trays other guests left, but then realized the Ample logo might tell her killer that the person in this room was somebody who was being given special treatment. She put it in the minibar refrigerator.

Justine took a Band-Aid from her purse and stuck it over the fish-eye lens in the door to free her of the suspicion that somebody in the hall could get a half-distorted notion of where she was—bed or chair—and fire through the wooden door. She sat on the bed and turned on the television set.

She had not watched much television since childhood. It wasn't something she'd had time for in college, and since then her job had kept her out almost every evening, so she did some exploration of the channels now. There seemed to be a number of things that could hold her attention, but her mind was too agitated to stay on any one program or movie for more than a minute or two. A couple of times she stopped on dramas, whether movie or television series she didn't know, in which one of the actresses was somebody she had protected. Each recognition was a reminder that she didn't work for Spengler-Nash anymore, because she had been fired. She kept changing channels until her eyes were tired from changing their focus with each click.

Justine turned off the television and used the toothbrush, dental floss, and mouthwash in the hotel's kit, spending an inordinate amount of time caring for her teeth, rubbed face lotion on her face, and then let herself sleep.

26

Leo Sealy had expected somebody from Smallwood, de Kuyper & Fein to show up at Le Chateau d'Or within a few hours after the press performance that Aaron de Kuyper had given. He had expected they would send a woman, but he hadn't thought she would be a high-ranking lawyer like Marina Obermaier.

Justine Poole probably needed clothes and things, and only a woman could go into the right stores and make the right selections without attracting attention. But he had seen her and the white Tesla she had turned over to the valet parking attendant, noticed the vanity license plate ended in ATTY and then heard her say the name Marina Obermaier to the parking attendant. He typed it into his phone and learned she was one of the company's stars, a lead lawyer who had won a lot of big cases, including acquittals in criminal trials.

He attributed her selection to the psychological cunning of law firms. They loved to establish rapport with new clients so they would be docile and accepting when the time came to manipulate them. The non-lawyers in a firm couldn't be sent out on something like this, because they had actual grunt work to do to keep the place running. A big lawyer was probably there partly to judge the client and decide how she could be used in her own defense. Was she quick or slow, articulate or tongue-tied, honest-looking or shifty-eyed, attractive or plain? That kind of thing mattered in any human interaction.

He had put on his KN95 mask and followed at a distance when Marina Obermaier had walked into the lobby and gone directly to a corner to pick up the white courtesy phone. As he walked, he turned on his cell phone, set it to video and aimed the lens at her while he held it up to his face and talked to it. Recording her dialing and talking took no more than ten seconds, and then he turned and walked toward the hallway that clearly led to a restaurant.

He ducked into the men's room just inside the restaurant doors, and a minute or two later he left the restroom and walked to the front door and out to the lot. He walked to his latest rental car, got in, and watched the video. He could see her fingers pushing the buttons on the old-style push-button phone. He drove a few blocks away, parked, and looked at his cell phone. He whispered to himself something that one of his elementary school teachers used to say: "Numbers will be our friends if we spend some time playing with them."

Again, he watched Marina Obermaier pressing the keys of the hotel phone and then talking. The image was too small to read the key numbers. What he could see was her fingers. He pressed the symbol on his phone that showed a phone keypad, and then ran the video again. Her finger moved left to four. Down the middle to eight. One space to the left of there. That's seven. Four-eighty-seven. The hotel phone didn't connect to an operator if you didn't dial 0 for one. You could dial the room by number. He watched the video again. Four-eighty-seven.

Leo Sealy had been thinking about the problem of hotels since yesterday morning. The reason hotels had always been a favorite place to hide protected people was that it worked. Every inch of those places was under surveillance, and nobody wanted to be recorded. The simple arithmetic made it difficult. A hotel could have hundreds of rooms, and a shooter had to find the one that mattered.

Leo had cleared the first obstacles easily. He had found the right hotel in a city with over a thousand of them. He had found the right room. The next parts were not going to be so easy. It wasn't that there weren't a lot of ways. People had been taken out by rifle fire to a hotel balcony or window. They'd been shot by a person who worked for the hotel with a pistol at close range. They'd been killed in explosions set off in public spaces in hotels. But how feasible were any of these against a woman who had worked in the security business for years?

Justine Poole was not likely to go out on a balcony, or even open her curtains. She was not likely to let a man into her room she didn't know in advance was coming. She wouldn't go downstairs to accept a package or even to meet with another lawyer from Smallwood, de Kuyper & Fein without calling Marina Obermaier first. She wouldn't go to the hotel restaurants for a meal or the bar for a drink. Even if he tried the most difficult method, preparing to trigger a large explosion in a public space, she would have to be in that space at the right moment. It would be nearly impossible to lure Justine Poole into any particular place at this point. He had to try something else.

Rooms in hotels were usually set up according to a few templates—single bed, double beds, king, suite, with the furniture almost impossible for a guest to move. He could try to find pictures of the various types of room in Le Chateau d'Or, and then figure out which kind of room 487 was. If he converted the picture on their website to a diagram, he could probably tell by inches which section of the room was occupied by her bed. The fourth floor wasn't very high up, so if he found a building nearby that was taller, he could occupy a space on the fifth floor or above with a window that faced room 487 of Le Chateau d'Or. He owned a couple of top-quality military sniper rifles fitted with folding bipods. It wouldn't be too difficult to estimate what downward angle would allow him to place a shot through her window and into her bed. The best tool for his purposes would be his M24, a marine sniper rifle based on a Remington 700, comfortable for him because he'd owned his for a decade. He had a couple of ten-round box magazines for it and some Lapua Magnum .338 ammo that he'd bought years ago. He could walk ten rounds across her bed and around her room faster than she could get out of bed and make it out the door to the hallway, and he had the advantage of knowing that was her only route to safety. With a military-grade sniper rifle he didn't have to worry too much about hitting a fatal spot. Almost any hit to her center mass or some places on limbs would make her bleed out in minutes.

He didn't remember the tall buildings around her hotel. He had found the place and rushed to it to get there in time to spot anyone from Small-wood, de Kuyper & Fein, and that had been his sole focus. He opened the Google Maps app. He started at the hotel and moved the display to see a continuous picture of the part of Wilshire Boulevard where the Chateau d'Or was. There were a number of apartment buildings to the east of there, and the advantage of his Remington was that it was effective at 1,500 yards. The problem was to find a clear sight line from above. There weren't any buildings along the north side of the street that would do, so he tried the south side. He couldn't get up high enough. He switched to Sixth Street and moved past the hotel. There was no suitable building there either. He had a moment of hope for the huge Park La Brea complex that occupied the space between Third and Sixth, because there were eighteen apartment towers, all of them thirteen stories. But he knew the process of renting an apartment took weeks, and vacancies were few.

Another problem was that Justine Poole's hotel room would have to be on the north side of her hotel to be visible from Park La Brea, and the room he fired from would have to be on the south side of a tower and at least five stories up. If his perch was too high up, he couldn't hit anything that was more than a foot or two in from the window. His shooting platform had to be between the fifth floor and about the eighth. He knew that the idea that he could find all of the conditions he would need was insane. He spent another few minutes on the plan because he had already invested so much time and thought, but then abandoned it.

It was probable that Justine Poole would live by ordering room service. Was there a way for him to know when she called in her order so he could poison her food? The only way would be to divert the room service waiter and deliver the actual order she'd called in, because otherwise she wouldn't eat it, and she had to eat it.

He needed a circumstance he could produce and control without being caught in the act or captured before he could escape, recorded on security systems, or shot to death. He needed it badly and soon, because Mr. Conger was getting impatient to have his swift revenge while the offense against him was still fresh. This also had to be unerring revenge with no more random victims, only Justine Poole. Everything had to be right.

27

Justine heard pounding. Her mind tried at first to incorporate it into her dream. What entered her dream was a team of big football players running down a long corridor that led out onto the broad green playing field. They emerged and there were loud shouts, maybe from the people sitting in the stands, and others from the players themselves. "Open up! Open up!" Her brain couldn't fit this into the dream, so her eyes opened.

There was a stamping of feet, and she realized she had been hearing that too. It took her a second to place herself in the hotel room, and then the telephone on the nightstand rang far too loudly, and she realized it was all the phones on the floor ringing at once. She snatched up the one beside her.

It was a pleasant female voice, a recording. "This is an emergency. If you're hearing this message, you must immediately leave your room and make your way to the nearest stairwell, which is marked with a red 'Exit' sign. Do not attempt to use the elevators. Leave all luggage and personal belongings. I repeat—" Justine hung up. It was obviously a fire. She stepped into the new pants she had laid out for tomorrow on the desk, tugged the top over her head, stuck her feet into the new walking shoes and wriggled into them, and slipped her purse over her shoulder.

The invisible men reached her door a second later and pounded on it. A man shouted "Police! We're evacuating the building! Come out now!"

Justine put her hand on the doorknob gingerly, her mind still clouded but aware that it might be hot, found it wasn't, and opened the door. What she saw was motion. The cop had already moved on, replaced by a stream of people of many sizes and ages, not stampeding but walking at a brisk pace from left to right across her doorway. She saw a break between a big man with a mostly bald head whose gray side-hair was standing up so it looked like animal ears and a woman who was wearing a long, graceful blue bathrobe with padded shoulders and a narrow waist like a 1930s gown, with stack-heeled shoes. Justine stepped into the gap and adjusted her speed to the procession, leaning to the side to peer around the tall man to see what was ahead.

The squad of police officers had moved out of sight already, but there was one standing under the "Exit" sign holding the stairwell door open and using a sweeping arm gesture to direct people into the stairway. "That's right, everybody. Keep it nice and orderly, and go down carefully. Watch your step, and hold onto the railing. Help anyone who seems to be having trouble. The officers in the lobby will direct you."

A man about forty-five years old who had a wife and a teenage daughter stopped in the doorway and said, "What's the emergency?"

The officer said, "The officers at the bottom will explain," and he adjusted his next sweeping hand gesture to guide the man through the doorway. "Eyes forward and watch your step, ladies and gentlemen."

Justine was aware that it was best for her not to be recognized, so she followed more closely behind the big bald man and kept her head down as she reached the stairwell entrance.

She had to be careful to merge into the stream of people already coming down from the floors above. The first steps onto the staircase where an unpleasant surprise. Each section of the structure was a freestanding flight of steel steps that went from one rectangular landing to the next, followed by another flight aimed in the opposite direction. The whole structure seemed not to be well anchored to the walls, so it was shaking with the heavy footfalls of the dozens of people hurrying downward.

She started to look upward to see how the staircase was held together—bolts? welds?—then caught herself and conceded that it didn't matter because the decision had been made long before now, but that made her wonder how long ago it had been.

She concentrated on the downward motion. Stepping down put people in the position where she wanted them. The ones in front were looking away from her, and the ones behind could only see the back of her. The one place where she had to look away was on each landing, when everyone had to walk in a semicircle to the next flight down.

One of the things that puzzled her was that she wasn't noticing anything she had expected in a fire—hearing an alarm sound, people coughing. She didn't smell any smoke. She was glad, of course. Maybe all of these people could get out before things got ugly and life-threatening. Her mind searched for an explanation—they had found an electrical fire right away and ended it, but had to be sure it was the only one, or there had never been a fire. Were they allowed to run fire drills in a hotel with real, paying guests? She'd never thought of it before, but it didn't seem possible. A more likely story might be that the fire had been real, but small, and they had decided to avert a panic by getting everyone out instantly. None of these ideas satisfied her.

She had been avoiding an idea that had been nagging to be recognized. The cops had said "emergency," not "fire." The emergency could be a man seen on the premises with a gun, an active shooter. This idea was now seeming the most likely, and the probable suspect would be her killer. Marina Obermaier had warned Justine that somebody would figure out she was staying here, but she had been speaking about a reporter, not a killer. Justine's next thought was that it didn't matter what anyone talked about. What mattered was what happened.

This was Justine's fault. She had been trying to stay ahead of the killer for three days, but she was the only one who knew how tenacious and skillful this guy was. She had tried to get Sergeant Kunkel to understand how urgent it was that the police go after him, but they'd already known, and then she'd realized she'd blown their sympathy by having called a lawyer instead of waiting to reassert her rights.

She looked at the number "2" stenciled on the wall by the door on the next landing. She was elated because she was almost to the ground, and then she felt frustrated, because she was almost to the ground and had spent her time thinking in the present instead of planning. In one more flight she was going to be out of the stairwell and in the open. She kept up the pace because she had to. There were people behind her who were terrified and descending faster to escape what they probably thought was a fire.

When she reached the concrete floor at ground level the door marked "1" was propped open and she heard a deep, authoritative male voice saying, ". . . bomb threat. The call has been deemed credible, so please keep moving. Don't stop until you and your party are on the far side of the yellow police tape."

It had not occurred to Justine that the rush down the stairwell could have taken more than a few minutes, but apparently the cops had been here long enough to cordon the place off. During the evacuation descent she had never been near anything but solid windowless walls, but as soon as she stepped out into the lobby, she faced the glass side wall, where she saw the rotating blue and red lights atop police cars; red, white, and yellow flashing lights on fire engines and ambulances; spotlights sweeping the street and the grounds of the hotel. She could see vehicles of several sorts moving around at the periphery. Staring made her move too slowly, so the flow of people from the stairwell engulfed her and swept her through the brass-framed doors onto the sidewalk.

Once people were outside, there were more police officers and firefighters to direct them away from the building, but most people went a hundred feet, stopped, and began to coagulate into thick crowds. They seemed assured that the emergency—at least for them—was over.

A few times, Ben Spengler had included visits from members of the police bomb squad in his training curriculum, because events involving people like Spengler-Nash clients—concerts, galas, awards ceremonies—were possible targets. The bit that came back to her now was that when there was a chance of high explosives, they had advised that a bodyguard move everybody at least five hundred feet from the probable device. She reminded herself that what she'd heard was that this was a bomb threat, not necessarily a bomb. One of the bomb techs had mentioned that only about a third of LA bomb calls resulted in a device that could even cause an explosion. That had seemed like few at the time, but tonight a third seemed like a lot. And the man who was after her wasn't some nut or prankster; he was a pro.

She began scanning the crowd, looking for her killer. She saw knots of people who were obviously hotel guests roused from sleep—couples, some middle-aged and some young, clinging together, while others seemed to see this as a social occasion, talking with animation about what they'd heard, seen, or felt. There were children, some so young that their parents were trying frantically to keep them in hand, or at least in sight as they strayed among the taller adults. The older ones seemed deeply bored and put out by the experience, but the attitude was a pose, because in spite of their flat expressions, their eyes were always moving, flicking from one sight to another.

Justine had trained herself to expect the threatening person to be less than obvious, and tonight he'd have to be very careful, because these cops would know enough to look for the man who had made the call, expecting him to show up. She raised her eyes to the tops of the nearby buildings, then the darkened windows, trying to spot an open one or a balcony that had anything on it that could be a man or hide one. She knew a professional killer must be good enough to pick her out in this crowd and make a head shot.

The cops were now making progress in herding the evacuees across the wide pavement of the boulevard to the opposite sidewalk and the recesses in front of the buildings there, and the lanes of the street were filling with emergency vehicles. She saw the fire engines with the long extension ladders were moving closer in case there was any need to fight a fire, but the ambulances were a bit farther away. She spotted the big rectangular bomb squad vehicle near the side of the building and the round steel containment vessel on a tow rig behind it. They were taking this bomb threat very seriously. As she had the thought, she realized that she wasn't—not the bomb, anyway.

She was almost certain that the caller had been the man who was hunting her, trying to flush her out of her hiding place in the hotel so he could get at her. She had stayed in the crowd as much as possible since she'd been awakened, trying not to be alone or to present a clear target. This had given her time and opportunity to study the evacuees and the nearby buildings. The people she'd ignored were the first responders.

There were dozens of cops at the fringes of the crowd. Most people—including Justine—thought of them as protectors. What if her killer had come dressed as a cop? She was sure that anybody who killed for a living must have at least considered using that disguise. Maybe her killer had done it tonight. She looked hard at each cop she could see, trying to find the man. As she looked at face after face, the idea seemed more likely. There were about ten thousand cops in the LAPD, and they couldn't possibly all recognize each other, especially when there were so many brought together in an emergency. And why not a fireman? There were dozens of them here too, most wearing helmets and turnout coats.

She noticed that an increasing number of the other evacuees were looking at their phones. She took her phone out of her purse and slowly turned around, making a video of the scene. Then she repeated it in reverse, taking a still snapshot every few degrees. If the killer managed to get her this time, maybe he would be recorded on her phone. She knew the police took pictures of bystanders watching arson fires. She assumed they did it on bomb threats too—better photos than hers—but at least she was doing something.

Some people were talking on their phones. She wouldn't stand out if she called someone. Who could she call? She looked at the time on her phone: 1:10 A.M. The people from the Spengler-Nash office had been warned that if they spoke to her, they would be fired. She knew that there were plenty who would ignore that if she asked. This was a tough choice. She was sure she was vulnerable; she was sure she was defenseless. But was she positive that this threat call was the work of her killer? She felt that it was likely, but it could easily not be.

Most of the Spengler-Nash agents had worked there longer than she had and were older than she was, meaning that they were likely to have people they were supporting and were less likely than she was to find new jobs. The older they were, the higher up they were, meaning the jobs they would lose were mostly supervisory. She couldn't throw somebody's career away because of a suspicion.

She admitted to herself that there was only one person she could use to get herself out of this. She pressed the picture of a telephone on the little screen.

28

"Hello?" Joe Alston's voice sounded dry, almost a croak.

She almost pressed the red circle to hang up, but thought ahead to the emptiness she would feel afterward, and spoke. "Hi, cutie," she said. "It's me, Anna. I'm sorry I had to leave without saying goodbye yesterday morning, but I had to go before you were awake. I absolutely couldn't help it."

He seemed to collect his thoughts quickly. "Did you just wake me up to apologize for not waking me up yesterday morning?"

"I guess I did," she said. "But I'm also in need. I have to ask you for another really big favor. Then I promise I'll take my time and thank you properly for all the favors at once."

"What's the new favor?"

"I'm standing across the street from the Chateau d'Or hotel on the Wilshire side of it with all the other guests. They had a bomb threat called in, so the police woke us all up and evacuated us. What I want is for you to zoom in and drive me to your house. I hate to ask you, but—"

"Are you in danger?"

"I think I am, but only if I stay here. This area is jammed with police and fire trucks, so you can't get to the hotel. I'd like to meet you somewhere a block or two away, and I think that will keep us both safe."

"All right," he said. "I'll be in my car heading in your direction within a couple of minutes. Call me as soon as you've found a place where I can pick you up."

"Okay," she said. "Goodbye." She began to make her way through the crowd, staying within it for protection. She chose the direction of the side of the hotel where the bomb squad truck was parked. There were several cops nearby in coverall versions of police uniforms, each with a badge embossed or embroidered over the left breast pocket instead of a metal badge. She supposed those guys wouldn't want any extra metal on them to conduct stray voltage or a spark.

She was judging the flows and currents within the crowd of people and moving with them instead of against them. She was able to move toward the bomb squad because a stream of evacuees was drifting in that direction, drawn by the universal human urge to get close enough to witness anything and everything that might be important. It didn't have to be safe or even easy to identify or interpret. It only had to be what was happening at the moment.

The bomb squad had disconnected their containment vessel so they could lower a ramp out the back door of their truck, and now a bomb squad officer was using a remote-control panel to make the squad's robot move on its treads down the ramp. The robot was only about four feet high. She remembered it had a human name, but right now she couldn't remember what it was. Andros? Its name was Andros. The robot had grippers on the ends of its arms, cameras that fed a display on the pilot's remote panel, and the ability to fire a shotgun shell to obliterate an explosive device. As the pilot walked along behind the robot, two other officers went ahead to open doors. The robot was a big attraction, and Justine's group was drawn to it, craning their necks to watch it move into the hotel lobby.

Cops in standard uniforms arrived at that point to prevent civilians from moving any closer, and Justine joined the swirl of people diverted past the bomb squad truck and away from the building. Justine walked along with them, then paused for a moment to look in every direction, trying to judge which one was most likely to be safe and lead to a spot where Joe Alston could pick her up.

Now that she'd seen that the police were about to search the building, she knew she had to move more quickly than she'd anticipated. Searches took time, and people who stayed at hotels like Le Chateau d'Or were not the kind who would stand patiently outside much longer than they already had, waiting for the police to let them back in. People were already activating Uber and Lyft apps or calling cabs. She had to get out of the area before too many others did and there wouldn't be enough people to hide her.

He was winning. He had found the hotel where her lawyers had hidden her, and he had scared the police into evacuating the hotel so all the occupants were standing in the open and unprotected in the night. In a minute she could be dead, and he would be driving to get out of sight before anybody had any idea what had happened.

Why wasn't she dead already? The thought seemed to have an energy of its own, making her shoulder and back muscles tighten and a wave of heat rise to the back of her neck. She knew he must be nearby doing something to make her death more certain. She looked around her again and still couldn't see him, so she kept looking.

She heard a quick *beepbeep* horn behind her and saw a knot of people part to let a police car crawl past, and on the far side, following in the wake of the black-and-white car, was the killer. He was wearing a black baseball cap, a dark pair of pants and shirt that matched, and a green-and-white reflective vest. He had a lanyard around his neck with a piece of laminated plastic that implied identification but could have said anything. He turned and she could see the back of his shirt had white letters on it that were mostly obscured by the safety vest, but looked to her like the upper parts of the word "SECURITY."

She considered trying to get to the police car, run in front to stop it, and point him out to the cops, but the car was moving faster now, only delayed for a few seconds. She could never catch it. Instead, she began to circle toward the area where the bomb squad truck was. That was the center of things, and there were cops nearby to keep people away. As she approached, she saw there were more police cars parked on the far side of it now. After a few more steps she could see one with a shotgun upright in its holder behind the center console.

She veered toward the car and kept her posture stiff and upright. She only moved her right arm a few inches to grasp the driver's side door handle. It was locked. She walked on, looking for the next patrol car. There was one near the yellow tape, one of the units that was still sitting at an angle with its doors open, but it was much closer to her killer than it was to her, and the space she would have to cross was now less crowded than it had been, so she would be in the open all the way. She dismissed the idea.

As she moved away from the hotel she felt as though she was seeing more clearly. The killer was wearing emergency gear and she wasn't. If she had pulled a shotgun out of an open patrol car and pumped it, somebody, maybe even her killer, would have shouted, "Gun!" and the nearest half dozen cops would probably have opened fire on her.

She walked faster away from the front of the building, where most of the light and activity was, and toward the north side. In that direction she could get off Wilshire to Sixth Street and head for dimmer, emptier streets where she could meet Joe Alston. She stopped to look back and didn't see her killer, but she was already feeling that her plan to have Joe swoop in and take her away was ill-formed and foolish. She knew her impulse to steal a police shotgun and fight the killer off had been desperate and crazy, but walking away to get picked up was too easy for the killer to defeat. It was also the only chance she had left. It was time to text Joe. "I'll be on Fountain, east of Crescent Heights." She pocketed her phone and kept walking and looking.

Some of the other hotel evacuees might have rides on the way, but so far, she hadn't seen any car pull up near the hotel that wasn't official, and she hadn't seen any of them open a car door and get inside. It was entirely possible that the police had roadblocks on all of the streets leading to the hotel. As she thought about it, the idea seemed obvious. It would be insane for them to allow cars to enter this area if they had reason to believe there was likely to be an explosion. She crossed Sixth Street, and looked back to see she had left the crowd behind. It was time to run.

She began to trot, increasing her speed gradually for the first block so she didn't strain a muscle or turn an ankle. She turned to the north and kept goading herself to add more speed. Much of her attention had to be on the sidewalk ahead—both for dangerous obstacles and for unexpected human beings. It was after one A.M. There were men in the city who would see a woman like her running alone as a gift from the universe, a perfect victim. She had just seen the killer minutes ago on foot by the hotel. She hoped that meant he didn't have a car nearby either. If he was on foot, she at least had a chance to outrun him. She had to try.

Justine glanced over her shoulder a few times to see if her killer was running or driving after her, saw a few sets of headlights and realized there would be no way to spot him in a car until it was too late. Her best

strategy had to be to get off the major streets, so she put it into execu-
tion at the next opportunity, took a left and then a right to head north
toward Fountain. Now she was on a street with apartments, where an
assailant couldn't just overtake her and trap her between the street and
an unbroken wall of locked businesses. Here she would be able to pass
between buildings and disappear into darkness. This part of Los Angeles
was a long slope that began in the hills that separated Hollywood from
the San Fernando Valley and swept down all the way to the ocean. North
was all uphill, and she had chosen that for a reason too. Hunters didn't
have as strong a motive for running as their prey had.

The street began to change after a few blocks. More apartment
buildings appeared as she moved closer to Third, then she saw Santa
Monica Boulevard farther uphill. She turned to the east, then picked a
north-south street that was even more dense and the apartment buildings bigger.

As she crossed the next street, she looked for a route that would keep
her invisible for one more block and noticed a place where two buildings
each had what looked like a new layer of gray façade. She could see a
narrow walkway between them, and above it a strip of starry sky that
was beginning to be obscured by wispy clouds. A dark, narrow walkway
was a risk, but far ahead she could see nothing but darkness, which
meant that the end, where the walkway led, was probably an intersecting
walkway and another building rather than a street. If she was being followed, her killer would almost certainly be in a car by this point, and
this walkway was only wide enough for a person. It was a perfect way to
leave him behind, like a mouse running into a hole too small for a cat.

The first stretch of the walkway was about six feet wide, so she could
run along it at the same speed. In the next stretch the space between
the two buildings narrowed to about three feet, nearly shutting out the

faint glow of stars overhead and making it darker. As she ran, she felt her left shoulder scrape the wall, overcorrected, and a few seconds later her right shoulder bumped the right wall. She began to have nightmare images of the space narrowing until she would get stuck. She didn't let herself stop moving ahead, but she went more slowly now, both hands up so she could prevent any more contact with the walls.

She heard something. It sounded like distant footsteps. She held her breath to be sure the sound wasn't just an amplification of her own steps in the space of the walkway. No, she could still hear it, and it was behind her. Somebody had run into the space after her.

She couldn't go back toward him, so she went on, now with more careful steps to keep from making noise. If it was him, he would certainly have a gun. Could he fire it in her direction and let the bullets carom back and forth from one wall to the other and hit her? It was a remote possibility, but the bullets would lose velocity rapidly. She turned halfway around and stayed sideways to keep her silhouette small. She couldn't see him, but she had noticed even as a child that it was easier to see things in dark places if she looked to the side of them, not straight at them.

She leaned forward and moved her head from side to side, listening, then leaned backward to see if the change of angle helped. She rested her back against one wall, and held herself steady by bracing her walking shoes against the other. She had just discovered something, so she tested it. She raised her right shoe against the wall and pressed. She raised her left foot into the same position against the wall, and pushed harder. She pressed both hands against the wall behind her to bring her back out from the stucco surface, and found she could use her legs to push her weight upward a few inches.

She came to understand the way it worked—her legs and arms pushing upward during the seconds while she kept her back from touching the wall, and then letting her back press against the wall to hold her there while she took a step and prepared her arms to push off again. She began to walk herself up between the walls of the narrow passage.

Justine was up five feet in three steps, ten feet in six steps. She kept at it and began to improve her technique. By fifteen feet she had learned that if she rolled her back slightly to the right against the wall when her left leg was stepping and rolled to the left when her right leg was stepping, she could alternate arms and climb faster. Maybe she could get to a window, break it, and crawl into it. There were no windows. All they would look out on was another windowless wall. Could she make it all the way to the roof? A few feet later she heard something and paused to listen.

It was him. His breaths were quieter and slower, but he was moving closer. She held herself where she was, absolutely still. She wanted to look down, but she couldn't move her head without dislodging her back from the wall. If he looked up, he would see her and if he saw her, he could kill her. Was he looking up already? She waited, terrified.

Justine's uncertainty made her fear her muscles were weakening. How hard did she have to push with her legs to stay up? Was she still pressing hard enough? She searched for reasons to believe she would live through this. People were better gatherers than hunters, and part of the reason was that when they were in forests they seldom looked up, so they missed plenty of sights. In jungles, leopards and jaguars had no trouble waiting on tree limbs and dropping on humans passing below.

She heard her killer passing under her. She held her breath until she was afraid of making herself dizzy and then took slow, deep breaths. She heard him moving along the passage ahead of her. He kept going for a while. Had he gone all the way out to the next street? She wondered if it was safe to try to walk herself back down. She eased down a couple of steps, but then she heard footsteps again and froze.

He moved more quickly now, stomping as he went back the way he had come. She waited until she decided that the steps had faded, not merely paused, and then strained to reverse her climb. It felt harder than the climbing had, partly because her muscles had become so strained. She forced herself to descend slowly. Dropping from fifteen feet, or even ten, could break her spine as easily as twenty.

At last, the time came when her left heel touched the ground. She eased her body down so she could sit for a few seconds. She was so relieved that she felt her eyes welling with tears. She stood up, brushed her hands across her eyes and began to move forward. In a few seconds she was moving more quickly. Something had stopped the killer and made him go back. Had he just given up the idea that she had come this way?

She kept going, working up her speed as her leg muscles stretched and loosened. Then she could see the end. It wasn't a perpendicular walkway. What she had been seeing was the plain, darkened side of a building. She moved up to the end. The owners had planted a set of vertical bars into the concrete pavement that narrowed the opening to about ten inches, so a man couldn't get through.

Justine slowly eased her left leg into the narrow space between the last bar and the building, facing the bar and squatting slightly to hold both legs sideways to slide her pelvis out through the space, felt the stucco scraping against her bottom, but kept going. She turned her head to look along her shoulder to present the narrowest silhouette of her head. She exhaled deeply to compress her rib cage, rotated her body to half-twist around the bar, and squeezed out.

She was on Fountain. She looked up and down the street. She was east of Crescent Heights. Now if only Joe would come.

29

Leo Sealy emerged from the space between the two buildings where he had entered it, and ran for the street. He had seen Justine Poole go into the passage, and he had been sure he could catch her in it, but he had underestimated her speed again, or maybe this time he had underestimated several things—her alertness, her stamina, and her ability to fit herself through a space designed to block a person. It had looked to him to be the kind of space where children got stuck and had to be rescued by firemen, but that had to be the way she had gotten out. He ran downhill, around the front of the building and up the street to Fountain, turned to the right to look, and saw her running far ahead of him.

She ran east on the sidewalk and then suddenly veered out to the curb. There was her voice, shouting. He couldn't hear what she said, but it made a man in a car pull over sharply and stop. She ran, flung open the passenger door, and threw herself inside. He could see her fiddling with something in front of her—maybe moving something out of the way of her feet. As she slammed the door shut, Sealy saw something white fall from the car to the pavement. The driver pulled away from the curb and accelerated. Whatever she was telling him put the spurs to him because the car kept gaining speed, going slightly nose-upward as it went.

Sealy stopped running. He had no hope of getting close enough to the car to fire. He also had no chance of running back to the parking lot two blocks from the hotel where he had parked and driving back here in time to see where the man who had picked up Justine was taking her. He could only be sure they were heading east, but that could already be changing right now. When he got to his car he would go in that direction, because every other direction had even less to recommend it.

First, he had to see whether he had been imagining what he thought he had seen when Justine Poole had gotten into the rescuer's car. It had been a flash of white, like a piece of trash, falling from the car just before Justine closed the door. He kept going, moving slightly slower because he wasn't chasing her now. He kept his eye on the approximate spot where he had seen the white object fall. He decided that the best move would be to get off the sidewalk and run beside the curb at the edge of the street, so he would be less likely to miss it and go past.

Soon after he had moved to the edge of the road, he heard something, a hum that was just above a whisper—a car coasting along behind him, its rubber tires hissing on the asphalt as it came up on him. He glanced over his shoulder while maintaining the cadence of his steps, as runners did. He saw a pair of headlights, and behind them the unmistakable shape of a police car. The light bar on its roof was dark, and the car was moving barely faster than he was.

He wished he hadn't been running. That didn't look good after one A.M. He had taken off his reflective vest and the rest of his gear and discarded it as soon as he'd seen her cross Sixth Street—except his pistol, which was in his right pocket, the side away from the street. Now he wished he'd kept the vest. A lot of nighttime runners wore them, and looking as though they wanted to be seen at least made people assume they weren't doing anything illegal. The cop drove along beside him for about a hundred feet, looking at him closely, and then rolled down his window and called, "Run on the sidewalk, not the street."

Sealy waved, stepped up onto the sidewalk and went into a slow trot, and the cop sped up slightly and drifted past. The police car approached the spot where the other car had stopped to pick up Justine Poole, and then the cop appeared to get a call. The car's light bar came on, the lights spinning and emitting blue and red flashes as the car accelerated sharply. As it passed over the bits of trash in the street some of it blew and swirled in its wake, including the white rectangle, which spun and then blew close to the curb.

The cop car was far away now and the cop had other things on his mind, so Sealy ran out into the street again to reach the spot before some sudden breeze could pick up the paper and blow it anywhere. When he got there, he found the white rectangle lying in the gutter among the dust and leaves. He stomped his foot on it to hold it down, not daring to trust its permanence even for the time it would take him to bend over and pick it up. He squatted and tugged it out from under his foot. It was an envelope, the kind that companies sent inside their solicitations for subscriptions or donations. He turned away from the nearest street lamp and held it up so he could read it. *Harper's Magazine*. There was a preprinted square in the right corner that said, "No postage necessary if mailed in the United States." There was no space asking for a return address, but one of those address stickers had been stuck there anyway. He read it. *Mr. Joseph Alston, 327 Corcoran Way, Los Angeles, CA 90046.*

Sealy folded the envelope and slipped it into his left pants pocket, then started to trot back toward the corner where he had first seen Justine

Poole running for the car. After a hundred paces or so he changed his mind and slowed to a businesslike walk. Running was a risk. The cop who had passed him had probably not entirely acquitted him of being up to something. He had just been giving all of his attention to his radio call. That must have seemed serious, because he had sped off immediately.

Sealy had no further need to run. He sensed that the rules of the universe had suddenly reasserted themselves. The fact that she had flung open the car door and accidentally brushed the envelope off the dashboard or seat or pushed it out the door with her foot was amazing—but no more amazing than her eluding him for the past three days. Things seemed to be normal again. The race damned well was given to the swift and the battle to the strong.

30

Justine turned in her seat to look out the back window. The street behind them sloped downward, a long double string of street lamps that marked its course beneath the now clouding and half starless sky. Beyond that it diminished into an indistinct part of the smear of hazy illumination that in turn vanished into the blackness of the Pacific. She did not see the car she was looking for.

She knew that Joe had been waiting for her to say something, and she was aware that she was going to have to, but she had not yet decided what it would be, so she let the delay go on.

She had made the big decision already, and she was still surprised by it. She watched the darkened buildings slide past, and she thought that it was not unlikely that she would be dead before the city was light again.

Her killer was a pro. He had managed to get himself close to her at least three times. That was something she had been trained to avoid in her own profession, and she had successfully eluded dozens of stalkers and obsessives and aggressive paparazzi who had wanted that million-dollar too-revealing shot of a client. Nothing she'd done this time had worked with this man. He had been able to take every turn she took, and sometimes it had seemed that he had read her thoughts and anticipated her moves.

Justine had tried a dozen logical, sane ways of surviving this threat. She had been denied the help of Spengler-Nash or any of her friends who still worked there. The police had never tried to protect her, and calling a high-end legal firm had alienated the police completely and had made her next hiding place possible to find. The cops had confiscated the weapon she'd carried at work, and the ten-day waiting period had made it impossible to take possession of the replacement she'd bought. Her well-meaning neighbors the Grosvenors had inadvertently endangered her by giving her photograph to a television station, and by opening the locked door of their shared building and giving her killer a chance to corner her. The sane ways had failed.

She glanced at Joe Alston. He was a stranger, but he was the only person she had turned to who had been of much use to her. She had chosen him as a convenient dupe, a man whose presence at the right time and her immediate impression of him had made him stand out. She had grabbed for him like a drowning swimmer raising her head above the surface by climbing up on the person beside her, even though her weight might push him under.

She looked again. She couldn't help feeling affection for him. She supposed that the quality that had made her pick him out in the coffee shop was simply being approachable. It struck her as a shame at this moment, because he didn't deserve this. If things had been different, she might really have been interested in him. Now those things—relationships with men—were over. Probably everything was over.

She said, "Thank you for picking me up, Joe. I really do appreciate it."

"How could I not pick you up?" he said. "You said you were in danger."

"I was," she said. "But one of the things I find kind of odd about certain kinds of men—the kind you are—is that it doesn't seem to occur to you that if I was in danger, you would be too. In this instance I'm glad, though. And I'm grateful." She leaned close and kissed his cheek, and then retreated.

"You are, huh?" He gave a faint chuckle.

She realized she had made him suspicious again. "I'm not offering to sleep with you. I'm going to give you what you really want."

"What's that?"

"The truth. When you went out, I read what you're working on, so you don't need to pretend you don't know who I am. You're trying to write about me. You can, and if I'm around, I'll give you an exclusive interview and tell you everything."

"Why?"

"Because you helped me," she said. "It comes down to the fact that some people will, and some won't."

"Good enough. When do we start?"

"Tomorrow, I guess. It's too late tonight." She hoped he didn't pick up some hint of the guilt she felt for saying that. He didn't know that she had intentionally changed everything.

He said, "Is there something I can do for you?"

"I don't know. You're an investigative journalist. Maybe you can help figure out who is behind this. The boys with the guns aren't the problem anymore. The one I need to catch is the one who hired them and hired the man who killed my boss and is trying to kill me. I think that one place to start might be by finding who has a previous connection to the lawyers who organized the picketing at my building and downtown."

"I'll try," he said. "I really will."

In a few more minutes he was turning into the driveway by the big house. He followed the pavement around the corner of the house, pressed the remote control, and glided under the rising door into the garage. Then he set the remote control into the drink holder at the front of the console and parked. They walked to the guesthouse and she watched him spend a minute doing the things that people did when they came home late at night—glancing at windows and adjusting the thermostat and looking around to be sure everything was the way he remembered leaving it.

He said, "We'll set you up in my room, and I'll go camp out in the main house again, since you seem determined to resist my many attractions."

"Don't feel disappointed," she said. "Tonight I would make a better doorstop than girlfriend."

"At least you'll have clean sheets, since you washed them. I dried them and put them back on the bed."

"Good for me. Thanks."

He went to the door. "Good night."

"Good night." She almost faked a yawn, but sensed it would look fake. She watched the same lights go on in the lower windows of the big house and then go out and new ones appear on the second floor. After a few minutes they disappeared too. It was time to get to work. Her killer could already be on his way. Justine turned out the lights in the guesthouse and sat back down in case Joe had decided to watch her for a few minutes to be sure she wasn't up to something secret that he should know about. She was.

Justine used the time to evaluate her situation. She had been sleeping for hours before Marina the lawyer arrived, then more hours before the pounding on the doors of the hotel rooms had roused everyone and begun the evacuation, so she was probably much more rested than her killer was. She'd had a good dinner. She had run, but he had run too.

What she had done after that was crazy, but she had realized that she had already exhausted the rational and normal ways of staying alive. The killer had found her everywhere except one place. The only thing she'd done that had helped her was to use poor Joe, who was a giant sucker because he was a writer, and that made him a slave to his nosiness.

She knew she had reached the end of Joe's usefulness. Things were now beyond his capabilities, and all she could possibly accomplish if she accepted more of his help was to get him killed.

Justine had become convinced tonight that the hunt was not going to end in her favor. When her opponent had the only gun, there wasn't really such a thing as a defense. There were only hiding and running. Being under police investigation made it illegal to do either, and she was out of effective ways in any case.

She waited for her eyes to get adjusted to the darkness in the guest-house. She wished for her grandmother. She had often remembered things after she'd grown up and wondered whether she had merely imagined they had come from her grandmother. Some had seemed to be things no grown-up would ever say to a child.

"We were cozy and warm and safe until one day our parents and our aunts and uncles started to whisper. If one of us wandered into a room where they were whispering, they would stop. Then one day, my mother was a different person. The other adults were still whispering. I had begun to sneak around and listen, so I already knew plenty.

"She told me more. There had been a battle miles and miles away. The best regiments, the ones who would never give up an inch of ground, were in it. Later I heard some of them really never did give up an inch.

There were so many heroes that the enemy had needed to bring up earth-moving machines to bury them all.

"Afterward there were still men who taught us to fight. We had no weapons, so they taught us to make the world a weapon—dig ditches and put spikes upright in them, ruin roads, bury food, weaken the wood floors of houses so they'd fall through. Later, when people stole bullets from the bodies of enemies, we made what they call in English 'zip guns' from pipe and wood handles and rubber from tire inner tubes. One shot only, and then half of them blew up or fell apart. Some people learned to make bombs. They used them for traps, but some of the makers blew themselves up or burned to death. But we made the world a terrible place for invaders. It was all we had the power to do."

Justine judged that she had remained still as long as she dared. She could see much better now. It occurred to her that she was also less frightened. She was used to night. Since the age of twenty-one she had spent more of her waking hours after dark than in sunlight. She had worked those hours to make some famous client or other safe to step into the electric glare that came with attention. She had been good at taking them out of the light with her afterward.

Justine had already thoroughly searched Joe's bedroom, but now she went looking for other places where he might have hidden something. She was hoping to find a gun, longing for one, imagining one as though to prepare herself to detect its shape. She was choosing to search in places where a person might hide one—in a drawer under dish towels, in a covered pot or pan, under a couch, in the back of a file drawer. She opened the coat closet and ran a hand over the surface of the high shelf, and felt inside the three shoe boxes he had on the floor. She swept her hand among the jackets hanging on hangers to detect anything hard and heavy.

Justine knew that people tended to hide things as close to them as possible, with the bedroom the favorite place. She could barely accept the fact that she had been luckless in her search for weapons, but she had no more time. She would have to use what there was. She went to the butcher block on the kitchen counter and pulled a few knives out part way to learn what was beneath the identical handles. She rejected the bread knife, the chopper, and both the large and small butcher knives. She selected the boning knife, which had a narrow, rigid blade about eight inches long. It was very sharp, had a pointed tip, and a bit of a widening at the bottom of the handle to give her fingers some hope of a stable grip.

Now she was armed about as well as she could have been three thousand years ago. Maybe she could do better. The guesthouse was a reflection of Joe Alston. He was the kind of man who was able to throw a laptop and a change of clothes into a bag and go find out about something happening ten thousand miles away. He wasn't very interested in possessions. When he could, he put them in drawers and closets so he didn't have to look at them. What he had that she might be able to use was a friend who wasn't like that.

He was living in the guesthouse of James Peter Turpin, who was a producer and director. Joe had told her nothing of the story, but she'd met Turpin once at some event. She'd noticed the two men were about the same age, were both physically fit but no longer athletes. They had the same Norhteastern inflection. She guessed they had been friends somewhere before they'd both reached LA—probably in college or some early job.

James Turpin was rich, and he was famous in the only way that mattered to serious men. People who made a difference in the entertainment business knew him, but to other people his name was just one of fifty or a hundred on a rolling list of credits. Looking at the house and grounds told her that Turpin was not Spartan like Joe. He bought cars and furniture, had people keep every plant trimmed and watered, the buildings in repair and painted.

He had made a few successful movies in which the characters were all bent on murdering each other, so it was possible that somebody might have given him something dangerous as a souvenir. Male movie people were always doing that kind of thing—giving a sword or dagger or something that had been used as a prop to the person who had made the luck that was enhancing the others' lives. She didn't dare waste her emotion hoping for a pistol, but she knew Turpin had made a movie set in the Amazon that had featured blowguns with poisoned darts. Even one of those would be an improvement over what she had. She had followed that train of thought as a way of calming herself, but it was so close to the truth that it made her admit to herself that with the passing of time she was beginning to feel afraid.

When Joe had driven her here the first time, she had seen that the far space in the garage had been occupied by an antique sports car that was half hidden by a dust cover, probably something Turpin had bought intending to have it rebuilt. It showed her that he had enough of that rich people whimsy that he might own something else she could use.

She moved across the dark living room to the side facing the main house, unlocked the door leading to the pool, and stood motionless for a minute to be sure that her killer hadn't arrived yet. Then she opened the door and stepped out. She made her way in the silent, dark night to the side door of the garage. She had seen Joe open this door without a key, so she entered and closed the door. There was a light switch on the wall, so she turned it on. There was a long workbench along the back wall, and on it were battery-operated power tools, all charging from a row of outlets on the wall. They were not the sort of mismatched tools that workmen bought, one at a time over a period of years as they were needed. These were a set, all bought at once. There was also a lot of irrelevant stuff in this area—a couple of cigars and a pack of matches, baseball caps on hooks, some receipts, a putty knife, a bottle opener in the shape of a hula dancer.

She walked to the old car parked in the far space. She pulled back the tarp. The finish made her pause. It was dark blue. The car must be about ninety years old, but it gleamed. She knew it was the kind of paint that had been sprayed on and dried, then rubbed by hand with extremely mild abrasives, painted again and rubbed again, maybe a dozen layers so it had depth, like a gemstone. But pulling back the dust cover allowed her to see something else. Under the chassis was a large sheet metal pan, about an inch and a half deep. It was obviously placed there to catch oil drips. The pan was large, probably manufactured for professional shops, not for a sportscar that wasn't much bigger than her own compact sedan. She noticed that there were some other things in the big garage. There was a low rectangular device about the size of a steamer trunk that she judged to be an emergency generator. It wasn't hooked up to anything, so it must be here for the aftermath of the giant earthquake everybody had been waiting for since she was a child. A few feet away were two large metal gas cans, and she supposed they were for the generator.

Her killer was coming. She had made sure that he knew where to find her, and he was almost certain to be here before daylight. She had to use what she could find here. She looked at the wall above. There were two black heavy-duty extension cords about eighty to one hundred feet long hanging there on hooks. They probably had something to do with the generator too. She unhooked one and took it to the workbench. She used a pair of wire cutters to snip the socket off the end, and then split the two copper wires that were exposed, and stripped about four inches of the insulation off them.

She went back to the old car. The front was facing out, so she knelt in front of it and dragged the sheet metal pan out from under the car and stood the pan on its side against the garage door. She found a two-wheel dolly, brought it back, got it under the pan, and wheeled it out the side door to the yard.

She knew exactly where she wanted it. There was a space where the path from the garage to the main house narrowed and ran between the pool and the tropical garden. She placed the pan there. Then she stuck the bare wires in the pan and held them in position with small clamps from the workbench. She used a trowel to dig a shallow trench through the tropical garden and lay the long extension cord in it, then covered the cord with a little of the dirt. She took it all the way to the guesthouse, and left the plug directly under the outdoor socket. She used the hose to fill the pan with water, and then covered the pan with the dust cover from the sportscar so the water wouldn't show. Then she went to the green trash can to see if there were any grass clippings. There were. She rolled the can to the pan, scooped out the grass clippings she could reach, and sprinkled them over the dust cover, then rolled the can back to its space behind the garage.

She looked at what she had done. All of the things she had found—the drip pan, the dust cover, the extension cords, and everything else, were pieces of luck. They weren't major ones, but they gave her more of a chance than she'd had. The last preparation, the one that made her most nervous, was the electricity. She walked to the side of the guesthouse, picked up the plug of the extension cord between her thumb and fore-finger, placed her feet on the single flagstone that kept her from making contact with the ground, and pushed the plug into the socket. Nothing happened that she could see, but she knew everything had happened.

Her killer was smart. He was well-practiced and calm. When he hadn't succeeded right away, he'd immediately thought of other ways to get to her. In persistence, at least, he was a bit like Justine. She stepped back into the garage and looked at her watch. It was after three A.M. She had worked quickly and efficiently, but she and her killer had used up the night. In the next hour or so, her killer would be coming for her. This time he would find her.

She took one more look around the garage for things that might help her. She had seen the killer a few times and tried to develop strategies for evading him or outthinking him. She had thought about him for days—the way he looked, the way he killed and kept from being caught. There was no more time for Justine—or for Anna. She saw a carpenter's hammer among the tools hanging on the wall. She took it down and tested its balance and weight. It was good. Almost any average-sized man could kill a woman with his hands. A woman swinging a hammer like this one would be a very different story.

Justine turned off the light, stepped outside, went along the pool deck to the end of the guesthouse, turned to walk under the umbrella shapes of the big trees where the shadows were deepest, and then between the tall green shrubs that had been planted for privacy. When she reached the front of the big house she turned again and found a sheltered spot beside a hedge, set down her hammer and boning knife, lay behind them on the grass, and stayed there, watching the street for the arrival of her killer.

31

Sealy drove up the quiet street toward the corner with only his fog lights on. He switched off even those and let the car's momentum carry it into the turn onto the street where Joseph Alston lived. He accelerated out of the turn and took his foot off the pedal to coast the last block in silence. As soon as he spotted the right house he pulled over to the curb and parked.

He looked at the clock set into the dashboard. It was already after three A.M. The delay he had run into had been maddening. By the time he had walked back to the lot a couple of blocks from the hotel to get his rental car, things had changed. While he'd been chasing Justine Poole, the police had received so many reinforcements that they had greatly widened their security perimeter and made it impervious to vehicle traffic. Hours earlier, when he had called in the bomb threat, he had been certain that his car had been parked far enough away to be outside any perimeter they might set up.

The phone conversation had been a tricky one. He had needed to tell them enough to persuade the bomb squad that he could do real damage. He had needed to distinguish himself from the lunatics and from the amateurs who used black powder or dynamite. He had mentioned a few ingredients of military-grade high explosives. That had brought out many more backup units and convinced the commanders that they needed a much wider margin of safety. He had needed to wait over two hours for the police to finish their full search of the hotel and roll up the yellow "Police Line Do Not Cross" tape before they opened the block where his car was parked.

The bomb threat call was an instance of Sealy getting in his own way, but it had happened long before the shift in the current of the universe. Things had begun to improve while he was at the hotel.

Since then, it seemed to him that the universe had begun to correct the imbalance that had allowed the girl bodyguard to survive this long. Sealy had failed at everything tonight and risked making Mr. Conger cut his contract short, but here he was.

Justine Poole was undoubtedly in that house over there, and after all the running she'd done tonight she was almost certainly asleep. The man who had picked her up on the street had been tall and slim and appeared to be in his thirties. He had to be Joseph Alston. He was probably her boyfriend or somebody who wanted to be, so Sealy had to be prepared to find him in the same bedroom and needed to be prepared to kill him too. Mr. Conger would certainly not consider him a bystander but an unavoidable obstacle. It would take two shots instead of one; not a big deal.

Sealy made one change. He had been planning to take the .357 Magnum revolver for this visit and use it on the girl so he wouldn't have to deal with brass being ejected all over the place by the Glock. Now he decided it would be best to take only the Glock. It was lighter and slimmer than the .357 Magnum, and even the two spare loaded magazines wouldn't hamper his movement because he could separate them in two pockets. He reached into the console between the front seats, took out the Glock, and put it in his right jacket pocket.

It seemed a bitter irony that after an eight-year career of extreme care and professionalism, he found himself suspected by a repeat client of having become overconfident and careless. He gave his head a small involuntary shake and reached back into the console to adjust the position of the revolver. He wanted the muzzle pointed downward and the grips upward just under the lid of the console. He wanted the pistol there for insurance. There was a possibility, however remote, that he might be driving away in a few minutes with an empty weapon or feeling the need to make someone think he was, when he actually had a loaded revolver ready to go and in easy reach.

He also had a knife in his pants pocket and a strangling cord with two wooden handles in case he had the chance to work silently. Working in a big city meant there was always somebody close enough to hear. He looked at his car's clock. He had been parked here for almost five minutes. The average emergency call to the police brought a car in about that many minutes. They always said it was three, but it was more like six. He gave it another two minutes before he was sure nobody had seen him and called. This was just another item on the checklist in his head.

He opened the car door. The dome light didn't go on because he had turned it off before he'd headed to the hotel. This time was going to be it—the final visit. He got out and closed the door without slamming it, locked it with his key fob, and walked toward the house.

Justine lay on the grass and watched her killer walking toward the house. What the hell could he have been doing sitting in his car all that time? He had looked as though he was busy moving things here and there.

And then she knew. He was a pro. He had not been doing something stupid like using his cell phone to talk to somebody. He had been preparing his equipment. He'd been doing what she would have done—putting each item he needed in the right place on his body so his hand would go right to it when he needed it.

It was at that moment that she understood something else about him. Yes, he had been loading his pockets with the things he would need. But he had been fiddling around in the car so long because he had equipment that he wasn't bringing. What would that be? She didn't dare to let her mind jump at what she wished it would be. Instead, she left it open for her observations and instincts to work their way to it. She kept her eyes on him as he walked the last stretch of sidewalk, crossed the street to James Peter Turpin's driveway, and turned into it.

He was wearing a lightweight black windbreaker, dark pants, a dark-colored baseball cap, and a black surgical mask. She knew he'd worn it to keep his white skin from reflecting light and making him visible. She regretted that she didn't have a mask too.

Justine slowly and quietly emerged from her position among the shrubbery and stood up, listening. She heard no sound of her killer backtracking to see if he was being followed or hurrying forward to come around the house to appear behind her. She went away from the house to the front gate, out to the sidewalk and across the street. She made the rest of her trip by maintaining the maximum distance from the house, ready to hide or run or freeze. If he saw her now, the hammer and boning knife she'd brought were nothing. If he shot her from the driveway, they would just be two things to drop when she fell.

When she reached his car, she took out her phone. The license plate was undoubtedly stolen, and she knew she was taking a risk, but she had a faint hope that she could leave one more lead for the cops if she died. She set her phone's camera, moved her body so the faint light from the street lamp would not be blocked, and took a picture, then ducked below the car's side, crept forward, waited, and listened, holding the hammer and knife. She sent the photograph to Detective Kunkel's phone. She was protected, for the moment, by the car's engine block and right wheel.

She crouched, ready to spring, and stayed that way for thirty seconds before she peeked out past the car's grille at the house. He wasn't coming, so she raised her head to window level and looked down into the car. She couldn't see anything on the seats or the floor, even when she used the glow of her phone's screen. She knelt beside the right front tire again and poked the side wall of the tire with the boning knife, applied both hands to the butt of the handle, and pushed hard. The blade went in, she tugged it out, moved to the rear one and stabbed that too, then dared to come around for the other two. She heard the hiss of the air escaping and saw the car beginning to settle slightly as the tires softened.

She looked at the big house. The guesthouse wasn't visible behind it. She knew that her killer might look for her in the main house, and if he did, Joe was in trouble. She couldn't put off the next part any longer. It had never really been a choice.

Justine stepped to the car's passenger window and swung the hammer. It hit the window with a bang and pounded a spray of small cubes of glass inward onto the seat and floor. She reached inside to the armrest and found the door handle. She opened the door and knelt on the seat, opened the glove compartment, found it empty, reached for the console, and flipped the top open.

The gun's handgrips were more than a shape she had been hoping for. They had a texture that made her hand feel good as it gave her hope of living another few minutes. She lifted the revolver close to catch a little light, saw that there were rounds in the cylinder, drew herself back out of the car, and began to run.

⚔

Joe Alston woke up, swung his feet off the bed, and moved to the window. What was that noise? It had sounded like a car accident—a bang of an impact and then glass. There was nothing visible from this window, only the roofs of the garage and the guesthouse, and the dark foliage of trees and the lawn. He sensed that he shouldn't be in a rush to turn on any lights. Justine had been in terrible danger tonight, and there was no reason to believe that had changed. He couldn't imagine that a gang of young thieves had found her here, but he couldn't assume that they or the professional killer hadn't.

He stepped out of the room, across the hall to the bedroom that faced the street. He moved the window's curtain aside and looked out. A couple of houses away there was a car parked by the curb. That was unusual for this neighborhood. All of the houses were big, with enough driveway and garage space for the inhabitants and their guests to park.

He was looking from above, so he couldn't be sure, but there seemed to be something odd about the car. The chassis looked very low to the ground, as though the suspension had been custom-modified. Maybe it just seemed that way because there weren't other cars to compare it to.

He moved his face closer to the glass and looked up and down the street. There was nobody on foot near it or visible anywhere, but he was still uneasy. He left that bedroom and kept going to the big sitting room at the top of the stairs.

There were big windows here that looked out over the yard, but he had already looked and seen nothing out of place in that direction. He still had the feeling that something was up. He turned and stepped to the bookcase, pulled open the section that was built into it to hide the door, slid the pocket door aside, stepped into James's safe room, and closed both doors behind him.

He turned on the light. It was time to test his theory about the last owner's guns. If James had been stuck with them, they would be here in the safe, and James had told him where he kept the combination. If there weren't any, then he was sure that he had seen baseball stuff in a downstairs closet, including a bat. He would go outside and take a look with that.

⚜

Justine had to assume that her killer had heard her break the car window, and if he had, he would be on his way. He certainly knew what he had left in his car, so he would not come out into the open driveway. He would come around the back of the house to ambush her from roughly the place where she had chosen to wait for him to arrive. She forced herself not to wonder whether he would step into the electrified pan of water and kill himself, because she needed to think about what to do if he didn't.

She dashed up the driveway, running on her toes to keep her steps quick and quiet. When she reached the five-car garage she veered to the left to reach cover quickly and go around the back of it. As soon as she was beside it she stopped and then moved forward slowly. Both the left and right sides had human-sized doors. She gave the doorknob of the one beside her a gentle half-turn to be sure she had left them both unlocked, and then kept going, turned right at the end of the wall and continued around to the back of the garage, then moved along it toward the backyard.

⚡

Sealy had been sneaking along the side of the main house studying it for openings and vulnerabilities when he had heard the bang. Instantly he'd been certain what made a noise like that. Justine Poole, or someone, had broken a window of his rented car. He had to assume that in a fancy neighborhood like this one it hadn't been some unrelated vandal or thief. Justine Poole hadn't been asleep after all.

She had broken into his car, which told him several things. She had seen him coming, because otherwise the car could have been anyone's. If so, she must have sat waiting for him to arrive. Worse, if she had not been armed before, she was armed now. The bang meant she'd tampered with his car, and he was probably not going to be able to use it to leave. Had she known or expected he would find the envelope with this return address on it? Could she have swept it out of the car to lure him here?

Sealy knew he had to take each of the obstacles, one at a time. She had probably made his car inoperable, but he could solve that. When he had arrived, he hadn't seen the car she'd driven before, but there had to be one nearby. As soon as she and any housemates were dead, he could find any keys in the house and use them to locate and start the car they went with and get out of here. First, she had to be dead.

She was more of a problem than most. The reason she was in her predicament was that she had been called to the yard of a big house at night and shot two attackers to death before any one of the five of them could shoot her. What that probably meant was that she had been patient and controlled while they had been aggressive and stupid, thinking if they fired enough rounds in her general direction, some of them had to hit her.

He would need to be smarter and more patient than she was to win. She was probably away from his car by now, beginning to make her way toward him in the dark. He needed to make a few preparations before she arrived. His first move was to step along the side of the big house, looking hard for something he knew had to be there. He found it about where he'd expected, on the end of the big building away from the driveway. He saw the distinctive shape of the meter first, with the glass dome. Beside it was what he needed, the main circuit box. He opened the metal door and held up his phone to get a faint, weak light from the screen, found the main power circuit breaker, switched it off, and shut the door on the box. He had brought a padlock for this, and he closed the latch on the box and padlocked it. He moved his phone close to the meter so he could see the little wheel inside. It wasn't turning now. He pocketed his phone and moved on beside the house.

⚜

When Justine heard the *clack* sound of the circuit breaker her breath caught in her throat and she crouched where she was, behind the garage in the dark. This had never occurred to her when she had been preparing, but it had been the first thing her killer had done. She was enraged at herself for not thinking he would cut off the power to the house. He wasn't going to step in the pan of water and electrocute himself. Her trap had instantly been turned into nothing. He must have wanted to be sure he didn't set off some motion-sensor floodlight and suddenly be lit up in the open. Had he thought he'd neutralize the alarms? No, if he was a pro, he would know that the systems had a battery wired in, and the newer ones also sent wireless mobile phone signals to the company. It had to be the lights that he was afraid of.

Didn't he know that she would hear the sound of the circuit breaker? Yes. If he hadn't before, he knew now, after he'd tripped it. Maybe that had been his own kind of trap, and he'd wanted her to hear it. He could be crouching in the dark near the main circuit box with a round in the chamber waiting for her to come check it. She had to rely on what she knew about him, which included what he knew about her. He would know that she wasn't completely inept in a gun fight at night. He knew she'd broken the window of his car and taken his revolver, so he knew she was armed. He had decided that his chances were better if there was no light. Justine had to make light.

⋆✦⋆

Sealy was moving along the side of the house that he believed was farthest from the bedrooms, at least the ones most likely to be occupied. The big master suites were most likely to be on the upper floor at or near the wings, where it was easiest to set aside large spaces and preserve privacy. He chose a set of French doors. It was impossible to see anything inside, but their position in the back near the middle of the building was promising. It might be a dining room or a conservatory, since there was a kitchen door only a dozen feet farther along the wall.

The fact that Justine Poole had just tampered with his car proved she was outdoors. That meant that right now, for this moment, at least, the alarm system was disarmed so she could get back in. He had a choice of going inside to wait for her to return or going after her. He decided that waiting inside was too dangerous unless he knew more. He hurried along the side of the house to the corner near the driveway and stopped. She would be coming back up the driveway to get in one of the two back doors. He looked at the guesthouse or pool house or whatever it was. Maybe she would be heading there when she returned instead of the main house, but it changed nothing. He was at a choke point between the pool deck, the main house, and some kind of exotic garden. If she came up the driveway he would hear her and open fire.

⚜

Justine was behind the garage again in the darkness. She had knelt here a few minutes ago and tried to remember everything that she had seen in the garage earlier when she'd had light, and then she had gone in the side door and walked straight to them, a blind woman walking in a memory. For a moment she had considered trying to restore power by starting the generator, but only for a moment. The generator had a gasoline engine, and that made noise. Instead, she had picked up the two gasoline cans stored beside it, stepped out the far door and made her way behind the garage to the spot where she stood now.

She wasn't quite certain where her killer was. She had been listening since the moment when she'd returned to the yard, but he seemed to be as careful as she was about making noise. She lifted the nearest five-gallon can to the back corner of the garage and set it down. She looked up at the sky again, but couldn't see the moon or stars because of the thick layer of clouds. In LA summers, the nighttime clouds and haze almost always burned off by noon and the sun took over. It occurred to her that she might not be alive when that happened this time. She would try to be. She adjusted the revolver in her waistband and unscrewed the cap of the can. The fumes of the gasoline seemed to engulf her, and she worried that in this motionless night air her killer would smell it. She tilted the can to let a thin stream go out into the trench she'd dug in the ground, pouring it slowly so that it didn't make a *glug-glug* sound. It wasn't collecting in a puddle, so it must be flowing away from her, and when she'd poured more, she guessed it must be moving past the grass in the direction of the tropical garden. She knew she couldn't keep pouring much longer than a minute, or he would smell it and figure out what was going on.

She closed the cap, set the can aside, and took out the book of matches she'd taken from the workbench. She held it in her left hand and tore off a match with her right. She struck the match and released it, and as she pulled her right hand back, she was already reaching for the revolver.

≈≫≈

Sealy heard the *skritch* sound, and then a huff like a breath of wind, and then the whole yard behind the big house turned bright—first an explosion of blue, and then a wall of glaring orange fire streaking across the yard toward him. He tugged out his pistol, but the fire arrived and he jumped back to evade it. He had a sense of where the fire had started, so as his feet landed on solid ground, he fired five shots along the corner of the garage.

***

Joe Alston heard the *pow-pow-pow-pow-pow*. He snatched up the pistol
he had just loaded, ran to the sliding door, and stepped out into the sitting room. The big windows were a single wall of bright orange light
from flames as high as the second floor. He sprinted out to the upstairs
landing and then ran down the staircase, turned at the bottom and ran
for the French doors that led to the backyard. He stopped for a second
to look, saw nothing that made any sense, but pulled the door open and
stepped outside.

***

Sealy felt pain, looked down and saw that the left calf of his pants and
his left jacket sleeve had been lit by the fire. He slapped at the flames,
but his vigorous movements only made them grow and flare brighter.
He dashed to the pool deck and dived. There was a wild, bright moment
of flight, and then his body arced downward and plunged through the
water's surface into the cool, quiet world beneath, now illuminated by
the flames billowing into the air above it.

***

Justine ran, closed her eyes, and covered her face as she jumped through
the wall of fire to the pool deck. The heat behind her told her when to
open her eyes. She caught herself, stood at the end of the pool deck, and
raised the revolver.

She could see her killer under the surface of the water. He was moving
his legs and arms to stay upright, but going nowhere. His right hand

still held the pistol he had just fired. He let out some air that bubbled to the surface, and she saw what he was trying to do. Without the air his body sank. He brought his legs together and pointed his toes. When he touched bottom he bent his knees, pushed off, and began to rise. She watched him straighten his right arm and move his finger into the trigger guard as he rose.

Would his pistol even work? She gripped the revolver and watched him. Should she try to get back and take cover, and did she even have time? He was only about two feet below the surface now, and his right hand with the gun was coming up above his body. His legs gave a strong scissors kick.

Justine aimed the revolver at a spot about six inches below the surface and forced herself to wait until the very top of his head broke the surface, then fired. The bullet churned the water and threw up a splash so she couldn't see him for a second, but then she could and what she saw first was blood. It was coming from his head, a swirling red cloud.

⚜

Joe Alston was running toward the gunshot noise, and he saw something through the veil of bright flames. He stopped at the deck with the gun in both hands and aimed at the only figure standing. The figure turned to look at him, and he saw that it was Justine.

⚜

That was when Justine heard the first sirens. It occurred to her that what they were responding to probably hadn't been the shots. It had to be the fire. The flames didn't seem to have caught anything else yet, but they were high and bright. She set the revolver down on the pool deck and said, "Put it down, Joe. They'll be hoping to see a man with a gun." Then she walked toward the guesthouse, unplugged the extension cord, and headed toward the driveway to meet the firemen and police officers.

32

Mr. Conger said, "All I was doing was trying to take care of my own guys. I still have two dead men, and three others sitting in county jail for almost a week, waiting to see if they'll even get bailed out. What I did was to make sure they knew I wouldn't abandon them. I wanted them to be respected while they were locked up, and they would be if I let people know I stood by them. The guy I hired to do that was a first-rate guy, and he was taking care of it. You all knew Sealy. What happened to him was a fluke."

Noore was much younger than Mr. Conger, but he was very large, at least six feet six and three hundred pounds, and that gave him a sort of aristocracy conferred by nature. "You went after Jerry Pinsky. People love Jerry Pinsky. He isn't some little jerk who's getting above himself wearing a two hundred thousand dollar watch and driving a Rolls to the supermarket. The minute you sent a crew to rob him you made sure the police weren't going to be able to ignore it. What happened to your guys doesn't matter. You brought trouble down on all of us."

Mr. Conger believed he could still gain control of this. He assumed a smile and turned it on each of the others, one at a time. He felt the solution was to rely on his reputation and reassert his authority. "I've been here for a long time. I know what works and what doesn't."

Ducky Sanders spoke up. "What's been working is making them believe the robberies were being done by small groups of young guys who were friends and happened to see all the rich bastards sitting at outdoor tables in the afternoon drinking wine under umbrellas. Now they think we're the Mafia."

Mr. Conger said, "I get your pitch. You think I'm going to pay all of you damages for bringing you bad publicity. I'm not going to do that."

Mick Noore, Ducky Sanders, and Vaughn Pineda all suddenly held pistols in their hands.

"What is this?" Mr. Conger said. "Some kind of joke?"

"No, it's like a firing squad," Pineda said. "When it's over nobody knows who fired the shot that killed you. Nobody's to blame. Nobody's a hero."

33

James Peter Turpin's house had been healing itself over the past few weeks like a big living organism. The burned parts of the grass and garden had begun to grow back in as soon as the charred areas had been scraped clear and replanted. The five 9-millimeter rounds that Leo Sealy had fired at Justine Poole had been dug out of the garage wall and a couple of trees by the police forensics people, and then the wall had been spackled and repainted.

The swimming pool had been drained, and while it was empty Turpin had hired the Augustino Brothers Pool Service to replaster it and replace the scorched pool deck with a surface of caramel-colored sandstone set off by streaked rocks big enough to sit on, so the pool didn't even look like a pool. It looked like a boulder-ringed oasis.

Justine Poole was lying on a chaise longue in a bathing suit. Her sunglasses were big and dark, and she was wearing a wide-brimmed white hat, so the effect was to make her seem small. Joe Alston sat under the umbrella at the big round table a few feet away with his laptop open. He said, "I've only got a few more questions. I promise I'll finish it by tomorrow."

"That's okay," she said. "I'm not your editor. I don't care when you finish it."

"Since this happened to you, the papers and other media have all apparently agreed that you're a heroine."

"I don't love that term. It always sounds like it means the hero's girl-friend, not a girl hero. That or the drug."

"I'll make a note of that. How do you think that's going to change your life?"

"I hope it will get me a job. It's all a blizzard of bullshit, though. Whether or not you believe it is a test of your common sense. I don't mean heroes aren't real, but heroes risk their lives for other people."

"That's just what you did."

"Not really. I'm glad it ended this way because he had killed Ben Spengler, a good man I owe a lot to. But Ben was already dead by then, so I must have been doing it for myself."

"What do you mean? You didn't have to be there at all. You could have left."

"I did it so I would still be me."

"Did it work?"

"I'm still me."

"Does that feel like enough?"

"The water in the pool is like a bath. When the sun shines on me it makes the water evaporate and cools my skin, but makes it feel tight and clean. The sky is that deep, perfect blue that makes me feel as though I'm looking all the way up into space. I have these great new sunglasses, so you can't see my eyes, but I've been able to watch you typing and I've noticed that you don't take your eyes off me even then. It's sort of flattering."

"So you're saying that is enough?"

"For now," she said. "But we're only here for now."